THE DUCHESS DILEMMA
A. Nichols

Special Thanks To:

June Weston, Editor
Sarah Bowell, reader; Angel Weyandt, reader

PROLOGUE

He stood on the rise and looked out over his vast lands. It had been ten years since he had seen them; the Crimean War had kept him away. Few people would recognize the strong man from the gangly, twenty-year old who had set forth with wide, starry-eyed wonder to fight. What he had seen had changed him irrevocably, and he would never be the same.

Alexander Roberts, the 7th Duke of Winterbourne, heard the horse before he actually saw it. It was cantering at quite a clip on the road below and behind him. He could peer down through the trees onto the dusty path that ran parallel to his own, and he did so, wanting to know who was hurrying at such a breakneck clip. Whoever it was would end up in the lake if he weren't careful. The path was narrow, and the slope of the path that ran down to the water's edge was quite a steep pitch. He looked over his shoulder to see horse and rider come into view. He thought he heard the sound of laughter.

He drew his own horse in tighter and slowed him to a walk. In seconds, he could see them; the horse was a daunting creature, nervous and built for speed, its hooves beating out a rhythm that was almost to a full gallop now. Its coat was pure white with a flowing mane and tail. A rider clung fluidly to the horse's neck, urging the animal on and moving as one with it; the rider appeared to be a small boy. How in the hell could anyone allow a boy that small to ride that spirited animal? Alex cursed at the sight even as he urged his own mount into a canter.

He heard laughter ring out again, filling the air; it was melodious rather like that of a small child. He moved his own mount into a gallop to make sure he didn't lose sight of the running animal and fearless rider. The boy's breeches and white shirt with billowing sleeves made him easy to follow. The body sat astride as easily as one could; he was bruising rider.

One wrong step and horse and rider would pitch down the hill only to slide and disappear into the cold, dark waters of the lake below.

Suddenly, the horse was drawn in quickly, rising on its back legs to protest the halting of its forward motion. Its hooves rent the air, and its rapid breathing could be heard, but it dutifully stopped after a series of steps forward. Alex stopped his own steed with an experienced grasp at his reins. The rider below held the horse tightly, and he patted the animal. The boy jumped down from the beast in quick order, leading the animal to a small clearing on one side of the dirt path. He looped the reins over a branch that would allow the animal to graze and pulled out a cloth of some kind from a packet on the side of the horse.

Alex, too, pulled his horse to the side of the upper path so he could better see what was going on below. By the time he had tied the animal, he turned once again to look. A boy's hat and clothes dotted the clearing; a shirt and breeches lay strewn by the side of the animal. What had happened to the boy? The man scanned the shoreline of the lake, only to see the pale backside of a small body with legs that went on forever enter the water—but this person also had long, streaming black hair. The observer's breath stuck in his chest; it wasn't a lad at all, but a young girl with rounded buttocks and pale skin. The loud splash and the delighted cries indicated she had found nirvana in the lake. That image and those sounds permeated his mind.

She must be a village girl; there was no other way to view this excursion into a questionably unsafe environment. The wooded area was home to any number of wild animals and perhaps even hunters. No well-born lady would ever do as what she was doing even if it was on estate land. He needed to see more of her, so he crept silently though the vegetation to the lower road, stopping to pinpoint her splashes in the water. His years as a military man made this a simple task. His movements caused barely a sound as he advanced on her.

As he edged closer, he stilled. He didn't want to frighten her, but she had no business being out here in the forest on his land, unaccompanied. Anything could happen to her. A lesser man would take her in a second if she were ripe for plucking. His eyes focused as she made swirls in the water with her arms, and then a sweet voice rang out as she sang and cavorted in the water in a dance, moving gracefully. His eyes lit up as she stood with the water lapping at her waist; he was granted a picture of her high breasts, pale and glistening in the fading light…this was no child. Then they were gone as she sank gracefully into the water again and pushed her dark hair out of her face.

He was in an awkward position. As an unwed duke, he could not take a chance of being caught in the snares of a woman of ill repute, but he wanted her out of the water. The currents in the lake were difficult to fathom, and she could be swept out into the center. Finally, in resolution, he pulled himself upwards to his full six foot plus height and waited for her to spot him. It only took seconds. Her eyes widened, and with a cry, she sank down into the dark blue waters to her shoulders. Her expressive face was elfin-like with large green eyes and even more perfect features. She was beautiful beyond any woman he had seen.

"Sir." Her wavering voice caught him. "You have me at a disadvantage. Please turn your back, so I may come out of the water." She added in a breathy, commanding tone. "I am cold."

He retained his serious expression. "You didn't seem to mind the cold water as you were dancing in it." Her eyebrows went up at that comment, and she wondered how long he had been there and much he had seen; what would she do if he tried to capture her? Her knife lay among the clothes on the ground.

"You, sir, are no gentleman." She made this pronouncement in disdain.

He advanced several steps on her. "And you, Miss, are no lady." He couldn't help the smile that turned up the corners of his mouth. He hardened his voice to make her see the error of her ways. "What are you doing here? This is not your property."

"No, it is not, but it is not your property either. It belongs to the Duke of Winterbourne, and he hasn't been home in years." He was surprised that she knew of him. He didn't think he had ever seen her before. "Sir. Let me get out. Turn your back. There is a drying cloth beside my horse. Place it on the ground by the water's edge and turn your back."

It was a staring contest. "Are you always this demanding, little one? You need to learn some manners."

She muttered something under her breath. "Really? From you? Who is in the wrong here? I would get out of this water--Sir." She modulated her tone to that of a sassy tavern wench to further allay his suspicions. "Move your ass, if you please."

Alex stepped back. How dare she use that tone of voice with him? Then he recalled that he was not dressed as a duke, but rather as a working laborer. He wondered if she might be of noble birth; she certainly spoke like it when it suited her. He could see her shivering body and hear her chattering teeth. It was time to end this impasse, and unless he wanted to wade into the water and chase her, it would have to be him. He crossed nonchalantly to her grazing horse and found the drying cloth. He picked it up and turned to her once more.

"Your drying cloth, my Lady." He placed it at the water's edge and made a show of turning his back. He did, however, remain close to the shoreline.

"Do not look. You promised."

He frowned at her reply but did not turn around. "When did I promise?" He heard her scramble out of the water, and the cloth that lay on the ground was mysteriously gone. He heard rapid movements behind him, and he gave her just enough time to get wrapped up in it. Then he slowly turned to face her. Now she was swallowed in a shroud of white cloth, and she trembled. Her wet, black hair hung down from a perfect face with an upturned nose. She should be taught a lesson for her own protection; he moved closer, and she backed away from him. The tops of her breasts peaked at him from the drying cloth. She was well-formed to his very knowing eyes, but a handful to be sure.

"Keep your distance…" she intoned.

"Or you'll do what?" he countered. "You are at my mercy."

"But you won't touch me." She straightened her shoulders, and damnation, she was right. No one knew he had returned from the wars on the peninsula, and he wanted it to remain that way for the time being.

Alex frowned. "I want your word that you will dress, get on that damned horse of yours and go home to your father. In addition, you will promise never to come back here again unaccompanied."

Her pointed chin went up as she considered his words. "I suppose I can promise." She took in his rough appearance. He must work the lands for the Duke, and she was lucky that he was letting her go unscathed. Her pointed appraisal left him feeling uncomfortable. She took note of his dark eyes, his rather long and unkempt black hair, and his clothes that had certainly seen better days. He had an arresting face, angular and now set in annoyance. His body was that of a sporting man, used to hard labor, his upper chest and arms powerful. As he turned away from her, she saw the size of his shoulders that tapered to a trim waist and strong legs. Alex was quite a man's man. His harsh voice caught her as she catalogued him.

"Stop gawking. You have very little time before I forget our bargain. Get out of here." He turned his back once more, and he heard her sharp intake of breath and a scrambling from behind him as she gathered and quickly dressed in her boy clothes. He stood close by, his eyes facing the woods, his legs set apart, and he waited. Several long minutes passed. Finally, he heard her voice. "You can turn now. I am getting on my horse and leaving."

He took one last long look at her--a gamine, fey creature of the woods. She was bold in her actions, and her body was far too tempting, even dressed in men's clothes. "Go," was all he could get out.

She jumped up on the dancing mare and was gone in seconds. Damn, he hadn't even asked her for her name, not that she would have given it to him. He ought to have it to tell her father or brothers that she was out looking for trouble. He walked towards the lake and saw a scrap of lace on the ground; when he picked it up, it was a lady's handkerchief with initials neatly embroidered in one corner—E.L.W. His fingers closed around it. A subtle lilac scent rose from it; it was the handkerchief of a lady.

Alex climbed the hill and took the reins of his own horse. He was already late for the meeting with his two best friends, but the episode had brightened his day. He would do some investigating on his own. She had to be from around his property. How many ladies with long dark hair could there be? Her age was another matter. Was she fifteen or twenty-five? And why that mattered to him—that was another story. He was already engaged to be married.

Alexander turned the horse towards the palatial home that awaited him. There was something funny going on among those who tended to his estates, and he was determined to find out all the facts before he revealed himself to anyone. The war had left him darker, fitter and more skeptical than when he had gone. Spying was not an occupation for just anyone, but he had reveled in it during the war. The search, the mystery, the unmasking of those who cheated...that made it all worthwhile. Ten years was a long time to be away. It was time to take up the running of his estates and his life again.

And the new *thief* of his paths and waters would be found. Of that, he was sure.

CHAPTER 1

Alex leaned on the balcony of the second floor of the Earl of Dunaway's mansion. It was a crush of perfumed, over dressed women and their escorts, each trying to outdo the other. The noise of hushed conversations and delightful diversions did nothing for Alex's well-being. He had come to dislike the social conventions that now dictated his life. He was not a man to mill about eyeing ladies' bosoms and attempting to steal kisses in the back gardens, although he could make love with a married woman with the best of them. The issue was all the unmarried, gauche young women who were being paraded in the marriage mart. That peacock parade left him cold. He shifted on his feet; thank goodness he could not be recognized. He had come to the party through the back door and through the goodness of the woman who held the fete. She was only one of a few who knew he had returned from the war. It gave him a chance to reconnoiter in the hallways. He found his spying skills came in handy.

Alex was searching for the lass who had bested him on his own property several weeks ago; no matter how many inquiries he made, no one knew of her. There were no known white horses anywhere near him. His eyes scanned the crowd once more looking for a body type or long black locks. Many of the women dancing and preening wore their hair powdered making any identification even more unlikely. He had stopped at several of the posting inns in the area looking for a commoner who matched her description. Nothing. It was as if she had disappeared into the woods she roamed.

"Alex." He turned to greet the man who was bounding up the stairs towards him. John, Earl of Essex, had been his best friend both at home and in the war. His smiling face was a welcome sight.

"John, or should I call you Essex now?" he asked, stepping forward. "It's good to see you again."

"The Duke returns then, right?"

1

"No, I am not back yet, at least not officially. Few people have even recognized me. I am here only as an observer, supposedly to help the new Duke get settled. When I am asked where he is, I merely shrug and say I haven't seen him yet."

"Clever ploy. You know it will not work for very long, but you are correct—ten years is a long time."

"There are a number of strange things going on at my estate; the land manager is a domineering sort of person, not well liked by the men who work for me. They remain pretty close mouthed about him, almost as if they are afraid of him. I need to find a way to break into their ranks and get the truth. I have checked the accounting ledgers, and I can find no discrepancies in the accounting. But who knows what is going on in the estate proper? I don't like it. Being a worker on my own estate may help me."

"What can I do to help?" John asked.

"Do you know of a dark-haired young woman who rides astride a white horse? I would think others had made note of her."

"Astride? Hell, no. If I did, I would be taking some action. Do you think she knows something?"

"I have no idea what she does or doesn't know. We had a bit of an altercation on my land, and I sent her on her way. She thought I worked for the Duke." The look John gave him was a comical mix. "Some men are just stupid, right, to send a fair lass on her way?" Alex countered.

"You can beat yourself up, but I will not help demean a friend." John paused for a moment. "Father Crenshaw might know if anyone has seen your young lady. He knows most of the families in the area, and he could give you some guidance." Alex nodded his thanks. "I'll make arrangements to see him." Alex's eyes still scanned the dance floor, but she was nowhere to be found. Then he found himself drawn to a stir at the far end of the elaborate dance floor. Someone new was entering.

The crowd parted just a bit to allow him to see a young lady. Good God—who had dressed the poor thing. The gown was too big, too gaudy and too colorless to be anything but a fright, and the young woman in it had a pale complexion and hair pinned tightly to her scalp...Alex had never seen anything more frightening in his life. The dress spread out in all directions making walking with anyone close by a tripping accident waiting to happen. Who in the hell was she? A niggling sense of recognition swept up over him, and he looked more closely. A slow smile lit his face—he knew damn well who she was....

The petite woman who sailed across the room like a great ship with her entourage following settled into one of the overstuffed armchairs at the side of the room. The flounces of the oddly colored puce gown settled in waves around her. The dress must have weighed a ton. She might have been a floating ark.

"Do you know her name?" Alex's question startled John.

"That, my friend, is the heiress of the century—Lady Elizabeth Weston. Her father has passed on, but she stays at her uncle's townhome. She should have been auctioned off in marriage to the highest male bidder by now, but there's a small codicil in her father's will; she cannot be affianced except with her permission. She must approve of the groom. Her huge dowry is in cash and jewels, but mostly in prime land."

"She looks like a gigantic circus tent," was Alex's comeback.

"Well, there is that, and her complexion is so wan. She almost blends in with that putrid color she is wearing."

"Does she have any idea of how she looks?" Alex thought of the snap of the eyes of the young girl he met, and the fluid movement of her body when he had last seen her riding away; the two images just didn't mesh. "Could this be a part of a game she is playing?" he mused out loud.

"I don't know, Old Man," John replied. Both men watched her stand and take the arm of a gentleman who led her to the dance floor. This, Alex had to see. It was bound to be an unmitigated disaster. It was like watching an uncoordinated romp between a giant vegetable and an accommodating beanpole; he thought it was a supposed to be a waltz. The dress flew everywhere, and Alex had it in his heart to feel for the poor man who tried to manage it. The dancer lost his footing several times, and the two participants came perilously close to landing on the floor in a tangle of arms and legs. Others steered clear of them both. Alex closed his eyes. This lumbering lady was a travesty, but he knew it was the young woman he had met.

Alex spent the next two hours watching Lady Elizabeth and her sycophants wend their way through the massive crowd; she seemed to be heading for the retiring room near the evening's end. He moved his position strategically to the side of the wall where she would pass. It was time to renew his acquaintance. He had questions to ask.

Elizabeth drug her exhausted body through the men and women that surrounded her. Her neck and back hurt as did her legs from holding up the weight of the billowing dress, yet her outward demeanor showed little of her fatigue. She had a headache from her tightly braided hair, and. she had already called for her coach with plans to exit the ball as soon as she could. If she smelled one more popinjay's heavy scent, she would expire on the spot. She sank into a semi curtsy to her followers, and she entered the narrow hallway towards the retiring rooms. If she could just sit down for a moment, all would be well. She pushed in the sides of the light purple monstrosity she wore in order to navigate the tight hallway, quickly entering it, leaving her horde of followers behind. Turning another corner in the short corridor, she was stopped suddenly by a man's arm across the opening. She ran into it and stepped back in surprise. Alex stepped directly in front of her. "Hello, Baggage."

Her eyes opened wide and then became positively glacial. "You! What are you doing here? This is a private ball, Sir, and I know you weren't invited." She dodged to the left and tried to sweep by him, but the wide skirts of her gown caught on his legs, effectively trapping her. She jerked on the material. "Get out of my way, you Cretin."

Alex had to laugh. She really thought she could get through or around him. It wasn't going to happen. "We are going to talk, Little Lady, and it's going to be now." He grabbed her upper arm and pulled her further down the narrow hallway away from the retiring rooms. Rounding another corner, he found a wooden door and pulled her into a darkened room that was obviously not often in use. The only light came from a dirty window with disintegrating curtains. Shrouded furniture and dust mites were everywhere. She stopped right inside the door; her hand swung, slapping him smartly across the face. He rubbed his jaw and slammed the door shut behind him.

"How dare you?" she squeaked. "You are a Neanderthal with absolutely no manners. Were you born in a stable?" Her index finger poked him in the chest as she chastised him. His large hand immediately wrapped around her smaller one, and he stepped into her. She pulled back and to the side only to hear an ominous ripping sound. The back of her billowy dress had been caught in the door when Alex slammed it; there was an unforgettable, tearing sound. As she jerked around to pull on her skirts, the fabric gave even more. Alex couldn't help chuckling at the shocked expression on her face.

"Oaf! You have ruined my dress." She made one more hesitant pull at her billowing skirts, but the dress was firmly caught. Alex tried to extricate her from the situation by pulling her further into the room only to hear the sound of more ripping; the complete bottom flounce and entire train of her dress now was held captive by the door. The billowing material lay like a molting bird on the floor. She glanced down at her uneven hemline, and her small slippers peeked back up at her. She was horrified.

"You might as well take off all those petticoats and that hoop, too." As he enjoyed her discomfort, Alex muttered to himself, "This can be fixed." In response, Elizabeth anxiously stepped away, but she stripped off the extra garments and the hoop; his hand grasped hers to balance her. She pulled hard against his control, and one of the huge puffed sleeves tore completely off as the entire front of the bodice shifted to the right. Her hand caught the top of the dress before it fell further. "They don't make these dresses very well, do they?" Alex mused, his hand rubbing his chin. Her embroidered shift, her partial bodice, the pantalettes and the torn skirt were all that kept her pale body from his sight. The skirt of the dress was now little more than a rag, but it clung to her small frame. Alex's appreciative eyes followed that form. "That's what you really look like. I thought I'd remembered a different body."

Elizabeth's hands came up to better shield herself, and she positively spit her words at him. "Now what am I supposed to do. I can't go back out there dressed like this." She kicked at the petticoats on the floor with her foot and beat on him with her free hand. It was like trying to move a rock; he caught it effortlessly.

"Settle yourself. All is not lost," he argued.

But she was right; he had unthinkingly boxed them into a very uncomfortable position; he had been in bad situations before. He had to get her out of this room without detection. It looked like she had been 'compromised', and that was one awful word—he could end up 'hitched' to the little she-devil.

Alex looked around the room. "Here." He handed her paper and a quill from an old desk in the room. "Write a note to your hostess that you had to leave. Write a second one to your coachman to go home without you. I'll see that they are delivered."

"The ink is almost empty—I can barely see to write."

"It will do," he replied.

"That still doesn't get ME out of here."

"Well, Baggage, there is a perfectly good tree outside. We can make our getaway, and I'll see that you don't fall."

Her bitchy, sugary voice rubbed on his already raw nerves, as she punctuated her words: "By the way, Sir, I don't climb trees. I am a lady."

Alex gave her a hard look. "Ladies don't ride astride either, or bathe in a lake--*au naturel*." If looks could kill, he would be dead.

"If you have any other ideas, however, I will entertain them." She waited for his response; her dark eyes snapping back at him, but he could think of no other way out of the mess he had made.

"It's the tree, or we stay here for the night," he said.

The stand-off continued. Finally, she replied, "This is all your fault, and I won't soon forget it."

In minutes, the notes were on their way. Alex checked out the window. There was a large tree that would do for their escape, but they would be at least thirty feet from the ground below. He hoped she was the agile rider he remembered. The only good thing was that she wouldn't be wearing that Godawful dress.

"Now Lizzie, this is how it's going to be." He prepared to lay out his plan. Elizabeth's head tilted up at him, and she tightened her look as the sparks flew from her eyes.

"I can hardly wait to hear, and it's not Lizzie. We haven't been formally introduced. What are you, a laborer of some kind, some maniac who rides the property lines of the new Duke? Why was it my bad fortune to run into the likes of you?"

"I could say the same thing, couldn't I?" but her remark stopped him in his tracks. That's how she saw him? He settled his mind back to the topic at hand—escape. "We're going to climb out that window and use the tree to reach the ground."

Her eyes smiled, and a saucy grin crossed her features. "Does that mean if I push you off the limb, the ground will catch you?" she teased him.

"Bloodthirsty heathen," was his reply. He gathered his anger into resolution. "I will make sure that you reach the ground safely as long as you are civil."

Her expressive face became mulish. "Really? Civil? You ask me to be civil? I am not the one who caused this disaster, and I AM being civil." She paused for air. "I am still speaking to you." There was a dramatic pause. "I am not going out that window." She sat down on a box next to the dilapidated window frame and rearranged her almost non-existent skirt. "You can't make me."

Elizabeth was right, so Alex improvised. "Just consider it as an adventure. It will be successful when you reach the ground in one piece, and I promise to make sure that it happens." Her face told him the argument was a poor one. "Get up—please." Alex opened the window casement and measured the distance to the closest tree limb. The bark of the tree would scratch her delicate skin, so he looked for something to put around her bare shoulders. He tore off his jacket and waistcoat to undo the white lawn shirt he wore.

Her eyes were now wide open and then quickly shut, covered by her hands; Elizabeth cried out: "What do you think you're doing? You're not going down naked, are you?"

From where had the thought come, Alex wondered. "No. I'm going to give you my shirt to keep your skin from being abraded on the bark of the tree." He pulled on her shoulders to get her up, but she wrestled with him. In desperation, he shook her lightly, and when she looked up at him with surprise, he pulled off his shirt and pulled it over her head, pushing it down her body, and tying the ends in front of her. It was gigantic on her small frame, but it would do the job. She was staring at his chest—now bare to her. His eyes followed her wide ones to his muscled torso. "It's only skin, and my coat and shirt would make it more difficult for me to descend."

Her eyes slowly climbed up to his face and remained there as if she could make the vision of his naked chest disappear. Her cheeks were colored a bright pink; he knew she was embarrassed, and he knew she was a woman with little knowledge of a man. He only wished that he didn't have a direct, visual recollection of her body as a woman from their earlier encounter. The wind blew the shredded curtains into the room reminding him that they had to go. The dance would not go on forever.

"Give me your hand. I'm going to go out the window first, and then you are going to climb out after me. Don't look down. Look at the branch where I place your feet and keep hold of me." She nodded but didn't say a word. She eased herself slowly from the box and allowed him to pull her to the open casement. The tree loomed precariously close to the window. There was little light from the half-moon above, and the shadows ahead of her were deceiving. He watched her intently for any sign of rebellion. "Are you doing all right?"

"Why wouldn't I be? It's only a tree," she responded bravely. Alex smiled to reassure her.

"Remember that. Lift your foot and put it on the sill of the window. I'm going to back out and get on the branch. I'll place your foot where it should go, and you just hold on to my shoulders. That shouldn't be hard, should it?"

"Are you patronizing me because if you are, I don't like it." But her foot dutifully came out, and he took it and placed it on the relatively wide branch of the tree. She stepped out and put her other foot down, balancing with her arms on his wide shoulders. "How long before we go plummeting to the earth? I'd like to say my final prayers." He couldn't tell if she was serious or not; she went on: "And to think, I couldn't even find a man in all of London that I could stomach enough to marry," she murmured. "My family will be sorely put out, but they will give me a lovely headstone, I'm sure."

Distraction was what she needed, Alex thought to himself. "So, you are Lady Elizabeth Weston then."

"Fishing for information now? Who did you think I was?" He guided her foot further down the branch toward the trunk of the tree, making sure she was upright and secure. They moved gingerly across the branch to reach the trunk "I'm watching my feet as I was told to do."

"Good. We're going to go down the trunk to the ground. I'm going to go before you again, and I don't want to throw you off balance. Can you hold tight to this tree until I am below you? Then I'll place your feet in the right places again."

"Do you think I'm an imbecile?" There was a right answer to that question, but his brains were addled by her nearness. In a pained voice, she muttered, "Just go. It's chilly up here; there's a wind." He moved quickly and capably until he was on the branch below her. He reached up for her hand. She placed it in his and stepped down to the place he indicated.

"See, no problem." Her eyes told him he was an imbecile. What other lady would stand in a tree some thirty feet off the ground with a common laborer? And so, it went—step after step. They were almost to the ground when her slipper missed the branch, and she wobbled precariously, grabbing him by his upper arms and holding on for dear life. Her body came up against his in a rush, and he gathered her in, stabilizing them both. Her lilac perfume filled his nostrils, and her warm flesh came in direct contact with his chest. Her heart was beating frantically against him. "Steady, baggage. We're almost to the ground." Her breath rushed in and out for seconds, and then her back straightened, and she stepped back. She could see the ground below, some eight feet below.

He made sure she was holding on to the tree when he jumped to the ground. As he stood, he barely had time to turn and catch her as she careened off the branch and directly into his arms. Once again, he held the woman close; his body was not amused. Thank God she was a little thing. She smiled sweetly up at him and said, "Thank you for a most interesting evening. I don't guess we will do this again soon, will we." It was a statement, not a question.

HIs innate good manners came to bear. "You're very welcome." It was going on two o'clock in the morning.

"I will expect you at the back of my townhome at 8:00 this coming evening. I have something that I want you to show your Duke." Her voice spoke of an intrigue he didn't understand. It was an odd request, but she had climbed down the tree at his demand, so he was obliged to hear her out.

"All right."

"You can release me now." The whisper was near his ear, and her imperial tones told him he was taking advantage, but her arms were tight around him and sent him a different message.

Alex set her down carefully, took her arm and walked her the three houses over to her uncle's home; when there, he found himself reluctant to let her go; he turned to retreat to the other house when her voice stopped him again. "What is your name? I am Lizzie Baggage, and you are?" she queried. "I know you work for the Duke."

"My name is Alexander."

"Well, Alexander, consider us officially introduced. You may call me Lizzie, and I will call you Alex." She gave him a small curtesy and walked away from him towards the front door of the townhome, only to turn once more.

"You owe me a ball gown, Sir."

CHAPTER 2

John burst into Alex's bedroom in the Winterbourne townhome early the next morning just as the duke was washing up. Alex stood only in his pants. His friend poured himself a drink from the whiskey decanter and stared, just shaking his head. "You must have had an incredible night."

"What?"

"Your back, man. It's covered with scratches...she must have been..." and he was at a loss for words, "something else."

Alex shook his head and actually chuckled. "It's a long story, and no, it was a night filled with other pressing issues. Did you manage to get my clothes out of the upstairs room?"

"I did. The lady's dress looked like it had been torn off her." There was no comment from Alex. "I also removed it to make sure there would be no chatter this morning, but you need to know that there is some whispering among the ton. They need something new to gossip about—and Lady Elizabeth is so eccentric and rich that she is often the subject. You'd best be careful. Your intended will be here within two weeks for your wedding. Lady Estelle will not appreciate any talk of you with another woman." There was silence from the Duke. "You do remember you are engaged to Lady Estelle of Coventry Manor and have some need of her dowry until your investments are transferred to the Bank of England."

"I do know. The church is engaged as is the priest."

John cautioned him. "I am going to suggest that you do not see Lady Elizabeth again to quell all talk."

"It's too late for that. I promised to go with her on some jaunt this very evening. She says she has something she wants the Duke to know. I'm to be the conduit of this information."

"So, she still thinks you work for the Duke. When do you plan to tell her that you ARE the Duke. A bit of advice from an old friend? Don't go."

"I already said I would, and my word is my bond. My intended should know that. By the way, thank you for getting my clothes out of the house. What did you do with hers?"

"I tossed them in a box in the alley way."

Alex pulled on his shirt and began to dress in his work clothes. "I have another appointment early this morning." John's eyebrows went up. "It seems I owe Lady Elizabeth a new ball gown." Alex cringed at John's full-fledged laugh behind him.

His valet knocked at his door. "Excuse me, Sir, but this was just delivered to the back door for you. It has your name on it." Alex looked at the package wrapped in brown paper with something akin to fear in his eyes.

"Thank you, James. I'll take it." As his man exited, Alex unwrapped the paper to find a finely stitched, white man's lawn shirt; it was his. It had been freshly laundered, and there was a small repair on the shoulder seam sewn with tiny stitches. A note dropped to the floor. He picked it up and read, "I believe this is yours and I hope it reaches you at the Winterbourne address. I planned to keep it as a memory of our great adventure but decided that you would need it more, having few clothes and little means to get them. It has been freshly laundered and stitched by myself." Alex didn't quite know what to make of it—her scent still lingered on it. What lady would mend a common man's clothes?

The dress maker's shop was trafficked by a number of influential women; Alex climbed from his horse and tethered it behind the shop, using a small door in the side of the establishment. Marie, his dear friend, came running as soon as she heard he was there. She had dressed his women before but in another country. "My Lord. You are home for good?"

"No, Marie. I am not at home--yet. You didn't see me here today. I came because I have need of your services."

"Something to clothe your new duchess-to-be, perhaps?" she asked with a smile.

"Not exactly. I inadvertently ruined a ball gown, and I need to replace it." Marie's puzzled look made him realize what a ridiculous visit this was.

"I will need the lady's measurements," she said. He indicated with his hands--a waist size and then gave her breast sizes with careful, rounded motions of his fingers.

"She's about that size." Marie was intrigued because the duke was blushing profusely. "She's small. His hand once again measured her imaginary body against the length of his own. "I guess one could say she is slight of build and only comes to about here on me."

"But a true handful," Marie countered as a delighted laugh burst from her throat. "I will see what I can do, but this is a most unusual request."

"I know. Thank God you are my friend."

"What about her coloring, this 'slight' woman whom you desire to clothe?"

"She has long dark hair, the palest of skin and—long, long legs. They go on forever."

"You don't say," his friend replied with a knowing smile. Men weren't supposed to know that a woman had legs.

Flustered now, Alex put his hands down and just looked at Marie. "It's a long story, and I don't have time to tell it right now. I'll put myself in your capable hands. The ball gown must be exquisite and fitted. The one I ruined was a monstrosity, but I did ruin it. I shut the train of it in a door." At Marie's scandalous look, he further explained. "It was an accident."

"Really, an accident?" She waited for more of the story, but Alex just waited her out. "I will do what I can. I will assume the lady is not married and use more subtle colors, correct?"

"Correct."

"I would like a final fitting if that would be possible," she added. "I'll see what I can do. Cost, Sir?"

"No limits. I want it to be outstanding." Marie smiled and took his arm. They had met in Paris during the war, and Alex had managed to get her and her family out of that city and to London; then he had helped her set up her clothing establishment the year before he, himself, returned. "How are Phillipe and your children?"

"We are good, thank you. When do you plan an 'open' return to your estates as the Duke?"

"Soon. My intended will arrive in the city in the next ten days. She will visit your establishment for her wedding trousseau. Our event is very close, and the banns have been read twice already."

"I will look forward to meeting her." Marie wondered at the Duke's preoccupation with this new woman. While attentive to his bride-to-be, he didn't seem to have the same interest in her as in this 'slight' woman to whom he owed a dress. It was a conundrum, and the Duke seemed distracted even with the thought of her.

Elizabeth sat in the drawing room, listening abstractedly to her uncle drone on and on about the bills in Parliament. She only perked up when she heard the news that the Duke of Winterbourne would be returning within the next two weeks to take his rightful place. It was a good thing she was taking his 'man' tonight. She would easily get the measure of the Duke who was to come. Elizabeth winced as one of the small cuts on her hand pulled. Tree bark could be deadly on skin.

The daring midnight tree descent was a coveted memory, and she immersed herself in some aspects of it. Once they had begun, Elizabeth lost her fear, but she didn't tell Alex that. He was a man's man—his chest covered with dark hair that did a downward dive into the top of his breeches. She would have liked to explore that, but well-bred women shouldn't even know of such things. Her maid had asked for the lost ballgown this morning. Elizabeth had lied, firmly stating that she had thrown the dress out because it was so heavy on her body, and the damn thing was just that—way too heavy. Actually, she had no idea where the skirt was. She hoped it wasn't lying in the room of the house. Someone might recognize it.

Her dress today was a demure gray with a crocheted collar; she had slept late and told the butler not to admit any of her many admirers. Still, the bouquets of flowers came, and she would be obligated to write cards thanking each gentleman. It was a shame to waste all that beauty. This evening would be a different matter. Just wait until the Duke's man understood what was happening right under the Duke's nose. Would he man up, or would he allow the continued disruptions with the families on the estate? She might take her cue about the Duke from Alex's actions.

At eight o'clock, Alex sat on his horse in the back of Lady Elizabeth's townhome. Her bedroom seemed to be dark; perhaps, she had forgotten her challenge. Ironically, there was a tree right outside her windows. His horse moved restively under him sensing another animal near, and a white horse appeared from the hedges. "You are on time, Sir. I happen to like punctual men."

Her body was once again attired in boy's breeches and a peasant shirt with flowing sleeves, and she sat astride her horse. Alex hadn't forgotten how beautiful she was. She had her hair pulled back in a tie. "You will find I am usually punctual, Lizzie." She smiled at the use of their pet name.

"I have need of you to carry some goods on your horse. They are in a bag. Will your mount allow it?"

"He will."

"It's on the ground by the tree. Again, his eyes caught hers, and he smiled remembering her precipitous descent last evening. "Yes, it's the tree that leads to my bedroom window and the one that we are not visiting tonight."

"Good times, Baggage."

Alex retrieved the heavy satchel and placed it over his saddle. Then he followed the lady through the grounds and to a path that mirrored the main road but was far more secluded. It was getting darker by the minute. She rode with ease before him, and he liked the image of her as she did so. Her hips were neatly outlined as she sat astride, and her body flowed with the animal. He wondered what she would be like in bed.

CHAPTER 3

Alex was surprised when they crossed onto his property. There were several cottage structures on the edges of the lake that were used by the men and families of those who worked for him. Ten such cottages were clustered together in one of the farthest corners; why in the hell was she going here? She pulled up her mount in front of the closest cottage. The place had seen better days, that was for sure. She dismounted as a middle-aged man came out on the porch with a lantern. Small candles lit the interior of the house. "Robert," she called. "It is only me, and I have brought someone with me. May we come in? How is Anna this evening?" The man took a quick look at Alex, but he nodded as Elizabeth dismounted. Alex followed her lead and tied the two horses.

Elizabeth took the bag from her horse and handed it to Robert. "I brought some food for you." Alex also removed his bag and carried it to the porch. Up close, the cottage was in disrepair. The roof needed fixed, and several of the shutters on the windows were loose or missing. The slats on the front porch were cracked or broken. Although it wasn't cold, the interior of the cottage was not pleasant. An older woman sat in the corner with two small children. There was a bit of chill in the air, and there was no fire in the fireplace. "I'm going in to see Anna. I've brought some soup for her to help with the cough and cold," Elizabeth said.

"She will be glad to see you," Thomas replied.

Elizabeth turned to Alex. "Could you please get out the bread and stew for the little ones." The two weary little faces looked at him as Alex did as he was told; he emptied the bag on the table.

Thomas watched him work but said nothing. Alex tried to initiate some conversation with the quiet man. "Why don't you have a fire? The stew will have to be heated."

The man looked him squarely in the face. "I don't have the money to purchase the wood necessary to keep it going all the time. We tenants have to pay for everything now. Our wages have been cut

16

several times, and we must pay to cut our own wood on the property. I am even responsible for fixing the problems in the cottage, and the Duke will not pay for the raw materials to do so. Feed for the animals is all but non-existent, and the chickens and cows are hungry. The Duke is letting us slowly starve to death as the cottage crumbles around us. If my wife weren't ill, I would be pulling out and looking for somewhere else to work."

The scowl on Alex's face was notable. He was stepping into dangerous territory. "How long have you been working for the Duke?"

"Over twenty years. My parents farmed here, and I hoped to continue."

"Are you saying—that the Duke does not fix these dwellings or provide you with wood or fodder for your animals?"

"The Duke doesn't provide us with anything, and for our work in the fields, our wages are garnished for everything extra; we are forced to pay for the grain for our poor cow. She barely gives any milk now, but I can't bear to put her down. What kind of a man is this Duke? Do you know him? My parents said his father was a fair man, but the son was gone when I began to farm. He went to war."

Alex used measured words. "I don't think he is a man to let his workers suffer. Why haven't you spoken about this with the land manager?"

"I have—many times. Each time I complain, something else is taken from me. The other families here are in similar straits. We have nowhere else to go and no one else to take up our cause. We are good, hard workers, Sir; the estate books should show that the fields are well-tended and that the Lord gets a substantial return for the use of his land, but we have to be able to live." Robert's frustration was easily seen. Alex couldn't make sense of it all. He had ordered good pay for his tenants, and never in his memory did tenants have to pay for their wood, fodder and repairs. Something wasn't right; he could sense it.

"How did you meet Lady Elizabeth if you don't mind my asking?"

"She met us. She found our Melody in the woods when she was lost and brought her home. Elizabeth's been visiting every week, bringing treats for the little ones. When my wife became ill, Elizabeth came and nursed her. She's been a Godsend, and now she's brought you. How are you acquainted with her?"

"It's a long, awkward story that I would not share with you without her permission." Robert nodded. "With your permission, I'm going out and gather wood that is on the ground to make a fire for tonight. Your little ones will need a hot meal, as will this gentle, older lady who cares for them."

"You will have to go a good way into the woods. We've scavenged every piece of wood we can from the forest floor. There are ten families to sustain in these poor cottages, and we have no riding horses, only the team that pulls the wagons and plows."

Alex needed some time to clear his head, but it was quite obvious to him that he was being systematically fleeced by the man who represented him. "Get the stew ready to heat, and I'll be back just as soon as I can." He stomped his way out to his horse. No wonder the common men on his estate had been so distant with him. The land steward had no right to make new rules surrounding these men who had worked for his family. He took a quick glance at the other dwellings nearby. All were in desperate need of repair. In the winter, they would be impossible to heat. A glance at the back of the dwellings showed vegetable gardens that had been harvested to the hilt, but there were no new plants to set in the ground. This was unacceptable, and he would deal harshly with the man responsible.

The estate books would not show the side dealings that the Land Stewart was making—selling wood and not seeing to the cottages as well as no longer providing feed for the animals and plants for the workers. Those expenses had appeared; he was sure of it. He just didn't know that the tenants never received the goods. The landowner could pocket those amounts easily, and he had listed them as expenses for the estate—expenses that were put into his own pocket. If Alex hadn't come to the cottages, he would never have known.

He began to gather wood from the floor of the forest. He filled the food bags with smaller branches, and as many medium sized pieces of wood as he could. At least there would be enough to warm the food and to heat the cottage for the night. The workers tomorrow would find a new order--new rules and benefits for them. Both wood and supplies would be delivered to these people without cost to them, and Alex would deal with the Land Steward himself.

When he returned to the cottage, Elizabeth was waiting. He quickly built a fire, and she filled the pot with the food, stirring it until it was bubbling. It actually smelled really good—common enough fare for those who were in the lower classes. She pulled a loaf of freshly made bread and cookies from her satchel and placed the dinner on the table. Alex shared a glass of ale with Robert, and he stopped by the bedroom to say goodnight to Robert's wife.

The ride home with Elizabeth was a quiet one, but inside, Alex was fuming. "Why did you take me there?" he asked.

Because you needed to see what your 'great lord'," and she used the word sarcastically, "is really doing to those who work for him. I would so love to give him a piece of my mind, and who knows, perhaps I will have the opportunity at some point. I offered them coin, but they are too proud to take it." She stopped her horse and looked him directly in the eye. "I want you to pass along the information to the Duke. I know you have some access to him."

"How do you know that?"

"There is something about you, and you ride his lands as if they belong to you. I expect you to pass along the information."

"You expect me…really?"

"It is part of your penance for ruining a perfectly good dress." Her eyebrows went up as she chided him for his clumsiness.

"Ah, yes. That blasted dress." Her chin went up, daring him to make a further comment. "Very well, I will see that the Duke gets your message." They reined in at the back of the house, and he tried to help her down from her horse; she was having none of it, sliding out of the saddle herself; she landed in his waiting arms. Her horse walked towards the stable.

"Don't you dare try to kiss me," she whispered as she looked up into his eyes, her hands resting on his wide shoulders. "I will strike you if you do." Alex held her a little longer than perhaps was necessary. Her catlike smile said she had bested him, and Alex was flummoxed at his physical reaction to her. She was so unlike any lady he had ever known, and yet her compassion for others was appealing.

"You shouldn't tempt a man, Lady Elizabeth. In the near future, I will have you at a disadvantage."

"Well, that will be interesting, won't it? Good night," she said with a coy smile, and Alex let her go imagining what a kiss from her would be like. Would she be fire, or would she be ice?

Alex turned to go but stopped. "I will need to see you in the near future."

"That may not be possible," she countered.

He modulated his tone with her. "Could you possibly do me the honor of just a small amount of your time tomorrow? It is important. It involves a debt of honor."

"A debt of honor?" Her brows knit as if she was cataloguing her day to come. "I will send a note to the kitchen of the great manor and let you know a time. It will be late in the day, for I am tired."

"Yes, my lady. I will wait to hear from you." He gave her a small bow. She gave him a dismissive wave and a sweet smile. "Don't get used to commanding my time, Sir. It will do you little good; I have no time for most men." She turned and grabbed onto the lowest tree branch and swung herself up onto the limb. Alex's mouth hung open as she began to climb like a monkey. "Did I tell you that I love trees and have been climbing them all my life?" Her magical laugh came from high above him as his eyes followed her image until she crawled through her bedroom window. He shook his head at her. How dare she! But Elizabeth dared much, he discovered. Alex waited only until she was gone. How she must have laughed at him as he 'helped' her down the tree the other evening…the little vixen. He determined that this would be only the beginning of their skirmishes, and while he might have been bested in the first one, he would be victorious in others.

Somehow, he would bring her to heel.

CHAPTER 4

Alex could hardly wait to see the inside of the dwelling where his land agent currently resided. He would task his friend, the Earl of Essex, to set everything to right once he had his man. Samuel Wainwright, his current land manager had much for which to answer, and Alex would see him jailed on charges of fraud as soon as he procured the evidence. Alex walked into the rather large chateau the man now claimed for his own dwelling and began to look around. It was decorated in the height of fashion—paintings on the walls, the best rugs and ornate furniture, and warm wall hangings. No expense had been spared. Where would a manager come up with the funds to decorate in this manner? Alex didn't have to guess; he knew. A portly woman accosted him at the door of his own establishment; the Duke owned the house.

"Excuse me, Sir, but you must leave this house. It is not to be accessible to those outside Mr. Wainwright's circle of friends. I know I have never met you, Sir." The housekeeper with her nose in the air dismissed him completely. "Who might you be?"

"I have business with Mr. Wainwright, and I have a right to be here. I represent the Duke of Winterbourne." Her eyes grew large at that name. "Where is your master?"

The woman sniffed in disgust, looking up at him with pursed lips. "If you must know, he has gone to the local inn to meet with his friends."

The corners of Alex's mouth barely moved. "I will find him there. In the meantime, these men," and the door opened to admit four other men, "...will canvas the house and the records of your employer."

Now alarm filled her face. "You can't..."

"Oh, but I can. I suggest you get out of their way. I will speak with you again at greater length as soon as I find your master." She was flustered by his words; that much was obvious. He turned to the others: "See what you can find, gentlemen; bring all the records to the Main House."

"Yes, Sir." The men separated and began to move throughout the house, two to the bedrooms upstairs and the others to the library near the front hall. The old woman ran from the room, fanning herself in her timely escape.

Alex went to the library to look for false drawers in the massive desk he found there. The others were going through the books on the shelves. He was trying to remember the house. He had been here as a child, but his recollections were sketchy at best. He pulled the drawers from the desk and reached underneath it, looking for a false bottom. He found just what he was looking for. The panel slid, and he reached inside to pull out several official looking papers and journals. He sat down to see what he had found. It was all in front of him, separate contracts with dealers to get prices lowered for wood, grain and livestock, all of which had never been given to the workers of the estate. Rather, they had been resold at a profit. Alex was being robbed… and the amount of money lost staggered him. The dealers were non-descript, not ones with whom he would normally do business, so while the costs were high as if he had negotiated with the best men in the area, only half the money went to the nondescript sellers. He gathered the journals to take to the magistrate. He would see justice done not only for himself but also for the workers of his estate. They had been cheated in their wages as well according to the ledgers he found.

Alex would need a new land manager, and who better to consider than Robert, the man to whom Elizabeth had introduced him. Robert knew the land, and he knew the workers. Alex wondered how long it would be before the men trusted the new Duke. Nodding to the men who continued to search the premises, Alex gathered the incriminating information and prepared to leave the home. He stopped by the kitchen to question the old woman.

"Here, Sir. I don't know nothing about nothing. I just work here," was her excuse. Alex laughed. He noted that she was already gathering her belongings to make a quick getaway.

"Don't leave, Madam, or I will call the watch on you. You have some explaining to do." She stopped in her tracks.

"Please, Sir. I'm just an old woman who has no place to go. Mr. Wainwright promised me good wages, but I was to let no one near the house. Men come and go all the time, Sir, and there were some wild parties with wanton women baring their breasts and running through the house half-dressed. If I hadn't needed the money so bad and a roof over my head, I never would have countenanced the goings-on." She hesitated. "I can't go to prison, Sir. I have others to support."

"I would talk to you tomorrow. Remain here at the house. Your employer will not be coming home."

"Yes, Sir."

"I trust there is food in the place." Her head nodded, and she began to take apart the bundle she was making.

Alex wasted no more time. He had other places to be, namely the Rose Inn where he would accost his estate manager. He welcomed the encounter; he had been far too peaceful since the end of the wars.

Alex walked into the Inn noting all those who were present at the tables. Since he had never met his land steward, he walked to the innkeeper and asked him if Samuel Wainwright was there. The innkeeper nodded to a table of three men in the corner; they were laughing and making ribald comments about the maids who were serving, attempting to pinch or capture them as they walked by. Alex walked to the table next to them and sat down. Their language was loud and obnoxious.

"What say you, Samuel, is she not fetching enough for you?' The men craned their necks at the woman who brought their ale. "Or are you still eyeing that heiress with all the money. How anyone could want to bed her is beyond me. It would be like taking a plank to mount." The three men guffawed and slapped their thighs.

"Lady Elizabeth comes with plenty of money; that could make up for a great deal. She could be coerced to marry me if I stole her away and broke her to my will. I can put her in the country under guard as her husband and make free use of her money."

Alex sat up straighter. This was another angle he had not considered.

"Getting the Lady Elizabeth into your bed would be quite a sight, Samuel. Is your money source running out now that the Duke is coming home? Is that what this is all about?"

"I do not plan to bait the Duke. Marriage would be an easy way to feather my nest even more."

Alex moved to the table where the three men sat. "Mr. Wainwright, I presume?"

Wainwright looked him up and down, at his plain clothes and lack of finery, and he dismissed him accordingly.

"I do not know you, Sir. Don't bother me, or there will be a price to pay."

Four of Alex's men moved into the common area and took positions in the room. The men at the bar shuffled off to the side, realizing that something was about to occur. Even one of the men with Wainwright got up and moved.

Alex kept his voice low. "I would speak with you—in private. If you want your business to be discussed in front of these men, so be it, but I offered you privacy." Alex stared straight at his intended victim.

Wainwright looked around, assessing his situation. His men were obviously nervous, but the man's bravado would not allow him to back down. He stood and faced Alex. "I don't need no privacy to discuss anything with you."

Alex stepped closer to the man. "Allow me to introduce myself. I represent the Duke of Winterbourne. He is not happy with the information I have been gathering for him, and most of it involves you. I have charges to lay against you should your answers not be to my liking."

Wainwright laughed a little, but this response was one of surprise and dismay. How much did this man know, and how long had the Duke been watching him? "State your grievances. I have done nothing wrong. Then you will leave."

Alex handed him a written page with a list of his issues. "Perhaps this will refresh your memory. The constable is waiting for you on the front porch. You can go quietly with him to London to face these charges. I'm sure you will want to provide a reasonable explanation for the discrepancy in the funds."

London meant Newgate Prison with a Duke as his prosecutor; there was a tremor in Wainwright's hands, as Alex went on. "I believe you owe the Duke a hefty sum in back payments. You have systematically stolen from him and cheated his estate workers for years."

A sneer covered Wainwright's face. "You lie. You couldn't possibly have proof for such an accusation."

"The Duke makes no false accusations. It's all here in the records." Alex dumped several ledgers on the table in front of the man. He recognized them from those at his home.

A new look crossed his face, one of fear. Wainwright nodded and began to inch towards the front door. Suddenly, he bolted. His legs took him to the side door, and he wrenched it open, only to have it caught by the man moving behind him. Alex slammed the door in his face and turned him. "The side door was not an option." Wainwright swung at him, catching his cheek in a glancing blow. Alex turned aside quickly and threw several punches into the man's stomach, doubling him over. His right hand caught the man's chin in an uppercut, and Wainwright went down in a heap. Alex stood panting over him. When Wainwright didn't move, Alex grabbed him by his coat and hoisted him to his feet. Then he turned the man and grabbed him by his collar pushing him along to the front door. Wainwright's men stood in awe; not one moved to help him.

One of Alex's men opened the door, and the two men went out to greet the constable. "You have the material to hold him," said Alex. Another of Alex's men had gathered up the journals and documents from the table. At the constable's nod, Alex released him. Wainwright was still trying to recover his breath. "File the charges." With that, Alex walked from the porch towards his waiting horse. He had another appointment, and he was already late. The lady would not be pleased.

CHAPTER 5

Elizabeth chewed on her lip at the sight of the edifice that housed a dressmaker's establishment. It was in a poorer part of London, and the sign certainly had seen better days. Alex reached to help her from her horse, and she allowed him to lower her to the ground. She had opted for a riding garment that gave her some freedom of movement since she assumed there wouldn't be anyone from the ton to see her with the Duke's man. She could be wrong, so it was important to pay attention. A hat with netting surrounded her face, making her identification difficult. A quick glance around found no one of her acquaintance. Alex tied the reins of both mounts to the post and turned to her.

"Why are we stopping here?" Elizabeth asked.

Alex looked down at her. "Well, Duchess, I ruined an outfit of yours."

"I am not a duchess, nor will I ever be one."

"Consider it my pet name for you then. Elizabeth; this is a dressmaker's shop. I always pay my debts."

"People are staring at us." Elizabeth adjusted the veil of her hat lower and tapped her small foot. "You are not purchasing an outfit for me."

"Yes, I am." Her eyebrows lifted in a look of total disdain. Why had she agreed to this? Alex took her gently by the arm and guided her towards the door of the shop. "Marie will be waiting for us."

Elizabeth gave him a sharp look; he was bringing her to one of his floozy's places of business. He probably brought all of his lovebirds here. This would never do, so she drew herself up and stopped. "Take me home this instant."

Alex could feel his temper rise as he began to pull her towards the front door, and as she resisted, he turned on her angrily. "I can always pick you up and carry you in." He, too, set his feet. "You are going in there." Her hands came to her hips, and she challenged him with her body language and her flashing eyes. The foot traffic around them was light because of the time of the day, but the idea of being carried by any man left her cold. Her pointed chin went up, and she raised her hand and pushed him aside.

"Get out of my way, then, you uneducated lout." She walked daintily up the stairs and entered the small, working room. A dark-eyed woman with a soft smile met her. Alex followed her in closing the door behind him.

"Marie, this is Lady Elizabeth Weston, the one I spoke to you about. Lady Elizabeth, may I present Marie, an old friend and an excellent seamstress." He turned back to the woman. "We need an evening gown as quickly as possible. I believe I told you I ruined hers by closing a door on the train."

Marie smiled and curtsied to the petite woman who stood before her; she was not Alex's type at all. Elizabeth looked Marie up and down with a question in her eyes. A hesitant smile came to the woman's face, and she offered Elizabeth her hand. Elizabeth smiled. "It's a pleasure to meet you. I assume you know this lout in some fashion. He has forcibly brought me to you in a ridiculous attempt to make up for an accident that occurred at a ball last week. I do not need a new dress." Marie looked frantically at Alex to gauge his reaction.

The man's voice was firm. "The lady will have a new dress; that is not up for discussion." He turned to his unwilling companion. "I suggest you play along here and get something beautiful without a temper tantrum."

Alex watched the rigidity grow in her spine "Temper tantrum? You haven't seen a temper tantrum, and if I want to throw one, I will do so with or without your permission." She added in a disparaging manner, "You have the manners of a goat." That brought a quick smile to Marie's face, but she hid it again as Alex glared at her. Talk about putting a man in his place!

"What did you have in mind?" the woman asked Alex quietly. It was not often that a man spoke of his clothing demands.

Alex grimmaced. "Something that won't make her look like a giant squash with a small head sticking out."

The anger in Elizabeth's eyes caught him, and she turned on him. "Get. Out."

"Gladly, My Lady. But when I return, I want you to have selected a garment to replace the one that I ruined."

Elizabeth's eyes lit up in devilment as another thought crossed her mind. "Are you sure you can afford me?" she countered. "I have very expensive tastes."

"I can afford this garment." Under his breath, he muttered: "At least you will look like a woman. And don't do your hair in that tight bun, either."

"Perhaps you would like to come and style it for me." Elizabeth sashayed over to him, took him by his shoulders and turned his body away from her. Then she pushed on his back. "Go along, Alex. You are not needed here anymore." He didn't like being dismissed, but he wanted to get his debt paid, so he begrudgingly did as he was told, the bell on the door jangling behind him as he left. Elizabeth turned to Marie and said pointedly: "You don't look like a man's plaything."

"I am no man's doxy if that's what you are suggesting. Alex and I are old friends from the war. The man spirited me and my family out of France in the bitter days at the end. Without him, I wouldn't be here. My husband and I and our children are extremely grateful."

A frown crossed Elizabeth's face. "So, he's not your—your…"

"Paramour? No, my lady. Alex had other ladybirds I am sure, but I was not one of them."

Elizabeth's eyes moved to the bolts of fabric that lay on the tables around her. Perhaps it was time to give in gracefully. "Let's see what you can do with me, then." A smile lit her small face, and she reached out for the woman's hands. "I have a story to impart to you, one that you can appreciate", and Elizabeth told the tale of her efforts to resist the entanglements of marriage. 'If you make me too beautiful, my attempts to become my own person will fail."

"Perhaps you can wear the gown only for Alex then. He is a man used to having his own way, and he will not settle for a garment that is unflattering to you, nor would I. My reputation may be on the line."

"Then we will have to be devious." The two women put their heads together, and the dress design became a reality.

Alex cooled his heels in the local tavern across from the shop. He had no idea what was going on between the two women, but he trusted Marie's instincts with clothing. If Elizabeth wore her gown, perhaps others in the area would begin to patronize Marie's shop. He needed to see the finished product, of course. That went without saying. The idea of having Elizabeth dress in the clothing he provided for her made him uncomfortable, but he wanted to see her at her best. He would write a draft to Marie and just have the cost filled in.

He saw the door to the shop open across the street, and Lady Elizabeth walked out, pulling on her gloves. The dress design inside the establishment was a knockout; the idea that only Alex would see her in it was appealing, but she had another plan at her fingertips. She had been invited to a masquerade in the coming days; perhaps she would don the outfit and wear a mask that denied the truth of who she was. That could be amusing, and she dearly wanted to see Alex's face when he saw her. It was not good for her to enjoy him as she did; he was not of her class, but since she planned never to marry, he was extremely appealing. Perhaps there could be a history between the two of them at some point in time far down the road.

Alex was beside her in seconds. "I hope you bought all the accessories to go with the gown. I am good for those as well."

"Oh, I did." She walked to her horse and waited for his help. He did not disappoint, helping her into the sidesaddle. She glanced down at him with a half-smile. He wondered what that was all about, and knowing women as he did, he knew he would find out at some point, but only when she was ready to tell him.

He mounted and rode beside her, taking the side streets of the city to avoid those she might know. She walked her horse sedately beside his and began to probe. "I understand that the Duke's land manager is now in jail." He didn't even glance at her. "And that there are now supplies reaching the working men on the estate—lots of them." Alex looked down. "The men couldn't believe how much the Duke was giving them, and I'm sure I have you to thank for this. Robert said that he was to see the Duke when the man arrived and might be moving into a new position. Your Lord must mean a great deal to you, and you must have a great deal of influence on him."

Now Alex looked at her and smiled. "I hope all was to your satisfaction."

"Not yet, but it is righting itself. I look forward to meeting this Duke of yours when he returns. I understand he is to be married shortly, at least, that's the word on the streets of London."

"Yes. His bride-to-be is coming to town this week." Lady Estelle would be staying at her brother's house. Alex would have to pay his respects to her as soon as she arrived. Their wedding had been months in the planning; to say he was looking forward to his arranged marriage would be a lie. It was a means to achieving a dream of his, to have money to build the horse complex that he wanted.

Estelle was not lacking in any department. She was very ladylike with skin of porcelain and beauty of face; she was considered witty and flirted well. She was popular in his circle of friends, yet Alex found her conversation to be limited to her own interests, and she had an uneducated perception of the world; discussion of the historical events of the day seemed to be beyond her. She lived to be worshipped, and her brother had allowed her the bevy of suitors that she craved before he came home. The Duke of Winterbourne's title and his wealth were two things in his favor for the marriage.

The papers had been signed; he would receive her marriage portion the day of the wedding, and it would be a good exchange. She would take over the care of his many holdings, be his charming hostess, and bear his children. He had already signed the bill of sale for the rich pasturelands that he so desperately needed to add to his estate. Once his own funds were transferred from banks abroad, he could pay for the land himself. But the sale had come up quickly, and he had to buy before someone else did. Her marriage portion would be the difference. If he couldn't pay, the land would be sold to the next bidder. He added, "The wedding has been one of long-standing."

The banns had been read in church; the event was less than one week away, and the entire ton would attend, including the Queen herself. His clothes had been sewn, and the event was a coveted invitation. The wedding lunch would seat five hundred guests at his London estate.

Alex came back to the present only to note tiny lines of dismay on Elizabeth's face. "Should I ask where the two of them met, or should I mind my own business. Marriages of the ton are probably far different from those that you know. The ton supports mainly business mergers; that's why I decided marriage was not for me."

"Yes, My Lady. I suppose that is so." Alex inwardly quailed; he wondered if she would get her desire to control her own wealth; somehow, he doubted it.

"Well, the Duke has my felicitations, I suppose. I think I have an invitation, and you are probably working on that day to see that all goes as planned." She paused as a smile graced her lips. "And are you taken with any woman?" Elizabeth thought that it would be such a loss—he was a good-looking, intelligent man, and he listened—qualities that were not often found in the male species.

Alex hesitated only for a moment. "I am, your Ladyship."

Elizabeth sighed aloud. "Well, any woman who would have you has my felicitations and my regards." She added under her breath, "And please don't tell her that you saw me naked." Alex's face colored at that reminder since he could once again see her explicitly in his mind. How did one forget what he had seen? She was perfection and the devil incarnate in one package. His eyes had been full of longing at that memory, and he hoped that Elizabeth hadn't seen it. He would be a man of honor.

Elizabeth had noticed his reaction. His attention to her on that day was a cross between lust and need, yet he had not acted on either of those inclinations. She wondered why he was so reserved. She might have been at his mercy.

The two quickly returned to her estate, and Alex set out for home. The dress would be delivered soon, and he was anxious to see the creation and the woman wearing it. He hoped to see her in it; he would see her in it. He could be circumspect.

CHAPTER 6

Alex was working in the fields just beyond the great house; the men were digging a new well to provide water to the fields. He was dirty and sweaty; he could hear a horse coming at a quick pace. Now what had gone wrong, he wondered. He looked up to see one of his best men leaning low over the horse, urging it to an even greater speed.

"Your Lordship." The demand was loud and menacing. "We have a problem." The horse skittered to stop within ten feet of him as his man jumped down.

"What is it?"

"I need to speak to you privately," the man said, his eyes glancing right and left at the men working with Alex. "It is very important."

Alex lowered his voice. This man had been assigned to watch out for Lady Elizabeth. Something must have occurred to bring him here at this pace. "Is it…"

"It is, My Lord." The two moved across the working area to a stand of trees before the man spoke again. "The Lady Elizabeth had a message early this afternoon. She immediately got her horse and cart and set off at some speed. I followed her for two miles, but she never let up on her pace. She obviously had been summoned, somewhere, and she was approaching your lands, My Lord. Did you send for her?"

Alex wrinkled his brow. "No, it wasn't I who sent for her, but I don't like the fact that she is out on her own. She took no one with her?"

"No, My Lord. She seemed upset though."

Alex quickly took the horse's reins. "Send a contingent of my closest men to follow me. Give them the best directions that you can. It could be nothing, but the lady has a penchant for danger. I need to make sure she is safe."

The man nodded and hurried through the field towards the stables of the Main House. Alex swung into the saddle and urged the animal back towards the road leading into his property. Had something happened to the workers that they had visited? Was Robert or his

32

family in difficulty? He had no idea, but he planned to wring the lady's neck for going without a guard. The roads were not safe in the area for an unaccompanied woman. He felt himself tense with the thoughts of what might happen to her.

Elizabeth crushed the note in her hand as she guided her horse and cart down the narrow lane at a rapid rate. She was incensed that the Duke was infringing on her friend's rights. She would see this Duke and level him. He was probably a stogy, old man with a flabby chin and a bloated body. She would set him on his heels. She became aware of three men on horseback ahead of her on the road, blocking her path. She did not care for the look of them. Noticing a smaller road to the right, she turned the horse's head suddenly and took it. The three men immediately raced after her, spurring their horses on to capture her. She looked behind to find them gaining. A narrow bridge lay ahead, and they would not be able to go past her and stop the horse's movement. She whipped the horse up to a faster speed and measured the side to side space on the narrow bridge in her mind. She could do this.

When Alex cleared the rise on the road to his property, the sight that met his eyes was concerning. The lady was forcing her horse and cart onto a narrow path with a wooden bridge ahead, the pond some four feet deep and underneath it. Three men were in hot pursuit, and they were obviously trying to stop her. What did they intend for her? Who were these men, now entering his property? He urged his horse to a faster speed, hoping to stop what he feared was an attempted abduction. He remembered the men in the inn, laughing about making Elizabeth marry and controlling her money. Why had that hair-brained woman even gone from her safe home that morning; he would lecture her until she finally understood her role in society. He urged his horse towards the three men, surprising them. One pulled up and turned his horse to flee, but the other two continued to follow Elizabeth onto the narrow path. The cart could barely fit between the railings of the bridge, and she was not slowing. She went onto the bridge, her horse's feet making steady staccato sounds on the wooden planks.

Alex caught the trailing man and knocked him from his horse onto the road. One down, one to go. He urged his horse to a greater speed. The man closest to the cart was now attempting to maneuver his horse so that he could jump onto the back of the cart. Elizabeth pulled up on the reins to slow the careening horse and cart, and the contraption shook from side to side in an uncontrollable manner. Elizabeth stood on the cart and turned to slash her whip at the man; the man uttered a cry of pain, jerked and fell from his horse.

"Elizabeth," Alex called. He yelled in the hopes of getting her to sit down. The cart was completely out of control, and he had no way of stopping it. "Elizabeth, sit down before you fall." He watched in horror as she lost her balance and tipped over the edge of the seat, clearing the bridge railing but falling the short distance into the freezing cold water below. The cart careened wildly between the sides of the narrow bridge and crashed through the right railing, breaking the leads and freeing the scared horse. It slowed and stumbled to a stop, quivering, its reins tangled about its feet.

Alex brought his horse to a quick standstill and peered over the broken railing into the water below. What he saw astounded him. Elizabeth stood, waist-deep in the water, covered in mud and leaves and streaming rivulets of water. Her heavy, wet dress clung to her, outlining her thin frame; it made her movement difficult at best. Her hair fell around her shoulders in dark, wet strands. When she glanced up and saw him looming over the broken railing above her, she shook her fist at him.

"YOU. I knew it had to be you." She sputtered for the correct words. "You owe me another dress." The feathers on her morning bonnet drooped onto her pale and scowling face as she raged at him.

Alex didn't know whether to laugh or to cry; she seemed to be uninjured. He dismounted and hurled his body from the edge of the bridge into the cold water, sloshing to her and reaching for her hand. Her irate eyes followed his every movement. "What were you trying to do, Sir? Drown me?" She looked from right to left for the others. "Where are your other men?"

Alex reached her and took Elizabeth's sagging bonnet off her head, sweeping the wet hair from her face before grasping her hand to steady her in the pond. "They weren't my men. They were after you. Why were you riding on the Duke's property again without protection? Did Robert send for you?"

Elizabeth jerked her hand away from his and pointed her finger in his face. "You dare not remove him or his family from the land in the Duke's name, or the Duke will answer to me."

Alex was taken aback. "I had no intention of doing so."

"It was all in the missive I received this morning. The Duke planned to send Robert and his fellow workers away as early as this afternoon. I had to come to talk with Robert, and I will demand to see your Duke at the earliest possible convenience. When will he be at his estate? I have many words for him; I cannot believe that he has the balls to do such a thing to Robert and those who work for him. I have heard of his Lordship's shady dealings."

Shady dealings? Alex was astonished at her vehement words about him. What did Elizabeth know? The man reined himself in and asked for the note. She fished around in the water for her reticule and pulled the soggy vellum forth. "See for yourself." She thrust it under his very nose.

He took the note and scanned its watery contents. It did appear as she had said, an order signed by the Duke for Robert and his men to vacate their properties. There was only one problem—the signature was not his, but she didn't know he was the Duke, so discounting it would not be a smart thing to do.

"I do owe you yet another dress." It was a vain attempt to change the subject, but she was having none of it.

"Help me out of this muck. I must see to the poor horse who was pulling the cart. There is also that man lying back there on the road. I suppose we must also see to his welfare." She climbed up the slippery bank with his help and began wringing out her heavy skirt. "Oh, the hell with this. Turn your head," she commanded. She watched as he did so with a puzzled look on his face, and then he heard the sound of ripping. In seconds, her wet petticoats lay in a tangle around her feet, and she stepped out in only the skirt of her outfit. Alex could think of nothing to say, so he wisely stayed quiet. But he was laughing inside.

The two of them climbed the slope of the pond and approached the bridge. The man before them didn't move. Alex took charge: "I'll see to him. You check your horse." Elizabeth nodded and plodded down the bed of the bridge, sloshing as she went. He heard her murmur softly to the horse to steady it. Then she was checking it for injuries. He should be checking her for injuries; he caught himself. That was not a place for his thoughts to go. He had to figure out who had written this missive and attributed it to the Duke. He reached for the man lying on the bridge. He nudged him over and shook him slightly. He determined the man was alive and then slapped his face to bring him around from his fall. The man moaned.

Alex grabbed the front of his shirt and whispered menacingly to him: "Why did you accost this lady?"

The man looked up into hard eyes and swallowed. "She's an heiress, ain't she? That's what Samuel said. "We was to get her and take her to him."

"And the name of the man who sent the missive that brought her from her house? Do you know?"

"Viscount Myers sent the letter. He said he was to marry the lady, and he'd give us a cut of her money when he got it. Ya ain't gonna lock me up, are ya?"

Alex became more menacing. "Did you know that the Viscount pretended to be the Duke of Winterbourne and falsified his signature? That's a hanging offense--to pretend to be someone you aren't."

"No, Sir, I didn't. Hal and me just needed some money, and this was an easy thing to do. How hard is it to kidnap a little lady?"

Alex smiled grimly as he glanced down the bridge to where Elizabeth stood, comforting the horse. "Yes, how hard could it be?" he replied. He pulled the man to his feet and pushed him in front of him. "We need to pick up your friend out there on the road." As Alex spoke, his own men rode up to him.

"Sir."

"Pick up that man back there and take this one as well. They are to be given to the watch and charged with kidnapping. I will come later to provide the details. In the meantime, send a rider to the main house at Winterbourne and tell Mrs. Knapp, the housekeeper to provide women's clothing in a small size to the Dowager House on the property. I, too, will need a change of clothes. Baths would also be welcome." Alex smelled like fish, and he knew that Elizabeth would as well. "We will arrive there shortly. Make haste." The men nodded and rode quickly away; Alex didn't want Elizabeth to seek any additional information about him.

As his men rode away, Alex turned and led his horse to Elizabeth and the cart horse. She turned as he came to her: "You will ride my horse, and I will ride the other since it has no saddle. We are going to go to the Duke's property. You need a change of clothes, and I do as well. The housekeeper at the main house will provide you with dry clothing.

Elizabeth was not be deterred. "I need to know about Robert and his family. We will go there as soon as we are dry."

"You have no fears there. Robert is fine for the present time. The message could be a fake; I certainly wouldn't act on behalf of the Duke until I ascertained that this is the Duke's will."

At Alex's words, Elizabeth adroitly changed the subject. "When will I get another new dress, Alex? You are systematically destroying my entire wardrobe. I have some ideas in mind for it." She smiled menacingly at him as he lifted her drenched body up into the saddle. He could smell wildflowers on her skin, and her body, even in the fishy, heavy ornate dress, was too close to his.

"Be careful of the horse; he has a mind of his own," Alex cautioned, struggling with her nearness. The statement was made for his own education.

Elizabeth's eyes sparkled down at him. "As do I," she replied as she took control of the horse. Taking a deep breath, Alex knew she had taken him in hand as well. It was not a good thought.

They arrived at the Dowager's House in half an hour. Elizabeth couldn't help the shivers that ran over her body from her drenching in the pond. Alex lifted her down from the animal, noting that her hands were blue and nearly frozen on the reins. "Let me help you," he said. His body held its own heat; he was like a furnace as he clasped her tightly to his own. He had to get her out of her clothes and quickly. They entered the house, finding their dry clothes already laid out; hot water was steaming in two tubs in the bedrooms above, just waiting for them according to one of his men at the doorway. Alex helped Elizabeth up the stairs, carrying her dry clothes with him. Pushing open the first bedroom door, he ushered her inside, and then he left her to go to his own room. As he pulled his wet shirt over his head and ditched his own hose and boots, he reminded himself to keep his hands to himself.

"Alex?" Her voice came from down the hall. "I need you."

His hands stopped undressing himself, and he dragged a wiping cloth over his wet torso and damp hair. His own clothes were still downstairs. What could she possibly need? He took a deep breath. "I'll be right there."

He padded down the hallway in his wet breeches and paused outside the door. Then he knocked tentatively. "Just come in," he heard her say in a waspish manner. What had he done now? Pushing the door open, the sight that met his eyes was stunning. She stood in her translucent shift, her heavy dress stuck at her waist, unable to move the material further down her body; the button hooks would not disengage. There were droplets of water on her chilled skin, and she still trembled with the cold. "I'm stuck in this rag."

Alex couldn't touch her, couldn't take the chance, but he also couldn't let her freeze to death. Swallowing hard, he crossed to her and turned her away from his sight, grasping the heavy material and ripping the buttons to pull it further down her soaked body. His bare chest came up against her as he attempted to take the dress from her. God—he had undressed women before. What was the problem now? His own body answered him, and he stepped back; the heavy dress finally fell in a wet pool all around her. Her shift covered little; it was as if it were painted on her skin, leaving nothing to his imagination. It reminded him of the first day he had seen her naked in the water. Elizabeth turned and looked directly at him, her nipples now pointed beneath the shift. "I need you to help me finish. The material is stuck to my skin."

The anguished words came from nowhere. "I can't."

"Can't what?" Elizabeth finally noticed where his eyes had fallen, and she began to understand his dilemma. "You've seen me before, Alex. It's just a body. You can close your eyes if you must."

"Really? That's kind of you." he intoned, his ingrained ducal heritage coming forth. The Duke was the man who responded to her suggestion. "Then you also won't mind if I enumerate what I want to do to you? I could manage any of those actions with my eyes closed; are you offering me carte blanche, Lady Elizabeth?"

Now her eyebrows shot up at his imperial tone, but she couldn't stop the corners of her mouth from smiling; he looked so out of control. Her own eyes meandered slowly down his naked torso, noting his arm muscles, chest and taut abdomen. His shoulders were broad, and his breathing somewhat uneven. Alex sensed another part of him was pushing to be freed of the wet material covering it. The odd thing was that Elizabeth appeared to appreciate his dilemma. What kind of a lady was she? Was she more seasoned than he thought?

"We do seem to find ourselves in a situation, don't we?" she offered, and she moved steps closer to him, almost as if daring him to act. She had to remind herself that he was not of her class, but she was tempted in her own way. But what could she offer him—money did not seem to be high on his list of needs. His peers would judge him unkindly on his high aspirations.

"Turn around." The command in Alex's voice was terse and domineering. She did so, turning her back to him once more, only to have him rip the shift from top to bottom from behind her. If she hadn't had her hands holding tightly to the front of it, it would have fallen to the floor. She heard him turn, and his footsteps moved quickly towards the bedroom door; it was wrenched open.

"Thank you," she muttered as she heard it slam shut. Several swear words rang out as those footsteps moved away. Now she smiled fully. There might be another course to be considered. She didn't want to marry; perhaps an affair of the heart would give the richness to her life that she was so sadly lacking. The cheval mirror in front of her showed her bared body as she dropped the torn shift to the floor. She wondered what Alex was doing...bathing, just like she would do, she supposed. She entertained the thought of going out that door and to him, but after his disturbing comments to her, she hesitated.

Another day, perhaps.

CHAPTER 7

Alex felt much better once he was bathed and out of his wet clothes, but that had been a close call. She was beguiling, seductive and innocent in her own way, and he was drawn to her; to say he wanted her was an understatement. Still, his life was laid out before him, his marriage less than a week away. His careful planning could not be undone by a small, unruly slip of a woman who wanted nothing to do with marriage or the careful constructs of society. Imagine a Duchess of his riding astride or swimming in the nude; it would not do. He would have to stay away from her until he married; that was all there was to it. Alex would have one of his men take her home as soon as she was ready. He would ride to see Robert to make sure he understood the threat to the two of them and to underscore that all concerns would go through him. If Robert had any questions, he was to seek Alex out to have them settled.

Alex dressed and hurried down the hall, stopping to tap at her bedroom door. "I'm going to Robert. One of my friends will see you home."

He heard water sloshing, and a sleepy voice replying through the heavy wooden door. "That will do. Make sure you tell him of my concerns though." Alex smiled; she was an over-caring, loyal little thing. Perhaps after he had been married for a time, he could see her again. She would be a free agent.

"Yes, Lady Elizabeth. I will do so. My man will be ready whenever you are." He heard no reply. "Don't go to sleep in the bath; you'll drown!"

Joyful laughter met his comment. "I promise you I will not; the water, however, is heavenly. Will you be at the masquerade ball in two days?"

Masquerade? Yes, he would, but his intended would be on his arm. Lady Estelle was arriving tomorrow, and he had already suggested that they attend the event. "I don't know. Perhaps."

"Thank you for your help even if you did destroy another of my creations. I shall look forward to its replacement. You will go broke dressing me." Now she did laugh out loud. "You had best go to Robert."

Alex thought of the ugly green garment that she had been wearing when she went into the pond. Her clothing choice remained ghastly. "Yes, My Lady." Without further ado, Alex turned and walked down the hall, wondering what was going on in Elizabeth's mind. He needed to stop wondering about her at all. She was not his concern—at least, not at the present time.

Lady Estelle had just climbed down from the coach that had brought her to London. It was Duke Alexander's coach, well-sprung with seats that were red velvet and plush as they could be. It had been a long trip, and she was tired. Her brother Henry met her at the door to his townhome, greeting her: "You've finally arrived. You were to be here three days ago. What happened?"

Estelle replied, "I was tired of traveling, so I stopped to visit some friends near Kensington. Our plans are basically in place, aren't they?" The two walked into the front parlor where they would not be overheard. Estelle untied her fetching bonnet and turned to her brother. "Well, are they in place? You have been able to put Alexander off on the final marriage contract settlements, haven't you?"

"I have. No moneys will be transferred until immediately after the marriage ceremony. But the man is getting bothersome. No one has seen him locally, so he must be holed up on his estate or still abroad just waiting for you and your influx of cash. The great man is about to brought down, Estelle. Father would be proud."

Estelle began to unbutton her traveling cloak. "Yes. I am ready for what lies ahead. The Duke has demanded that I attend a ball tomorrow evening, a masked one. Do you know of it?"

"Lord and Lady Caldwell are hosting it, and everyone who is someone will be there," Henry replied. "It will be the place to be seen."

"I'm not sure I want to be seen with Alexander at a gathering. It is becoming more and more difficult to appear to be the doting fiancée with him. I find him abrasive and controlling, so the less time I spend with him, the better I will like it. He has to be strung along, but I would like to limit the time I spend in his presence. He isn't truly in love with me, you know; oh, he likes me well enough, but he wants the money. I get his exalted name, some of his lesser estates, and his untarnished reputation—all things I can do without. Geoffrey, Lord Sinclair, is going to meet me at the ship in Cyprus when we arrive. Now there is a man I can love." She smiled.

"If it weren't for the vendetta between our families, I would be far away from here. I plan to beg off the affair tomorrow evening, but only after he has come to pick me up. We need to keep him guessing and in hot pursuit, now, don't we? I can't wait to see him brought low, his plans disrupted, his arrogance belittled."

Her brother answered her tartly. "We do need to keep him on his toes, and I won't mind helping you, but you need to bring him along. Let him arrive to fetch you, and I'll send him packing with some story." The man chuckled at the thought of the Duke of Winterbourne being sent away from his intended.

Alex glanced at himself in the mirror. He looked every inch the Duke of Winterbourne, his black coat, waistcoat, necktie, and black pants only softened by a pleated white shirt. He wore no jewels, only his ducal ring, as he didn't want to make a spectacle of himself at the masquerade. The ton was far too interested in his marriage affairs; there was little doubt of that. He had a mask that would alter his appearance a bit, but it would be removed during the festivities. Tonight, he would introduce his intended as the future Duchess of Winterbourne. He was looking forward to escorting her; it had been some time, and she was an attractive woman who knew how to act in polite society. Estelle had answered his brief note, asking him to arrive after nine to pick her up. She claimed she was looking forward to being with him once more. She was a very reserved woman who, thankfully, knew her place.

Imagine Alex's dismay when he arrived at the townhouse and learned that she was indisposed and unable to accompany him to the fete. She didn't even want him close to her in case she could be contagious. Illness was nothing to be sneezed at, but her protestations left Alex fuming. Her note had been delivered by a footman as he arrived at her brother's establishment, almost as if it was planned. Henry himself met the Duke at the door, invited him in, offered him a drink, and then expanded on his poor sister's illness. When Alex asked to speak with her, her brother demurred telling him Estelle would contact him as soon as she was well enough. Alexander then offered the use of his own physician, but the offer was politely refused. There was little that the Duke could say, so he left, assuring the man that he would be waiting for his intended's note. The Duke didn't see the smirk on Henry's face as he left the house.

Alex debated going home once again, but a small boy caught him as he exited the townhouse and handed him another note, this one from Lizzie, asking him to stop briefly at the Masked Ball if he could get away from his duties. What the devil could that be all about? A smile teased his mouth at the thought of being summoned; he was never summoned by anyone. He would certainly have to find out what she wanted. He urged the coachman to drive to the Masquerade. Thinking of their upcoming meeting put a smile on his face—what was she up to this time?

Elizabeth looked at herself in the mirror—the red satin dress was beautiful on her slender form. It draped enticingly around her breasts, only to fall in graceful lines to the floor; there was a slight train decorated with flashes of tiny seed pearls. The pearls also decorated the décolletage. The small sleeves accentuated her graceful arms., and she added long black gloves to the ensemble.

The red color highlighted the soft pink of her cheeks and the soft swell of her breasts. She pulled her hair from her face in curls, only allowing tendrils to soften her look. The red and black feathered and seeded mask hid her face, but her eyes blazed forth in a shimmer of green. No one would recognize her as the hideous woman known as Lady Elizabeth Weston. A complete siren stood in her shoes, and she wondered what Alex would have to say—that is, if he could get away long enough from his duties to see her. The grapevine twittered all day about the arrival of the Duke and his intended at the Ball, so she assumed that Alex might be on call. She wanted him to see her in this creation; it was, after all, his gift to her, and his friend had created it. She smiled as she thought of the bridge incident; now, he owed her yet another outfit from her dunking in the cold waters of the pond.

"That will do, Joanna," she said to her maid. "Fetch my wrap and tell the carriage that I am on my way." She picked up the invitation and slapped it against her hand. She would have to be careful that no one connected Lady Elizabeth Weston and the woman called Lizzie at the Ball. At least she would get to see the new Duke and perhaps even scold him for his betrayal of this retainers. She swept the train of the beautiful dress around her high-heeled shoes and began to plot in her head. She wanted a dance with Alex—looking as she did. She needed to see his reaction to her; in addition, she wanted him to kiss her at the ball. She wanted to feel his hard body against her own. Why, oh why, couldn't he be a man of her class. Then she mentally kicked herself. She had no desire to marry. She had less than two weeks to go before her dowry would belong to her to be used as she wished. But a moonlight kiss with a stunning man would not go amiss, would it? She could treasure its memory; Alex was memorable as a man.

Alex came through the gardens to reach the house. The music spilled from the venue, and there were carriages all around the hall. He stripped his ducal ring from his hand and swept silently into the corners of the ballroom, wearing his mask. He could not be recognized; he had sent a note to his host and hostess that Estelle and he would not be able to attend due to Estelle's illness. He steadied himself, looking for Lizzie. All he had to do was find the worst dressed woman here; then he could find out what she wanted and leave.

There was a strong swell to the left of him and a beautiful woman and man could be seen dancing the waltz. He turned to focus on the couple; they were the centers of everyone's attention, and he had to stretch his neck to see who they were. When the gentlemen and ladies surrounding the dance floor parted, he saw flashes of a stunning woman in a garnet red gown, her face covered by a feathered mask. The music stopped, the two curtsied and bowed, and there was spontaneous applause. The man led her to the side of the room as the men drooled over her.

Who was she?

Alex moved slowly towards the vision, stopping only a foot away. The sweet sound of her laugh met his ears, the scent of wildflowers filled the air, and soft green eyes met his own with a blatant invitation—this woman recognized him, and he instantly recognized her as well. Good God—it was Lizzie, her lithe body on display for all to see. His surprising need for her caught him unawares, and he reached out a hand, capturing hers—she seemed delighted to see him.

Elizabeth was sure it was Alex, even with his mask. The man pulled her close and whispered in her ear. "Lizzie Baggage. Is it truly you?"

His eyes wandered over her draped form, as his mouth curled into a seductive smile. "The dress is spectacular, but it is made all the better by the woman it embraces."

"Such words, Sir," she muttered coyly. Elizabeth pulled her hand from his; out loud, she said, "Do I know you, Sir?"

"I believe that you do, Madame. I believe I was promised a dance." He frowned at the men surrounding her. "I need to borrow this young woman for a little while. I promise I will return her." His protective words were not lost on the men who speculated as to who he might be.

"Sir, you can't take her from the dance floor," said one flustered gentleman.

"Oh, I can, and I will." He tucked her gloved hand beneath his own and walked her away from the group, glancing irritably at those who trailed behind. They finally took the hint and moved away, promising the charming lady that they would seek her out again.

Lizzie whispered to him: "You are making a scene, Alex. I know your employer is here, and I don't want to get you into difficulty." He looked as if he didn't understand. She went on. "The Duke. He is here with his intended, isn't he?"

"I believe they were to come; but I haven't seen them," he mumbled. Alex quickly turned her and opened a small door set into the side of the room. Pulling her along behind him, he climbed several stairs to another servant's hallway. There he rested, looking for a place where they could be alone. Spying an open room, he walked her into what was a private bedroom and closed the door behind him. Then he turned to look at her and pulled her in close. He whispered: "My God, Lizzie. You are beyond beautiful in that dress.

Elizabeth laughed. "Lizzie Baggage cleans up quite well, My Lord, does she not? Marie is an excellent seamstress. I will make sure to recommend her." Lizzie's breasts were tantalizingly near to him, and her breath was warm on his neck as she reached up and asked: "Why are we whispering? There's no one here."

"No, there is not." He was far too aware of the fact. He backed off and tried to get his mind around his own reaction to her. "So, this is the dress I promised you. I don't know what I was expecting, but you look magnificent. I do not care for the number of men's eyes that are watching you tonight."

Elizabeth smiled coyly and replied, "But you know I am not interested in anyone; you know that. I would like to waltz with you in this dress if you can find a way. It can be part of your repayment to me for the loss of my gown." He nodded, knowing already that it was a bad idea. What if he were recognized? She reached up to touch his cheek, but his eyes met hers straight on, and suddenly, his lips tasted hers. They parted under his assault, and he pulled her even closer to him; she could feel his hard body against her own, and her head swam with unexpected emotions. His tongue swept into her mouth; it was a feeling like no other she had ever had; she needed more. He sensed her capitulation to him, but it was a dangerous game that they played. A dance—that he could give her. But anything else was folly for them both.

"We will dance on the garden terrace in the moonlight," he said. She nodded her head, and he led her from the small room. They maneuvered themselves out onto the terrace. There was a sliver of a moon; the music of the string quartet could be heard faintly in the cool air. As the waltz began, she melted into his arms, and he moved her willingly along the terrace in the steps of the dance, her dress sweeping out, his body aligned with hers, his gaze on hers.

"This is sinful," she said.

"You are sinful, Lizzie Baggage. You make fools out of men, yet you are not as you seem, are you?"

She hesitated. "No, I am not." They moved even closer to each other. "You dance well, Alex. You should know that I come into my money in less than two weeks. Then, I can do what I please with whom I please." She was offering him a second invitation, but he couldn't act on it, nor could he tell her why.

"I wish I had the same path as you," he replied enigmatically, remembering his intended. His wedding was within the week, the Church secured, the guest list finalized, and the luncheon prepared for 500 guests. He would have a wife at his side to provide him with his heir, and he would finalize the money necessary for the lands he required to build the horse complex. All was ready—except his heart— it was singularly unengaged. This small woman caused him to hesitate, to rethink, and to reconsider the path he had planned for himself. His father would not be proud of his actions.

The music stopped as did their dancing motion; his eyes met hers one last time, and he reached down to kiss her. The world around him disappeared, as their breath mingled, the kiss becoming deeper. His tongue found the seam of her lips and she opened to him. It could have been seconds or minutes that they kissed before they broke apart. There could be no change for him, however. Lizzy touched his face and painted its contours with her fingertips; then she turned and melted into the shadows; she was gone before he knew it. He glanced around, but there had been no one on the Terrace to see them. At least he was safe in that.

CHAPTER 8

The last days ahead would be long ones, Alex knew. He needed to get his intended bride out in the public and introduce her formally to his closest friends and allies. John, the Earl of Essex, had met Lady Estelle, right before Alex had asked the lady to marry him. John approved of her to be Alex's future Countess. He felt she had the stature necessary for the position and wasn't that what Alex demanded—the perfect woman to grace his bed, his table, and his life? The idea wasn't nearly as grand as Alex had once thought—his thoughts were always turning to Lizzie Baggage. This waiting for things to unfold was killing him.

The contracts for the Horse Complex were ready; Alex made the arrangements to turn over the money from his intended's dowry just as soon as it arrived, but that money wouldn't be received until his wedding was finalized. Four more days. He was in an untenable position, but the land would be immediately sold to another if he failed to provide the funds on the given date. Alex determined to take his intended out and about. There was already some speculation about Estelle and the fact that she was not on his arm; when society talked, the rumors flew.

Elizabeth sailed forth very early on the next morning after the ball hoping that she had not been recognized at that affair. The news sheets were filled with descriptions of the staggering Masquerade Ball. A mysterious woman in red was mentioned, but there was nothing about a kiss on the terrace. The meeting of two strangers had been noted in the article—but Alex, too, had not been recognized. Their dance on the Terrace had been noted. It had been a magical moment for her, one that she would never forget. The kiss had not been noted; that was between the two of them.

Lizzie pulled out her boy's clothing, determined to go about in public to see what else she could learn. A trip to Marie's was also on the agenda. After all, Alex still owed her another outfit. The red dress hung discreetly in her closet; her new dress would have to outshine that one, and she wondered if Marie was up to the task. Pulling her hat lower on her head to cover her pinned locks, she swaggered to the courtyard to mount her horse. The doorman at her Uncle's gave her a wave as she turned to go.

Lizzie arrived at the small dress shop without incident. There were several barouches around, so she assumed the shop was busy today. She opened the door hesitantly only to find several ladies looking at the designs and material of the small dress establishment.

"I don't like this." A strident, unkind voice rang out in the room. "Take it away."

"But Lady Estelle, this is the finest French material to be had." Marie could be heard trying to sway the woman's thoughts. "It was sent especially for you."

The woman's face froze in a scowl. "It is my wedding dress, and you will make up what I choose. You overstep yourself, Woman. I wouldn't even be here if I hadn't agreed to allow you to design it. Your establishment is quite lacking in amenities."

A subdued Marie answered, "Yes, Miss."

"I like this material." Elizabeth glanced out of the corner of her eye at what Lady Estelle had selected. It was printed with gaudy flowers, almost see-through and very overdone; it glistened with diamond pieces. The woman would look like a walking mirror. Lady Estelle went on: "Make it out of this; I love it. You have my measurements. I'm done with this fitting."

"But you need to be remeasured Lady Estelle. I can make alterations, but I must have the dress fitted. Please, I want the gown to be perfect for you."

"You will make do. It must be ready on Sunday for the wedding. We can do any alterations there." The woman's thin mouth was pulled down, and she acted as if she wanted nothing more to do with her wedding dress. "The Duke will have to take what I like."

Elizabeth now guessed that this was the Duke of Winterbourne's bride-to-be; if so, she was not a very nice person. Somehow, Elizabeth was glad that the sharp-tongued vixen would be at the Duke's side. The two would match each other very well.

"I will do my best," Marie replied, but she looked very strained. She glanced at Elizabeth and recognized her through her boy's disguise; she offered her a tentative smile.

Lady Estelle flounced over to the side of the room and grabbed a finished gown off the rack. "I'm going to the fitting room to try on this delightful frock, though." The dress was a ball gown with sweeping skirts and a low décolletage. "This is far more to my liking. Come along, ladies." The blonde-haired beauty walked back to the fitting rooms with two of her lady friends.

Elizabeth caught Marie's hands and whispered: "She's a piece of work, isn't she?" and she chuckled at the relieved expression on Marie's face. The voices of the three in the fitting rooms were rather loud as they bickered over the look of the new dress. Their conversations were easily overheard.

"What is the status on your wedding, Estelle. Everyone is talking about the occasion. I'll bet you are excited," said one of the women in the back.

"It will be a grand affair." Estelle stopped, and then added with a laugh, "And it will host a huge surprise for the ton."

"What surprise?" asked the second woman. "Do tell."

"Ah, my dears." Estelle responded. "You will just have to go and watch the whole affair. I promise that you will be struck dumb at it all. The Duke will have a very surprising wedding day."

"What are you hinting at, Estelle?"

"I can say no more, Ladies. But the wedding will be like no other; that I can promise you. Help me into this dress at once." There was a flurry of activity and giggling in the room.

The two women listening outside looked at each other. "There is something wrong here, Lizzie." Marie spoke in low tones so that only Elizabeth could hear. "Lady Estelle has shown no interest in her own wedding gown, and now she tells the others of a 'surprise' at the affair. That is so strange; surely she understands that I can't make a dress fit without pinning it on her."

"I can help you with it, Marie. My body is slighter than hers, and I certainly don't share the bosom that she has, but I would be happy to stand as a mannequin for you. Did the Duke pick the material that you showed her?" Elizabeth really wanted to help the seamstress.

"He did, and I dare not disappoint him since he is paying for the wedding dress himself. The material was quite costly."

Elizabeth replied with a solution of her own. "Perhaps you could make up both dresses and take them to the church. That way, both of them have been served, and the Lady or the Duke can choose at that time. The Duke will just have to deal with it."

Marie looked thoughtful. "What a wonderful idea. Thank you, Lizzie. That would be far less stressful for me." Marie looked at the 'lad' in front of her. "We'll have to wait until they leave, but I would like your help." Lizzie nodded, as Marie went on. "By the way, why did you come today? Do you need help?"

Lizzie smiled brightly and clapped her hands. "I have another dress coming. Alex managed to drown me in a pond the other day."

"Drown you? What is that man thinking?"

"I know. What is it with that man and my dresses? I do have some ideas for the new one. And oh, Marie--everyone loved the red gown that I wore last evening. I made sure everyone knew that you were its creator." She paused, and a frown marred her face. "Marie, Alex can afford these outfits, can't he? I know he doesn't have a great deal of money...so if there is a problem, you must tell me."

Marie looked totally confused for a moment, but then said in a sweet voice, "Of course, he can afford it, or he wouldn't have offered." Marie was aware that Elizabeth did not know that Alex and the Duke were one in the same.

"Oh, that is a relief," Lizzie countered. "I do so like to see his face when he sees me dressed up appropriately. He can be a very demanding man."

An angry sound came from the woman exiting the fitting rooms. "Stop talking to that boy over there. I am a paying customer." The accusing voice cut through the conversation between Lizzie and Marie. Estelle flounced into the main room holding the dress she had tried on. "I'll take this one. It isn't nearly as nice as others I own, but I like the color. Put it on the Duke's bill." Marie nodded. "You, there. Boy! You will deliver this garment to this address, and don't damage it in any way and don't touch it. Make sure the wrap is around it." A paper with an address was thrust into Elizabeth's hands. "Make sure it is at this address in the next hour." Estelle left the small shop, without a backwards glance, chattering to her friends. As soon as she was gone, Lizzie broke out in peals of laughter, and Marie joined in.

Lizzie shook her head. "Don't worry, Marie. We can get to work on the gowns whenever you prefer. I feel sorry that you are forced to work for someone who doesn't appreciate the gowns you create." An assessing look came over Lizzie's face. "I will deliver this dress but only because it will bring money to you." She then picked up a quill and changed one of the numbers on the paper. "It will take me a little while though." She held up the paper. "The address is wrong. Imagine Estelle making a mistake like that." She smirked again, and then sobered instantly. "I said I would help you. Where would you like me?"

Lizzie stripped down, reminding Marie to measure a larger bust for the woman who had just left; Lizzie's body was trimmer in all areas. The two chatted amiably as Marie worked, taking measurements and draping the material over Lizzie's small body, pinning as she went. Elizabeth only glanced once in the mirror when the pinned wedding gown was lifted over her head—she was blown away by the look of the dress. Marie was correct; the Duke had exceptional taste. "It's beautiful," she breathed as Marie worked to take it in around her waist. She lingered over the mirror thinking that this was the only time she would see herself in a wedding gown. When Marie draped Estelle's chosen material over her, the dress was far too ornate and garish, meant to amplify the bosom; Estelle would look like a wanton, showcasing her wares to any who would buy; of course, that was only Lizzie's interpretation, and she did not have a favorable impression of Lady Estelle.

The two women moved on to select the material for Lizzie's new dress, a stunning light blue brocade that would accentuate her small form and beautiful hair and skin. Marie had been quick to find a pattern that they could use that would be innovative and fresh.

Lizzie left in the early afternoon, carrying the wrapped dress in front of her; Marie assured her she would continue the work on the wedding dresses. As she climbed on the back of her horse, Lizzie was looking forward to having an opportunity to see where Duke Winterbourne's wife-to-be resided. The horse broke into a delicious canter under her. Men had it so nice, she decided—no ridiculous side-saddles.

Alex spent the afternoon with his three best friends at the Swan and Trumpet, drinking well into the night with them. It was his last days as a free man. He had sent flowers around to his intended, and she had replied with a sweet note that said she still was not feeling well. She invited him to a small dinner at her brother's house in two days—only one day left before the wedding. Alex was beginning to feel shut out of her life, but the invitation did lift his spirits. He apologized to Michael and Jonas, who were to be his groomsmen for the wedding. Neither had met his intended, but both thought nothing of the situation; Alex, however, felt uncomfortable. He couldn't put his finger on why he felt that way. Something didn't feel right.

Estelle came into the library early that evening to meet with her brother and his two cohorts about the upcoming debacle; it was time to finalize the mission. The conversation about The Duke of Winterbourne commenced. "I'm going to make him a laughing stock. Alexander will be left standing at the altar when I don't appear. I'm sure it will be a stunning blow to his male pride. Imagine the expression on his face when he waits for me to come down the aisle in the sight of all his friends, and it doesn't happen." She laughed, and as she paced, she went on to detail the background of his fall from grace. His moneys were tied up in many ventures in Europe and the East, and he had entered into contract negotiations with several of the landed gentry to purchase tracts of land close to his estates. He did not have the ready cash for them; he had pledged Estelle's dowry money to purchase the lands. She, however, placed it into the marriage contract that he would not receive the notes until the two of them were officially wed, and she had no intention of meeting him at the Church. Imagine the guests, the gossip, the flow of information about how poor he was; in addition, he would lose the highly coveted lands that he desired to pursue his dream of breeding horses. The exalted man would be brought low— just as his father had driven Estelle's father into penury.

Estelle's mind revisited all that had gone before. Of the children in the family, she alone had held on to her dowry because it was inherited through her grandmother. Had it not been for that, Estelle, too, would have no dowry to offer any man. Her father's love of gambling had been hushed in the aristocratic community, but she and her brother had been made very aware of their reduced status. She had been assured that Alexander's father was the culprit, but she couldn't punish him; he was dead.

Estelle now sought revenge for the loss of her family's estates, and she had worked hard to bring Alexander up to speed, quickly accepting Alexander's offer of marriage. The man would find himself in the same position as she and her brother—ridiculed and shamed; he would suffer as she had for his father's deeds as she had suffered for hers. Both she and her brother had secured berths on a ship leaving London the very day she was to become Alexander's bride. Her dowry would go with her, and her new man was waiting in the wings.

Even though Estelle had been told that the old Duke of Winterbourne tried to stop her father's wagering, she gave it no countenance. When her father persisted in his gambling, the old Duke bought up as many of the man's vouchers as he could. She had been told that small sums of money had been returned to her mother to help with their small estate, but Estelle still felt slighted. Her father could not have been at fault in any way; he had blamed the Duke for enticing him into the games, and he had begged for his daughter's help. Now, the plans were in place to scapegoat the current Duke of Winterbourne by standing him up at the altar and destroying his dreams.

The delivery lad was shown by the butler into the main foyer of the town house and told to wait and not to touch anything. Estelle's dress was in his hands; Lizzie pulled her hat further down and smirked; he had no clue she was a woman. She could hear people talking loudly nearby, and when the Duke's name came up, she moved closer to the partially opened door to the library. Estelle was there with three other men. Lizzie looked around, and seeing no servants, she moved even closer. What she heard held her captive. Estelle was going to stand the Duke up; he was going to be shamed and shunned in front of the entire ton. Her tirade about his father went on and on, and her anger was palpable. Lizzie could no longer stand still and wait; she hung the dress on the doorframe and ran. She would have to get a message to Alex to warn the Duke, but she had no idea where Alex was. Her message couldn't fall into the wrong hands, so she decided to send it to Marie instead; someone had to do something, and it was obvious that Marie could get the information to Alex.

Duke Alexander visited his intended the very next day. She was sweet and willing, offering her cheek for him to kiss and expressing her delight at seeing him. Her brother served an impressive meal to the Duke, and the talk centered on the horse complex that Alexander coveted and the up and coming wedding. His bride-to-be was perfect, demure, sweet, and yielding to him. When he pushed her to come with him for a ride in the park to meet his friends before their wedding, she shyly explained that she needed to rest and be fitted for her gown. Surely, he could understand her reticence. She promised him that she would be delighted to do so at the wedding luncheon.

As he left, Estelle asked that they not see each other again until their wedding Day. She hinted that she was looking forward to spending time with him on her honeymoon, even allowing him to take charge of her mouth in an all-encompassing kiss; but she reiterated that packing and preparing for the wedding would take some time. He kissed her one last time and asked her to think about their upcoming wedding when she would be his wife in all ways. She looked down at the floor and smiled hesitantly, so he chose not to press her any more. He hoped that her reticence was just that of a maiden's fears. He would hate to have a frigid woman in his bed.

Inside, Estelle fumed. She couldn't stand his hands on her, and she had nearly gagged when he kissed her. She only wished that she could see the entire debacle, but she would be on her ship fleeing England by then.

Lizzie's note to come to her as humanly possible reached Marie. The wedding was only two days away. Instead of going to Marie's establishment, Elizabeth sent a carriage for her, asking her to her uncle's home and choosing to explain the visit as a dress-making consultation.

Marie arrived by noon, having closed her shop for the rest of the day. The two wedding dresses were hanging ready for the finishing touches. She had no idea why she had been sent for; she knew something terrible must have happened.

Elizabeth met Marie as soon as she was admitted, taking both of her hands. "Come in. Come in. We have a crisis, Marie, and I'm not sure what to do."

"What crisis? Is it the wedding dresses?" Marie responded. "I've been working on them every waking minute."

"Heavens, no. I must talk to you, and this may go no further. We both have to act. How do I get hold of Alex?"

"You don't. I believe my husband said he was leaving the city to visit his honeymoon estate in the next county. He won't be back until the wedding. Why do you ask?"

"When I went to deliver your dress to Lady Estelle, I overheard a conversation about the Duke. His intended, Lady Estelle, will not be at the wedding; she plans to sail from England early tomorrow morning and leave him standing at the altar."

The look on Marie's face spoke volumes. "I cannot believe that the Lady Estelle would do such a thing." She ran her hands through her hair. "I cannot go to his Lordship and accuse the Lady. We have no proof, other than your overheard conversation. Could you have gotten it wrong? Are you sure that this will happen?" That gave Elizabeth pause.

"No, I am not positive. But that is what she was saying. You know what that would do to the Duke and his credibility, don't you? The ton is an avaricious, self-serving entity, and I don't want Alex to be hurt because of his work for the Duke."

"I have no idea what to do to stop the whole thing. Duke Alexander wants to marry the Lady Estelle. It is what everyone has talked about for weeks. He has intimated as much to me. Are you sure, Lady Elizabeth."

"No, I am not. But something isn't right. I think we need to have a second plan in place in case the wedding is off. Who among the Duke's friends can we contact? Contingency plans could go a long way to staving off disaster," Lizzie said. "If I am wrong, then the wedding can just go on as scheduled. How far along are the dresses?"

"Both are nearly done. You have only to slip them on to make the final changes."

Lizzie sat down. "All right. I'm going to try to speak to one of the groomsmen. Their names are out there. If I cannot contact one of them, I'll come to you, and we will finish the designs. The problem will be when the Duke no longer has the funds to pay for his land. I will have to think about that."

Marie sat as well and took Lizzie's hands. "I think we are getting upset over nothing, but I will do as you ask. When you have a plan in place, call me and I'll bring both dresses for their fittings. I hope by then you discover that what you heard was wrong."

Lizzie replied, "I hope so as well. I'll ride to the Earl of Essex's townhouse and see if he will see me. I believe he is to stand for the Duke. Wish me luck, and the right words to make this all real."

Marie stopped her as she rose. "Go as Lady Elizabeth, please. I do not think you will be received as a lad." Lizzie nodded.

CHAPTER 9

The Earl of Essex could not believe the name on the calling card: it read Lady Elizabeth Weston. He knew of the lady and of the many stories surrounding her. Known to be standoffish and a very poor dresser and dancer, he had no idea of why she would be in his drawing room, waiting for an audience with him. She had come in her own conveyance with only a maid. He braced himself; something was amiss, and he hated to be taken unawares. His townhome was a single gentleman's establishment.

Then a thought struck him—the torn dress that he had thrown carelessly in a box in an alleyway to protect Alex. He had been told its tearing was an accident, that the train had been caught in a closed door. What if that wasn't the story? What if she had discovered his role in that strange affair? His shoulders slumped, and he had no idea how much he could say. His friend's plans were involved here, and he would be a party to who knows what. Alex had been known to 'sow his seeds' in the years of the war. What if he hadn't really changed? But then again, who would want this 'lady' as a lover? Nothing made sense.

John adjusted his cravat and straightened his shoulders. Then he walked slowly down the hallway from his study and turned towards the drawing room. "Lady Elizabeth. What an honor. What brings you to me this morning?" His heart was hammering like a drum.

The woman he addressed was walking agitatedly up and down the room, her ugly gray carriage dress dragging along the floor. There was too much dress, too much padding; the poor lady was overwhelmed with material as her poor maid crouched in a corner trying hard to be invisible. Elizabeth paused and pierced him with her green eyes. "Lord Essex. Thank you for seeing me on such short notice. I have come to speak with you about the Duke of Winterbourne." Surprise lit the man's face. Alex had done something; the Earl swallowed hard.

"What has he done, My Lady?" Deep down, he waited anxiously for her reply. What if the Duke had defiled the lady in some way?

What if he owed her marriage? The man had been distracted these last days, but John had placed the blame solely on the Duke's impending nuptials.

Lady Elizabeth went on: "I have news that will surprise you, and I need your help."

Oh God. Was she pregnant; could she know this quickly? He swallowed hard. "Granted, My Lady, if I can help in any way."

"May I sit?" she queried.

Appalled at his own lack of manners, John moved swiftly to offer her a seat. "Of course. Please." As she lowered herself and her awful outfit onto a side chair, John, too, sat—and waited for the axe to fall.

"I hardly know where to begin, Sir, so I'll just tell the tale and you can tell me what to do when I finish. Lord Winterbourne isn't here, is he?"

"No, Lady Weston. He is not. Is this about the dress?" he stammered thinking of the train and petticoats he had disposed of. "I can replace a dress." What was it about these men and dresses?

"You know about the dress?" Lizzie thought of the two completed wedding gowns that Marie now held. The Duke must have told the man who would stand for him of the creations.

"A little." The Earl did not meet her eyes as he spoke.

But she mustn't get distracted. Time was now the enemy to get things in place in case the worst happened. "Forget the dress for now. We can speak of it again." Elizabeth paused. "There is a plan afloat to hurt your friend, the Duke. I know you are to stand for him tomorrow at his wedding to Lady Estelle in the great Cathedral."

"Yes, that's true. The Queen herself is to attend."

"Well, Lady Estelle may beg off the wedding. She has said that she will leave the Duke standing at the altar and make him a laughing stock of the ton. Her money, of course, will go with her."

John's head snapped up. What was this woman really saying? "Estelle would never do that. The marriage banns have already been read, and the marriage contracts are completed. Why ever would she back out now?"

"It has something to do with retribution—her father and his father."

"Are you sure about this, My Lady? Who told you of this feud?"

Elizabeth looked down at the floor. "I overheard a conversation in a library when those in the discussion did not know I was present." She dared not tell him of her dressing often as a lad.

"How did you get into Lady Estelle's home?"

"I would rather not say. Just be aware that I did hear the lady and three of her friends, one her brother, discussing a plan. She has purchased tickets on a ship out of London early tomorrow morning. She will be gone before His Lordship can do a thing."

"You are saying she is running, and Alex will be left at the altar? You must be crazy. Who would turn down a great Duke with all his prestige and power?"

Lizzie's head came up, and her tone was harsh. "I might, given the right circumstances; it would all depend on the man. And if I am correct about the scheme? What then? Will you allow your friend to be so used?"

The Earl hesitated. "Tell me more. Why are you involved in this, My Lady?" the Earl asked suspiciously.

"I am protecting one of the Duke's men; he is a dear friend of mine, and any harm to the Duke will bring harm to him." She thought of Alex and his devotion to the Duke. "His livelihood could suffer if the Duke falls to this scheming woman. But I, too, will need some protection if I am to give my help, so you must explain the entire contract the Duke holds with Lady Estelle. If Lady Estelle comes to the church, all will be well. My friend will be protected as will yours. Will you agree to help me?"

John hesitated, only for a moment. "I will regale you with the terms of the marriage contract. The wedding must take place, or the Duke will suffer massive reversals in his plans to create a horse complex. He has given his word on the purchase of tracts of pasture land around his estate. The money is to be paid immediately upon his wedding. Lady Estelle's dowry money is to be used until the Duke's vouchers abroad are put back into his bank account. Then he could pay for them himself."

"So, if the Duke cannot pay these land vouchers, he will be kept from this endeavor; is that correct?"

"Yes, he has put a great deal of his own money into getting some of the land and the main building ready as well as in the new land contracts and the purchase of horseflesh. Others will be waiting to snap them up should he fail." He was beginning to see how the lack of a wedding could wound the Duke financially as well as socially.

Elizabeth pursed her lips. She had money to burn, but it was not in her control. "Here is my proposal. I can give the Duke the sums of money he needs to fulfill his contracts and more. But to do so, I will have to marry him; I am one week away from receiving my independence and fulfilling my father's will. I am not yet in control of my dowry." She paused as if thinking. "I need some assurances that I will have enough to fend for myself if the Duke takes the money and refuses to give it back. I have no assurance that he will return it, but I know he will not want to remain married to me. I myself have no desire for marriage."

John looked her up and down and understood her concern. He also knew Alex well enough to know that he would do the right thing; the lady would have her funds returned to her if Alex would consider an annulment.

Lady Weston went on: "I want you to be my insurance. Will you gift me a small tract of land and a house for five years and allow me a modest income should the Duke not return my money? You see, once I am wed, my money is his."

"So, you would marry the Duke in place of his intended to save a friend? How admirable," John said with surprise in his voice.

"I would, but only until the Duke could secure a annulment or a divorce. I know the Duke by reputation and through the eyes of my friend, but we have never met. I cannot sit by and allow him to be brought down by Lady Estelle for an old slight." She drew herself up and stared at Lord Essex. "What say you, Sir. Can we sign the papers tonight? They can be torn up if Estelle appears at her wedding. If the Duke returns my money, I will pay you for the inconvenience of this contract."

John thought he could see the lady tremble. She was trusting the Duke to restore what should be hers; her rescue of him could cost her everything. He admired her, and he would back her. It really was too bad she wasn't particularly good-looking. Alex needed the perfect woman, but he far preferred this one to the cold woman Alex was marrying. "I will see you have a modest sum upon which to live and a place to stay. Let me call my lawyer. You had best bring yours as well. I really don't feel that it will be necessary, however. Alex always knows what he is doing."

The two sat down and put their heads together.

Marie carried the two wedding dresses into one of the outer chambers at the church and looked for Lizzie. She said she would be there by 9:00. Estelle was to arrive at 10:00 for the final fittings of her dress. Her maid would then finish her hair and make-up. The church was filled with flowers—beautiful roses and white lilies were everywhere. There was no bride's bouquet to be found, however. That could pose a problem. Marie still felt that Estelle would come, but there was an unease in the beautifully decorated church. Guests were already beginning to arrive—to get the best seats at the elaborate affair, dropped off from their carriages, dressed in their finery. And the Duke, it was said, was already on the premises; he had stopped by to see Marie, letting her know how much he appreciated all her help.

Marie had to stop herself from telling Alex of the problem; what if Estelle showed up? What kind of a start to a marriage would that be. She settled herself and hoped that Lizzie would come soon.

Alex had checked out the church, and all was ready. His barouche was decorated with flowers, and the matching white horses had been well-groomed. His housekeeper was overseeing the luncheon at Winterbourne House, and Alex's lawyer had rechecked the papers required for the money transfers. John found him in the vestibule and greeted him: "I guess the groom is ready."

"I am more than ready. I don't like huge social gatherings."

"You look very nice in all your finery." Alex nodded. The bridegroom was in full dress wearing a dress coat, which was laced with white satin; a white vest; black pants; and dress boots. His hands were covered by white kid gloves, and a white cravat, carefully styled, circled his neck. He was very intense, second guessing his decision to marry Estelle. But he had committed to this undertaking, and he would follow it through. She was perfect Duchess for him, everything he thought a Duchess should be.

"I wish the ceremony were over. It feels like I haven't seen Estelle in months. Oh, I sent the bridal bouquet to my intended's house this morning; the delivery man said there was no one there, that the house was being boarded up as he arrived. I had the flowers delivered here instead. The bouquet is in the back. Could you see that Estelle gets it as soon as she comes in?"

A niggling doubt began to grow in Essex's head. Why would Estelle board up her home? His checks on the docks indicated that a boat had sailed at dawn for the Cyprus Islands, but he could not confirm any of those on board. Surely Estelle would arrive. "I'll see to it Alex. I may need to speak to you before the ceremony. If I do, it will be very important."

"We can talk later. This day has to be perfect," Alex responded. His dead father would be proud of him and of what he had accomplished. His mother, however, would not. She often complained about his singular view of what a true aristocrat's actions should be. But she had joined his father in death, so there was no one to take him to task.

Lizzie sneaked into the church by a side door, dressed like a boy. She had ridden her own horse and given it to one of her men to hold. She streaked down the corridor and ran smack into the Earl of Essex. "I say, watch where you are going, Lad."

John pulled the boy up and stared into Elizabeth's green eyes. Her hat had been knocked from her head, and her dark hair tumbled about her face. She looked very familiar. "I'm late; I have to go." She pulled out of his arms and zigzagged past him, leaving him with his mouth open. John struggled to come to grips with the slender, young woman who had left him behind. "Was that Lady Weston? It couldn't be, could it?"

Damn, Damn, Damn. Why did she have to run directly into the Earl of Essex? He would be scandalized at her behavior. Elizabeth flew into the last room on the left where she was to meet Marie. She wondered if Lady Estelle was already here. She hoped and prayed that she was. Otherwise, she was going to be a bride, something she swore she would never be—and her husband would be the infamous Duke of Winterbourne, a proud aristocratic prick of a man. She wouldn't be able to do anything but smile in her perfect dresses, and well, that 'other' thing, bearing his heir. She couldn't think about that. The divorce would happen.

"Is Estelle here?" she asked as she entered the room.

Marie turned and handed her the beautiful wedding gown. "No, and when the Duke's bridal bouquet was delivered to her home, no one was there. I'm afraid it is all going to happen as you said. Get your clothes off so I can fit the dress on you. We haven't much time."

Elizabeth turned as white as the garment she held. She couldn't do this.

CHAPTER 10

Something wasn't right—Alex could feel it. The church was filling rapidly with the ton of society. The queen's aisle had been marked, and the Episcopalian priest was getting dressed in his vestments. What had Alex forgotten to cause this unease? John had the wedding ring in his pocket, and the choir was performing a medley of appropriate hymns. It was going on twelve o'clock, nearly time for the wedding. He glanced out the doorway to the long aisle. Was Estelle there, waiting to begin her march?

At the back of the church, a panicked Elizabeth stood in the most divine creation she had ever worn; she was a vision in white. The gown was exquisite, following the lines of her body. The bridal bouquet was on the table, and Marie was ready to place the veil over her head. "What if the Duke stops the service? Lizzie asked. "What will I do. He will have to realize at some point that I am not the woman he thought would marry him."

"My Lady. I don't know what to tell you. Lord Essex said he would let him know that there would be some surprises for him, hoping to prepare him."

"Well, I am not prepared, and I think this is a silly thing to do. Has Alex been found yet? I would feel much better if I could just speak to him. He knows the Duke and how he will react. Why can't he be found?"

Marie looked guilty, but she said nothing. Lady Estelle still had not come. Elizabeth looked down the long aisle before her. Her uncle had been notified to come to the back of the vestibule as quickly as possible. She wondered what he would have to say. Of course, she would be married and to a very prominent member of society. Her uncle would love that.

Marie came to stand before her. "You look beautiful, My Lady, and this will all work out for the best. I'm sure of it."

"I wish I had your conviction. It is going to be a muddle, and I absolutely hate muddles, as you know. Well, maybe you don't know. Is he standing at the front yet? I'd like to see him before it all unfolds."

"No. No one has come out yet. Let me put on your veil."

"But then I won't be able to see him clearly." She sat down with a plop. "Maybe that's for the best though. Keep your eyes out for Alex. The monetary arrangements have been made; all should be well. If only Alex could be here; I know he could make me feel better about this undertaking."

Marie swallowed hard. "Something tells me he will not be far away, My Lady," she hedged. Marie gave her a weak smile wondering how Alex would react when he saw Lizzie before him. She hoped that Lord Essex had managed to warn Alex that there were great changes to occur. The wedding would not go as he had planned. There was a hush as the Queen entered the church and was ushered to her seat. Soft music played, and there was a great expectation in the congregation.

On the deck of the *Sweet Mary*, Lady Estelle leaned over the balustrade to view the water below. She was several hours out in the channel, and she hugged herself as the twelve o'clock hour came. How she wished she could be there to see the Duke struggle to make sense out of what was happening around him. She laughed, delightedly. Her friends would send her accounts of the wedding of the Century—or rather the debacle of the century. How Alexander would suffer. The perfectly correct lord would find himself mired in misery, in disgrace and in complete disarray. And even better, he would lose what he desired—his Horse Complex.

Geoffrey, Lord Sinclair, would meet her in Cyprus, and she would be a bride—the woman who walked away from a Duke; her dowry was safe with her; she would be wed to a Lord, and Alex couldn't touch her.

Elizabeth's uncle hurried to the back of the Church. "What is going on, Elizabeth? I don't understand."

She smiled at him. "I don't really either, but just escort me down the aisle if you will."

He looked solemnly at her. "Elizabeth? Do you know what you are doing?"

"Getting married to the Duke of Winterbourne." She looked at the hundreds of people sitting in the church. "There are certainly a great many people here, far more than I expected. I hope I don't fall on my face."

Her uncle's eyes widened as he took the time to really look at Elizabeth in her wedding finery, and to contemplate her words. "You look ravishing; why had I no idea of this wedding? The Duke never came to ask for your hand or to review your dowry. I thought he was going to marry Lady Estelle…" He broke off his statement, not wanting to upset his niece. "When did you meet the Duke?"

Lizzie chewed on her bottom lip. "I haven't really met him." Lizzie's thoughts went back to the first day, when she had splashed naked in the water before Alex, and he had yelled at her to get out of the lake and off the Duke's property.

She smiled up at her uncle. "Don't feel bad. You always wanted me to get married." She took his arm and kissed him on his cheek.

"This is highly irregular, you know," he stammered.

"I've always been highly irregular. Nothing has changed." Taking a deep breath and listening to the music, Lizzie began her march down the aisle.

Alex looked up, wondering why Baron Weston was with Lady Estelle. He felt a tug at his sleeve; John was staring at him intently. "Alex. You have to listen to me. There is going to be a surprise at this wedding. Lady Estelle backed out of the contracts. She has is not here, and she has left England."

Alex's wrinkled his brow, trying to get a better view of the lady in white coming towards him. "But she is coming towards me." Then Alex noted a disconnect—the bride was not buxom or of some stature; she was tiny and moved with a grace he thought he recognized. His entire body stiffened, and he turned towards his best man. "What are you saying, John. Spit it out!" He whispered it urgently.

"You are going to marry another lady instead of Lady Estelle. Your land vouchers have been covered by the new bride's dowry." The words slipped into Alex's mind, but he could not take in their meaning. It was Lizzie Baggage who was walking towards him, not Estelle. He stepped down to offer his hand to the dazzling lady in white. She was breathtaking lovely, her eyes downcast. "Elizabeth?" There was a question in her name. She nodded, and they moved as one to the Queen. Alex bowed low as Elizabeth curtseyed.

They turned together towards the altar before the bride managed to whisper, "Alex? Are you a proxy for the Duke?" Elizabeth's soft, mumbled words came to him. "Where is the Duke? I can't marry him if he isn't here."

Alex's eyes blazed directly down into hers. What kind of a game was she playing? "I AM THE DUKE. Why are you here, Lizzie?"

Lizzie nearly stumbled, but his hand caught her arm and steadied her. An intense anger swept through her; this man who stood before her—this man had played her for a fool. She had been willing to be bound in marriage to a man she didn't know, and it was all for Alex. Her body tensed, and he could sense her overwhelming rage. He leaned down and whispered into her ear, "Baggage, I don't know what is transpiring here, but we are surrounded by hundreds of people. Remember who you are, and do not make a scene."

She glared at him, wanting to stamp her foot down on his. "I do remember who I am, My Lord. I am nothing but a damned fool to have cared what happened to you," she whispered. She went forward to the altar, the ever-present shuffling and coughing of the congregation behind her. She did not look at him as she managed to say: "Tell me you are NOT the Duke."

Alex had to force himself not to react. Why was Elizabeth Weston here to marry him? Where was Estelle? Had the woman not wanted to be his bride? And why was Elizabeth so beautiful, so alluring? He noted that she was dressed in the material he had provided to Marie. Nothing made any sense. Without looking at her, he answered: "I cannot tell you something that is not true. I am the Duke." The priest gave them a look as they quietly bickered.

Alex caught the priest's eye and nodded for him to continue. The priest began the ceremony by blessing their joined hands and welcoming those who had come to be witnesses to the marriage. There was a murmur of surprise as the congregation realized something unusual was happening right before them. The Priest said the opening prayers, the candle was lit, the vows were intoned, and Elizabeth repeated them. Alex did the same. How long the service lasted, she had no idea. Alex helped her kneel and stand at the appropriate times; at the conclusion of the ceremony at the priest's admonishment "You may kiss the bride", Alex lifted her veil and kissed her fully on the lips.

That jolted Lizzie like nothing else in the service had. She brought her small heel down hard on his foot to show her dismay as he continued the kiss; he finally stepped back and threatened her with his searing look, but there was still confusion in his eyes. Alex accompanied her to church vestry to sign the marriage registry, and Lizzie angrily scribbled her name, as did Alex. Then the two of them turned and walked down the aisle of the great Cathedral to greet their well-wishers. No other words were spoken between the two. As she walked, her hand now held firmly in his, Elizabeth retreated deeply into herself and tamped down the rage she was feeling. She appeared to be a beautiful angel, a smile pasted on her face. Only her eyes were shooting daggers every time she looked at Alex.

Members of the elite society peopled the reception line. Lord Huntingdon kissed her on both her cheeks as she accepted his deepest congratulations. "Lady Weston, I mean, Duchess Winterbourne. You are a delight to the eyes. No wonder the Duke kept you from his friends. I have to admit, I am amazed to find the two of you together." She gave him a weak smile and thanked him.

A hard slap to Alex's back came from one of his other groomsmen. "You are a sly old dog, Winterbourne. She is the loveliest woman I think I have ever seen. I don't remember seeing her at the Balls leading up to this affair. I should have known you would ask her to marry you. Why didn't you tell us things had changed between Estelle and you? We never really liked her cold reserve, you know, so we are delighted that you picked up this little slip of woman who has some fire. Who knew what lay beneath all those hideous clothes." He caught his error quickly at Alex's dark look. "I beg your pardon, my Lady. I didn't really mean that." Lizzie had to catch her smile. "But it did leave the battlefield clear for you, my friend, didn't it? And you scored." The man caught himself again. "My humble apologies to the both of you."

Alex smiled tentatively as he waited for his bride's reaction. She didn't disappoint. "Picked up…little slip of a woman? Really, Lord Griffith. The Duke is true to his kind—a conniving man among men." Alex winced at the double entendre. But the consequent offerings of congratulations made him begin to relax. The ton thought that Lizzie was his chosen bride, and he wasn't about to tell them any differently. For now, Elizabeth played her part. It wouldn't last, and he hoped she didn't explode before the festivities were over. She was entirely capable of it, he knew. The entire aristocracy had turned out to officially welcome him back to his estates and to greet his chosen bride.

John gave him a tight nod from the front door, and Alex pulled Elizabeth to him. "We must give our farewells to the Queen, Elizabeth." He nudged her toward the open church doors where the Queen sat waiting in her carriage.

Elizabeth muttered under her breath, "Yes, let's say goodbye to the Queen, and then I can ditch this fiasco."

Alex grasped her arm firmly, and his voice became stern. "You are going nowhere, Baggage. This will all sort itself out, I am sure. You are just as dismayed as am I. We need to talk."

Lizzie turned to face him, her eyes now flashing. "Oh no, My Lord." She gave him a devastating smile and a nod of her head.; those around them thought them in love. "I stepped into this willingly, hoping to save a dear friend from damage. But my friend didn't need rescuing at all. He was a DUKE. Imagine that." Her acidic comments were not lost on him.

They said their goodbyes to the Queen and thanked her for coming to grace the ceremony. The Queen embraced Elizabeth, whispering her approval. She offered Alex the back of her hand for a kiss. As Alex walked Lizzie carefully to his waiting carriage, there was a flurry of flower petals around them. He helped Lizzie into the conveyance and told her to smile as well as to wave. Unwilling to meet the eyes of those around her, she looked shy and demure; the people were watching the two of them, sensing a commitment. The ton would wait for that with baited breath.

Alex could hear the warm comments about her person; the ton seemed to love and accept her as the new Duchess of Winterbourne. Her credentials certainly were stellar, but the woman was an enigma. As he climbed into the carriage, it began to move. He reached for her ice-cold hand and she tried to pull it sharply from him. The Duke inside him responded, catching her small shoulders and dragging her into his embrace, kissing her with passion. There was a roaring from the people on the streets and catcalls. Lizzie recovered her composure after his onslaught and looked for a distraction—any distraction. Glancing down at the ragged children along their route, she nudged him: "You need to throw coins, Alex. They deserve something for coming to see you wed." His compassionate lady—he immediately reached into his pocket and threw the change that he had.

"Michaels. Are there other bags of coins there? I thought I ordered them." The man nodded and handed several sacks to him. Alex opened them and began to pepper the crowd with coin. They cheered even more, and Elizabeth threw her coins to the little ones who stood along the roadside. They were so sweet. She felt like another being—why couldn't she have married Alex, the man? No—Alex had to be the great Duke of Winterbourne. He had allowed her to believe he was the Duke's man. This was all such a mess. What she wouldn't give for a wild ride on her favorite mount this very moment. She glanced sideways watching her husband wave as the carriage moved forward. He might put her aside if she asked him nicely. His vouchers would now be paid by her dowry, and Alex would have his dream. What need of her could the Duke now have?

But what of her dream—independence? What a ninny she was. She must halt the night that lay ahead if she were to get away; Lizzie began to plot as soon as the wedding luncheon began. She didn't notice her husband's eyes on her as her thoughts ran circles in her head. Alex needed to know how all this had come to pass and what the Lady's intentions were in the coming days ahead. He could not just dissolve the marriage; surely, she knew that. Why had he never seen what a beautiful woman Lizzie was? Or had he, and because of his engagement to Estelle, just not allowed it to register? She challenged him in every way.

The naked woman that he coveted in the lake was now his for the taking. It was a strange turn of events.

Lord Essex met him at the steps of Winterbourne Manor and welcomed him home. He whispered in Alex's ear that he had to speak with him as soon as possible. Alex nodded and escorted his lady into the great hall. Elizabeth had never been inside the Townhouse before. It was a grand place, beautifully decorated, if a bit ornate for her, and kept nicely. The entire staff welcomed her, and small bouquets of flowers were placed in her hands until she could hold no more. A maid took them from her as Alex led her to bride's table. He pulled out her chair, seated her, and filled her glass with wine. When the other guests were seated, Alex rose to toast his bride. It was beautifully done, and she colored with his praise. She raised her glass and drank deeply.

She uttered under her breath: "This is such a farce." She kicked his leg hard under the table in retribution. He jerked, but he maintained his smile.

"Be careful, Baggage." he whispered back. "I'm making notes on all your missteps."

Angry eyes boldly met his. "You would—you are an arrogant oaf. The only misstep here is your lie to me. I, too, am making notes." She dropped her napkin onto her lap and grabbed a roll.

"Is that a threat, My Lady?" His voice had taken on that menacing tone that men used to browbeat women. He speared a piece of ham.

Lizzie smirked back at him. "You don't scare me, LORD WINTERBOURNE, so just back off. This little one has claws, and you will soon feel them." She savagely buttered the roll.

"I am counting on that, My Lady. It is part of the foreplay to intimacy." Her knife tumbled to the floor making a huge clanking sound.

Her head swung around so quickly that she almost lost her balance on her chair. His smile said he knew he had upended her. "It takes two, My Lord, and I will be an unwilling bride. Don't forget that." She reached once again for her wine.

Alex looked away. She had every right to be angry with him, and it would take some time to bring her around. He would do it, though; she had to know that. He could not undo what had transpired. She was bound to him. Estelle was his past; this woman was his future.

They both reached for the same piece of wedding cake that was being passed among the guests. Their fingers collided, and Elizabeth jumped back. "Allow me," Alex said, and he held a tiny piece of the delicacy near her mouth. She could feel the stares of the guests around them; her heart began to beat more quickly, but she dutifully opened her mouth. His smile blazed at her as he put the piece in. She was caught in his mesmerizing stare. "Would you like more?" he asked. Elizabeth shook her head no, but she couldn't break eye contact with him. What was it about him?

After pushing the food around on her plate for most of the meal, Lizzie stood and spoke to Alex. "I have need of the retiring room, Sir.

I would like to remove my veil before we finish the sweets that were prepared. Are we staying here for tonight or leaving for our honeymoon later today?" Several of the guests looked at them as they overheard part of their conversation. Noticing the attention, Elizabeth laughed softly. "You did say you would surprise me." Her hand went to his chest as she spoke, the first time she had reached out to touch him. Alex found he liked her touch. The ladies went back to their personal conversations with smiles on their faces. He knew he had to talk with John as soon as he could, but his concern for Lizzie was centerstage. She was too quiet; was she in flight mode? She was his wife. He would stop her.

"I'll escort you."

"NO." The word was almost shouted. Then she relaxed and said more sedately, "I will be fine. Just show me the way." When his eyebrow went up, she added, "I won't be long."

The woman was going to run; he knew it, and he couldn't allow it to happen. "Don't you run from me, Lizzie Baggage. I will come after you. We can iron all of this out as soon as the luncheon is over. Promise me you will stay."

Lizzie moved from foot to foot considering his words. She knew he would come after her; his protective nature would not allow her to evade him for long. "I will consider staying until all the guests leave. Then you will have little or no need for me, and I will go. Is that understood? I also want you to tell me why you lied to me and led me on. You were no Duke when we were together."

"Ah, Lizzie, but I was, and there is nothing I can do about it. We will discuss it later. The room is down the hall and to your left. Go."

She swung around and fled, disappearing from the room. Alex felt himself relax for the first time all day. He could sue his intended for breach of contract, but he might have to take her back, and that, he could not do. He would not deny that he had called off the wedding to her and that she had left England. She probably would not come back, but he needed to know more of the story as to why she had gone; he wondered if she was meeting a man somewhere. If so, he could call that gentleman out, but he had no desire to do so. He found he no longer desired Estelle in any way. It was Lizzie who stirred his blood. Their weeks together had done something to him.

"Alex. Do you have a few minutes to talk? I want to explain what has happened here." John caught his sleeve.

"Tell the tale as briefly as you can." John explained Elizabeth's visit to his home, the tale of his intended and her brother's revenge and her suggestions to save the land sales for his horse farm. That would require some digging on Alex's part; he did not understand Estelle's tale, and why had Lizzie jumped the Duke's defense? John finished with: "Lady Elizabeth is so upset, Alex? What did you do to her?"

"I'm afraid I left the lady under the impression that I worked for the Duke, not that I was the Duke. I'm not sure she will ever forgive me for that deception."

"When Elizabeth saw you in the Church, she knew that you lied to her, and yet she went through with the ceremony anyway. She could just have walked out of the Church had she chosen."

Alex thought out loud. "But Lizzie would have destroyed my honor and my reputation. The ton expected a society wedding, and she gave them one."

"Her dowry is now yours, Alex. All of the sales were covered. The lady is immensely rich according to your lawyers."

"The dowry is not mine until I take the woman to bed. Only then will the marriage be complete, and that deed still lies ahead." He looked down the hall again. "I need to see that she has not run. I'll be right back, and should I have to leave, you will make my excuses to the guests that remain."

"What should I say?"

"Tell them I couldn't wait to lie with my lovely wife. That will have tongues wagging for the next couple of weeks."

"That really isn't Duke-like, Alex." John chewed on his lip and hoped the ton departed soon. He couldn't imagine himself telling that to the Grand Dames.

Alex laughed. "I will be forgiven by them. After all, I am the Duke." His mother would turn over in her grave if she heard him. Pride was one of her least likeable attributes in a man.

Alex hurried down the hall and then stopped, politely knocking on the retiring room door. There was no answer. He wondered how far from the ground the room window was—if he remembered correctly, it was not far. He pushed on the door, and he called her name.

"Elizabeth?" He heard movement inside and tapped. Pushing the door open, he could see that she was not in the room. A small piece of her wedding veil fluttered where it remained, caught on the window sill.

CHAPTER 11

The young girl in the retiring room jumped up at Lizzie's entrance. Her dress proclaimed who the woman was—the bride. "What may I do for you, Ma'am?" She curtsied to the Duchess.

Taken aback by the sight of her, Lizzie stammered. "I'm looking for some clothes for myself."

"The duchess's traveling dress would be upstairs, My Lady, in the Duke's rooms."

"That's not exactly what I meant." She thought quickly in her head. "I'm to go on an adventure with the Duke. We are stealing away from the nuptials. I need a boy's pants and shirt and shoes. Can you help me?" She looked to see how the young girl was taking the information; did she know Lizzie was running away? She would need help removing her dress because of the row of buttons in the back of it.

"An adventure. Really?" The girl's face lit up with excitement. "How romantic of the Duke." Lizzie thought of course, he would get credit for the plan. The girl stood. "I can help. I've been fixing my brother's clothes." Lizzie noted a sewing basket with clothes that needed repair. "I think they will do, Your Ladyship."

Lizzie brightened as the girl held them up. "Would you help me, then?"

"Oh yes, Your Ladyship." The girl turned Lizzie and began to undo the buttons at the back of her wedding dress, slipping them through the myriad of hooks. As the dress began to fall from her shoulders, Lizzie cast a look at the door; Alex would be coming soon. She had to get away. Grabbing the pants and shirt from the girl's hands, she quickly donned them. "I'm afraid my brother's shoes will be too big for you. Perhaps mine would do.

Lizzie could have kissed the girl. "Yes, please. I'll go out the window here. Is that one of the Duke's horses tied outside?"

"It is, Miss." Lizzie started to crawl out before she realized she was still wearing her bridal veil. It caught on the window casement. "Oh

Miss. I'm so sorry; it has ripped." The girl helped to extricate her, but there was a piece of the veil left on the window sill. "I will try to repair it, Miss. Honestly, I think I can."

"That would be lovely. And thank you. You have been of such service to me. I won't forget." Lizzie pushed herself completely through the window and dropped some five feet to the ground, grabbing the horse's reins. She jumped into the saddle, yelling over her shoulder. "Thank you, again."

"It was my pleasure, My Lady. Enjoy your adventure." Lizzie turned the horse and gave it its head. It thundered away from the Duke's home. Inside her own mind, she laughed; she had escaped.

As the girl moved to retrieve the piece of veil, a timid knock came on the door, and she heard the Duke's voice calling, "Elizabeth."

The girl arrived at the door, just as Alex pushed it open. "Sir? Your lady is already away on her great adventure." *Alex thought...great adventure? What was the daft girl talking about?*

"Where was she going? Do you know?"

"No, Sir, and I can't take sides in this. Having an adventure with one's lady is so romantic. I didn't think ye had it in you." The girl realized what she had said, and quickly covered her mouth. "I'm sorry, Sir. She has a good head start on you, and she has taken a horse."

Great, just great, Alex thought. "Thank you." *Now she was turning his life into a great adventure and turning his own staff against him if he didn't comply.*

The girl interrupted his thoughts. "I will tell you this. She has me brother's clothes. I never saw a Lady ride astride like that before. 'It was something else, Sir. Her ladyship is amazing."

Amazing? "Well she is something else, that's for sure," he replied drily. *Alex grimaced at the thought of his bride riding one of his horses astride in men's clothing. But it was so—Lizzie.*

His work was cut out for him. Alex grabbed Lord Essex and told him he was leaving the reception. Then, in a flash, he was gone. He managed to peel off his bridal clothes as he went opting for his work clothes, and he also said his goodbyes to the Grand Dames of the ton on the way out, suggesting he and his bride were having an adventure. While they scolded him for his impatience, they chuckled after him. Such a man.

Lizzie glanced over her shoulder, but there was no one following her. She had managed to get away. The clouds on the horizon were turning dark, and rain would be coming soon, even though she had had the sun on her wedding day. She crouched lower and urged the horse on. She had no idea where to go. If she went to her uncle's, he would quickly return her to her husband. She had no money and no food, and she was soon to be drenched. She thought of Robert's cottage. He would not be there since Alex had informed her that the Duke promoted him to land agent and offered him a house. At least the cottage would be a roof over her head, and it was getting darker as she rode. She didn't want the horse to fall; she turned its head towards the woods where the cottages lay.

Alex looked up at the sky; it was going to pour in a matter of an hour, and his bride was out there, somewhere running; he grabbed food from the wedding spread. He had no idea where she was going, but he was sure it would not be towards London. He knew she wouldn't go home either. He could only hope that she would use common sense and find shelter. But since when did Lizzie use common sense? He urged his horse on.

The rain began hitting Lizzie's face in big splashes. There was a rumble of thunder as well, and thank God, the cottage was close. She slowed the horse and trotted into the wooded area. She jumped down and pulled the animal into the stable. She could see that there had been repairs on the building, and it was stocked with hay and oats. She led the horse into one of the stalls. Even though she was now very wet herself, she rubbed the horse down and gave it food and water. She took off the saddle; it fell heavily to the floor, and she could not lift it over the fence railing. She pushed it to the side. The horse began to munch happily at the measure of oats. Lizzie looked longingly at the food.

She turned and walked into the small cottage, noting once again the number of repairs that had been done. The shutters were straight, the porch planks had been nailed down, and there was a new roof on the structure. Kindling wood was stacked on the front porch, so she gathered some to make a fire. She would be warm soon. She fed the fire until it blazed happily before her. As soon as its warmth reached her, she shed her shirt and breeches, standing only in her now translucent shift; she laid her clothes before the fire to dry. The only thing that was missing was food, and her stomach let her know she was hungry. She hadn't eaten much at the wedding luncheon. A blanket from the bed found its way around her shoulders, and she huddled in the rocking chair before the fireplace. She would not be a true wife today; a single tear slipped from her eye. Alex could annul the marriage if it weren't consummated, but what would that look like? The great Duke would be a laughing stock for his inability to bed his woman.

There was a crash of thunder that caused her to jump as she listened carefully to the rumbles echoing in the valley outside. The noise was unnerving, and Lizzie thought she heard something or someone outside the front door. She crossed to the closet where she knew a gun was hidden. Robert had shown it to her the first time she visited in case she ever had an emergency. It wasn't loaded, but an intruder wouldn't know that. She lifted it into her hands and held it pointed towards the cottage door. Men who were travelling were known to weather in the small, uninhabited cottages until they could continue their journeys. What if such a man were out there?

She heard the noise again. The front door pushed slowly open, and lightning streaked behind it; Alex stood outlined there. "Well. You've led me a merry chase." He looked around the small cottage. "So, this our adventure." His anger was controlled, but it was there, and so was he. Words failed her for the first time in her short life. He took in her weapon, but he never hesitated. "Planning on shooting me, Baggage?" Then he crossed into her space.

He reached down and gently removed the gun from her hands as she watched with wide eyes, her breathing erratic. He checked the weapon and noted that it was not loaded. "I think I'll take this for now. Where does it belong?"

She motioned with her chin to the cupboard. He walked to it and put it back; then he moved to shut the front door against the storm. Alex turned to her again, his back against the door, and a tremor shot through her. She was alone with her husband; he had, indeed, hunted her down.

"Take off your shift, Elizabeth." She froze at his command for seconds and then shook her head slowly back and forth. "Yes, Baggage. You won't warm up with it on—it's too wet."

She glanced down to see that her body was outlined clearly under the damp material. She pulled the blanket up to her chin. Swallowing hard, she commanded: "Turn your head, then."

Alex slowly turned and smiled when she couldn't see him. "Do it quickly, Lizzie." He didn't want her to have time to think.

"I have nothing to cover myself with but this blanket," she said frantically.

"Use a drying cloth and climb into bed." Elizabeth glanced towards the bed in the next room and swallowed. This was not going as planned. She did have a plan, didn't she?

"Where will you sleep?" she asked. He could hear her moving behind him, thankful that she was following his directions.

When he heard the bed creak and the sheets flutter, he answered her: "With you, of course. You are now my wife."

Lizzie was brave as she faced his back; she had climbed quickly into the bed and covered herself; his reply reminded her of her altered status. She spoke in a very loud tone and proclaimed her position: "We are not sleeping together, Alex. We have much to discuss before we can even consider such a thing. I would have those discussions now." She issued her ultimatum with some strength: "I want a divorce."

"Then it's a good thing you aren't in charge," he countered. He softened his tone. "Look Baggage, we can't divorce until we are truly married, can we? A discussion of what has happened will occur, but it will be at another time." He used a no-nonsense tone with her. "I'm going to make you some hot tea and give you some of the food I've brought. Then we can proceed."

"With what, may I ask?" Her tone was indignant as she rubbed her chilled hands together under the sheet. She was so hungry, but she wasn't sure for what—the man or the food.

Alex turned to see her sitting upright in the big bed. It was a sight, one that he had only imagined in his wildest dreams when he knew she was the woman who now wore his ring. The girl from the lake sat naked in his bed, the sheet pulled up as far as she could stretch it, and she was waiting. "What do you think I mean?" Her sudden intake of air was all he heard. Alex put water in the kettle and placed it over the fire. He sorted through the loose tea that he found in the house and prepared the leaves. "We won't have cream. I hope you don't mind. There might be some sugar."

Lizzie shook her head. Alex was worried about cream at a time like this? The man was insane, and what he was suggesting was even worse, that's if she really knew what he was suggesting. Her experience in these things didn't go far. She examined her predicament. She was sitting naked in a bed in a room with a very virile man who just happened to be her husband and a Duke, and he was worried about cream for her tea. Alex, in the meantime, had sorted through the foodstuffs that he had brought. There were some small cakes, slices of meat and cheese and some bread. He pulled a small tin plate from the sidebar and placed some of the food on it. Taking a deep breath, he turned to meet her eyes. "What say you, Lizzie? Is this not a grand adventure?"

She huffed in response and drew her line in the sand, as any maiden would: "You will not touch me, Alex or should I say, Lord Winterbourne?" Her chin came up a notch to make her point.

Silence swept the room, and then his voice filled it: "Oh, but I will, Lizzie." He pulled his own damp shirt over his head; his rippling arm and chest muscles were the only thing she could concentrate on; she had never really examined a man without his shirt except those working in the fields and that was at a distance. Alex's chest was covered in a dark patch of hair that went downward into a V in his breeches; she remembered it faintly from their precipitous climb down the tree.

"I will scream if you touch me," she threatened in a much softer voice, taken by the sight of him. She watched his strong hands as they went about the business of getting her food.

"Oh, I am planning on that, Lizzie. In fact, I will make that happen—many times before I'm done with you. I will welcome your screams of pleasure." His hands stopped filling the plate with food and turned to remove his boots and socks. He stood and walked to the fireplace, where he carefully reclaimed the kettle. His hands reached for a dainty porcelain cup, pouring hot water into it and putting in some of the sugar he had located, letting the tea steep for a minute or two. His hands cupped the vessel, and he said, "For you, My Lady." He was offering her something besides tea, but she wasn't quite sure what that something would be. She spoke without thinking.

"You mean to make me your wife tonight, don't you Alex? I've heard so many things from other women about that process."

"Forget what you've heard, Lizzie. You are mine now, and I would never let anything happen to you. I only want to pleasure you."

Lizzie took the teacup from his hands as if it were a snake that might bite her. She gathered it to her, the aroma teasing her famished senses. Only then did Alex release it. He turned and put slices of meat and cheese on the plate and some of the small cakes as well. The first sip of tea was heavenly, and the cakes looked sweet and sugary with nuts and honey. She ate hungrily and wiped her messy fingers on the bedsheet. Alex held up a piece of ham, and she took it in her mouth from his fingers, licking them as she did so.

He patronized her. "That's my girl."

Lizzie reacted by grabbing his hand and sucking on those fingers with some vigor and then biting one hard. Her tongue immediately soothed the bite as she teased him with her words. "I was hungry, and I didn't have anything to clean my fingers but the bedsheet. Your mouth was far better."

"So, sucking on my fingers before you bit me was all right?" She grinned impishly at him. "That shows you have some trust in me," he muttered. A tremor raced through her as she remembered Alex's lips on other parts of her body. What would happen if she just let go and experienced it all. Pleasure came from a man, but did that mean a woman could not contribute to it? Was she just a receptacle for his seed? Lizzie thought not; she would not allow it to be so.

Alex sat beside her on the bed and fed her another small piece of cheese and then another bite of ham. The room warmed as the fire blazed, and Alex continued to put small pieces of food in her mouth until she was finally full. She was mesmerized by his patience with her. The teacup was placed in her small hand, and she sipped daintily at it as if they were supping in a dining room. The two of them shared the intimacy of being together. Lizzie's body finally relaxed, feeling warm and soft again. What was Alex doing? Why didn't he plunder her as men were wont to do according to the romance novels she read? Of course, once the hero and heroine kissed, the chapter ended, so she wasn't sure she would know if she were 'plundered'. Alex should touch her, and she should be able to touch him. She felt better once she had decided that for herself.

Alex swept away the dark curls around her face with his hands and held her face still; then he leaned into her and kissed her upturned lips, nipping at them to open for him. "Lizzie Baggage. What am I to do with you?"

"Throw me back into the lake where you found me, Sir. I will never be the Duchess you want. I am too undisciplined and wild." Her tortured eyes caught at him. Even as Lizzie spoke, she found that she wanted to please this man. Perhaps she could give Alex her body and learn his, and then she could leave him to find his perfect Duchess. She would know what other married women spoke about in hushed tones.

Alex claimed his kiss, drawing her tongue and breath into his mouth as she melted into him. He pulled her small body up as he came down to meet her, and her tight-tipped breasts brushed along his naked chest drawing a deep moan from him. Still, his kiss went on, pulling her deeper under his spell. A strong feeling of need overcame her, and she moved restlessly in his arms. Surely, there was more to this joining of a man and a woman. This was her one chance to find out.

Lizzie pulled back and whispered in his ear: "I think I have changed my mind, Lord Winterbourne. I will scream if you don't do something to ease this ache inside me." Alex chuckled softly at her words. He had guessed there was deep passion within her because of the way she embraced life. Her uninhibited responses to him gave him hope for their future together. "But I seek Alex, not the Duke. Do you think that can happen?"

"Yes, Baggage. I think that can happen."

The Duke was far from a beginner in the bedroom. He craved the scent of wildflowers that came from her skin and the softness of her hair as he ran it through his fingers. It was easily bunched in his hands; he could control her sexual responses, and he was already growing hard. A sudden thought struck him—what if he were her first lover? Her lifestyle seemed free of temptation, but she was an enigma in all things. It wouldn't do to hurt her as he initiated her into the world of pleasure.

His lips moved slowly down her neck in small love bites, and he pushed the sheet aside helping her to lie down on the bed. She lay under his sight, not trying to hide her body. The world around her melted away until there was only the feel of his lips and hands and body on her own. Her skin grew tight and her nipples pebbled under his expert touch. Her body wept for him as her hands plucked at his hair, and her voice called out his name. Alex responded by sucking a nipple deep into his mouth and pulling hard; her body jolted, and her small cry was his reward.

There was no way for him to stop now. His body needed hers more than air, and she would be his. Lizzie's hands eagerly pushed at his breeches, searching for his warm skin. He stilled them and got off the bed, releasing his breeches and smalls and pushing them to the floor. In the firelight, she could see his chiseled body. He had wide shoulders and narrow hips, but what really caught her attention were his manly attributes. She drew in a lungful of air. He would never fit that inside her. She was a small woman. Alex felt her hesitation and slowed his pace.

"What is it, Baggage? What are you afraid of?" He placed his body over hers again, his hips now pushing to ease open her long legs, and he gently pressed his body down on her woman's mound. She could feel his manhood growing on top of her, and he felt enormous and very hard. His hands skirted the tops of her long legs with careful, circular touches and he touched her intimately.

A sobbing sound came from her lips: "Alex. I want to explore you. Now, please." She craved the feel of his skin, and her lips licked at his chest in the very spot that covered his heart.

Alex couldn't believe his luck. No aristocratic woman would be so free in her quest. He guided her hands to his length, brushing her fingers over him as he calmed her. At the same time, he thrust one of his own fingers deep inside her body. Her response was pure delight; she quivered under him; her muscles grew rigid, and her breathing strained. She was ungodly tight; there was no more question about her being with another man, but it posed a problem for him. He was sure to hurt her the first time with his size. He moved his finger slowly in and out, touching as many nerves as he could to prepare her for his entry. She relaxed, and her small hands continued to explore him; he was able to slip another finger deep inside her. She still mapped him with her uneducated fingers, stroking more firmly up and down along his flesh—feeling his girth and length. It was sheer torture to him, and he wouldn't last if she kept it up. He would explode if he didn't take her soon.

"Baggage. You'll unman me if you keep that up. I need to be inside you," he said.

Her wandering hands hesitated. "Inside me? You need to be inside me? What's stopping you, Alex?" Her posed question released the tight hold he had kept on himself. He placed himself at her tight opening and pushed forward. His head swooped, and his lips kissed her breasts. She cried out again in sheer pleasure, moving her own lips to kiss his body. As he moved further inside her, he shifted his hips to give him more maneuvering room between her splayed legs. She relaxed even more into his advances, concentrating on the flat planes of his stomach.

Her uttered words stung him into greater action: "Not enough, Sir."

"You're a demanding little thing," he replied.

"Oh yes, I am, and I find this delightful. Let me help." Lizzie pulled his arms out from where they held his body up, forcing him further inside her narrow opening. There was a small, pained rush of air from her lips as he pushed relentlessly into her, completely filling her, and yet it still wasn't enough; she felt that she was teetering on the edge of something wonderful. He pulled out and pushed in carefully, moving even deeper into her warmth; he had never felt anything so glorious. Her sheathe gripped him firmly, her wetness giving him freer rein in his movements.

Alex tried to hold himself as his release threatened, and Lizzie twitched under him, her legs wrapping tightly around his waist as if to bind him to her. "Shouldn't we be doing something more? We seem to have reached an impasse, and I want—I want…I can't quite get there."

Her question caught him, and he almost laughed out loud. His body blazed with need, and he answered its call by pushing deeply inside her in a new hard thrust and moving rapidly in and out of her slick opening. 'Alex. Oh. Oh. What I feel…" Her words flowed over him like honey, as she tightened around him. "I never knew—" He shut her mouth with his kiss as her body peaked sharply and splintered into shards of intense feeling as she screamed; the ripples went on and on, leaving her limp in his arms. His body pressed in deeply one last time until he found his own relief, crying out her name.

The rain outside continued to fall. Lizzie Baggage rested within the loving arms of Alex or make that the Duke of Winterbourne. Who could have known?

CHAPTER 12

Alex woke slowly to a warm, willing, naked body sitting on top of him. He was on his back, and his new Duchess was actually sitting astride him, her legs tucked along his sides, her fingers carefully tracing his broad shoulders and his muscular chest. She moved cautiously; she didn't want to wake him, but she had forgotten his training as a soldier. No military man could sleep though her tactile exploration of his terrain. Another part of Alex's body rose spectacularly in reaction to her soft rub, and she was obviously trying to figure out the connection between the massaging of his chest and abdomen and the sharp erection that she had called to life. What in the blazes was the woman doing? She was such an innocent; she had no idea of what she did to him. He stayed as still as he could. Lizzie was very intent on mapping each part of his male anatomy; she didn't notice his measured concentration was now focused directly on her, even though his eyes remained closed.

Her finger lightly traced the muscular alignment of his shoulders, and her small hands then circled his upper arm. It took both of her hands to do it; such strength and power rested there. Then, they meandered through and tightened briefly on his nipples, resting in the mat of dark hair that covered his chest; she followed the hairline with her fingertips, down past his waist and belly button to his rigid manhood; she leaned backwards and placed a small kiss on that appendage and licked its mushroom head as a cat laps at cream. It was already damp with a pearly fluid and it tasted somewhat salty; the look on her face was intense as she took in all of him.

Lizzie thought that Alex's body was wonderful in its complexity without an ounce of fat anywhere. He was hard where she was soft; he had muscles where she had little definition. Her hands slowly danced back up his taut stomach causing him to jerk involuntarily. She hesitated a moment to see if he would awake, and when he didn't open his eyes, she carefully traced and caressed his thickening member with a sweet smile on her face. Each of her touches caused him to grow even harder as if that part of his body had a will of its own. Lizzie seemed fascinated by it, touching with more pressure to increase its rigidity. Surely it couldn't work that way.

This was the first time Lizzie had ever touched or held a man's body; why could men explore a woman's body, but men's bodies were off limits? Women knew so little of them. She had been told to give in to her husband's demands and to lie still and think of England as she performed her marriage duties. Lizzie chuckled softly at that advice— and miss all the fun? This must be a state secret to keep ladies from running amuck, seeking pleasure where they could find it. She flattened her body along his, and her tongue made its own path, reaching as far as she could to taste the rest of him. It was almost too much for the Duke.

When she moved to sit upright, her hands again caressed his chiseled pectorals; she was perched in a haphazard manner directly on his manhood, and her body was responding to her forward movement against him with a gush of wetness of its own. She wondered if she could place him inside her mouth, doing for him what he had done for her last night. How would he react?

Placing a small kiss on its tip, nibbling a bit, and then stopping to see if he was awake, she spread her legs wider and positioned him where she wanted him to be, directly beneath her. Alex managed to withhold his smile, but he moved slightly, too, to see what she would do. She guided his rigid manhood towards her opening.

Trying to readjust herself on his very naked form, she kissed the base of his throat and began to slowly impale herself on him. Her hair fell over her shoulders to brush his body, her sweet scent surrounded him, and her pointed breasts rubbed against his chest as she did so. Her sweet nether lips taking him in were far too much for Alex to withstand.

His arms came up around her, and he caught her to a squeal of dismay. He quickly rolled her onto her back and tucked her under him, reversing their positions. She now lay open to his demands. "What can I do for you, Lizzie Baggage," he said in a sleepy voice. He gave her a sultry kiss, and her tongue slipped into his mouth. Her arms wound up around his neck, and she pushed her small form tightly into him.

Breaking away from his lips for a moment, she said, "I want to taste you, Alex, as you have tasted me. It is such a wonderful sensation."

Alex hesitated. "Well, baggage, it is not something that *ladies* often do." Her raised eyebrow reminded him that she did not believe she was a lady.

"Why ever not? Men seem to enjoy doing it. I know I enjoy it when you do it to me."

Alex had no idea how to explain it all to her. "I suppose we could explore your request in private in the coming days." He proceeded to suck on her breast and her stomach, causing her to giggle and protest. He didn't want to tell her that ladies of ill repute put their mouths on a man; the marriage bed was usually another matter. But explore it, he would, especially with her.

"You must say nothing about this kissing to your lady friends, Baggage. We must be agreed on that." Alex could just imagine how the ton would react to his wanton wife's stories of what he did to her, and she to him.

"As long as we continue to do it, husband, my lips will be sealed." She lay quietly underneath him, her wide eyes watching him.

"Are you sore this morning, Lizzie?" he asked.

"No," she said saucily; then there was slight hesitation. "Yes. But I think we need to practice so that my body becomes more used to your overwhelming power. I think now would be a lovely time to try." Her hands slipped to his backside and pulled on him. "You need to come inside me and move, husband."

His body heard her, but his mind played hard to get. "So pushy, Baggage. That will have to change."

"Never, My Lord. You will just have to deal with it." Her fiery kiss set him back, and he forgot what the conversation between them was. Fortunately, his body knew exactly what to do and within minutes, he had pushed deeply inside her; his explosion was quick and forceful as he filled her to her cries of pleasure. Foreplay had never been so fine.

They spent an enjoyable day together, mostly in the bed. Alex took her to the lake to fish. She looked adorable in her boy clothes, and she did catch a fish for their dinner. She refused to bait the hook, stating clearly that 'worms were not her thing.' She also pushed him in the lake, laughing hysterically as his legs went out from underneath him and he plunged into the cold water. He stood dripping as she turned tail and ran as if the demons of hell were after her. Alex wiped the water from his eyes and followed her in a far more leisurely way, wringing out his shirt sleeves as he went. Payback would be rich, indeed. He could wear some of the clothes that had been left in the cottage; she had only what she had stolen from his house. Of course, Alex used that excuse to make sure that she spent most of her time in her natural state. She had a perfect body, and Alex had much to teach her about the ways between a man and a woman. He threw off the dictates of his dukedom.

They spent a week in the small cottage; it was one of the best weeks of Alex's life, but he had duties to attend to with the estate and his place in society. Lizzie shut out the world and lived in the moment. Making love with her husband was high on the list of her priorities, but she knew it would soon end. She was far from ready to take her place in society as Alex's Duchess.

Her first days as the Duchess of Winterbourne were fraught with difficulty. She could manage the Great House well. She had been trained in that, but the restrictions on her personal life were chaffing. She could not run, she had to continually change her clothes—morning gown, afternoon tea gown, evening gown. Her hair was plucked and combed and combed again. She was not to ride astride any horse. (like that was going to happen, she thought). She must be polite, talk of matters that didn't matter to anyone, and be serene. It was too much for her to take in.

Alex had returned to his place as the Duke. That meant he and his bride must make house calls to those aristocrats to whom such things mattered. Many afternoons were spent attending to their duties. He also invited several prominent government officials to his home, reminding Elizabeth of the times and dates. Several weeks passed without a major incident.

Arriving home on Tuesday with the Prime Minister and two of his cabinet members for a scheduled visit, Alex was surprised to find the entire household in an uproar when they arrived. There was screaming and yelling and servants running everywhere.

"You have to catch him," he heard his young wife yell. She careened into the front parlor with her clothes amiss, water streaming from her, and her hair tangled following some kind of hairy beast. She brought herself up short when she saw the gentlemen observing her. A huge furry animal hurled itself at Alex, almost knocking him down and soaking him with water and soapsuds. The ministers dodged the animal as Lizzie tried to catch it yet again. She bounced off one of the gentleman's chests, muttering "Sorry" and continued the chase.

"Chauncey. Come here." The large, furry dog refused to listen, and it exited the front parlor to climb the stairs once more. "Megan." Lizzie screamed to the morning maid. "He's coming your way." Lizzie hiked up her skirts above her ankles and ran up the stairs two at a time after him leaving a trail of water and soap suds behind.

The Prime Minister looked at the Duke. "What was that?"

Alex tried to straighten his damp clothes while answering, "That, gentlemen, is my wife."

There were shrieking screams, running steps, and the sound of something breaking on the second floor. The crash indicated that something rather large had fallen. The visitors looked like they could bolt at any moment.

"I've got him!" Lizzie screamed, and her sweet laughter followed. "You are such a naughty thing." A door slammed, and an overwhelming silence ensued above; one could have heard a pin drop.

The door upstairs opened again, and Lizzie tripped down the steps dressed in one of the upstairs maid's outfits; the front of the skirt and bodice were soaked. She skittered to a halt before her disapproving husband; his somber look and scowling face said it all. "Lady Winterbourne, may I present the Prime Minister and two of his cabinet members, Lord Symthe and Lord Hescox."

Elizabeth's mouth made a small O before she sank gracefully into a full courtesy. "Welcome, My Lords." She couldn't help but see the displeasure on Alex's face at her costume.

"My Lords, this is my wife, Lady Elizabeth."

All the men bowed to her, being very careful to keep their eyes above her very wet bosom. Lizzie looked back and forth and stumbled into an explanation. "We were chasing a dog, Sirs."

Alex responded in a clipped tone, "Lady Elizabeth, the dogs are out in the stable."

"I know, Alex, I mean My lord, but we found a stray."

Now Alex positively bellowed at her: "That animal is stray? What is he doing in my house?"

Lizzie fidgeted. "We were trying to bathe him. He is very dirty from being outside."

Alex's voice was measured and cold. "He belongs outside if he is a stray. See that he gets there."

Lizzie countermanded his decision. "We cannot. He was hit with a cart in the driveway, so he was brought inside to see to his injuries."

Alex clenched his teeth. "The only thing injured here is my dignity. Get. Him. Out." He looked her up and down derisively. "And, put on some suitable clothes."

Elizabeth straightened her small shoulders under his very public scolding. She turned to the visitors. "Tea will be served in the drawing room presently. Please make yourselves at home. I will be down shortly." She turned on her heel and walked sedately from the room as Alex attempted to wipe more dirt from his coat.

His butler showed the men into the drawing room as he helped Alex remove his coat. "Would you like a clean one, Sir?"

"I would." The butler left with the offending garment in his hands. Alex watched as a tea cart was pushed into the room; the smell of fresh breads and scones made his stomach growl; the kitchen staff must have been baking today. He didn't remember a selection of pastries like the ones that lay before him. A maid asked if he would like her to pour tea until the Mistress came down. Alex looked at his watch.

"We'll wait for Lady Winterbourne."

"Yes, Sir." The maid made a perfect courtesy and left the room. The butler immediately entered carrying a new coat and helped Alex put it on.

"Will there be anything else, Sir?" the butler asked.

"No, Graves. That will be all."

Elizabeth appeared in minutes, her day dress immaculate, her hair pinned up in a pleat. "Excuse me for being late, gentlemen, and welcome to Winterbourne. It is a pleasure to have you." She sat demurely and began dispensing tea with or without lemon, cream and sugar and passing cakes.

"You have a beautiful home, My Lady," one of the ministers said.

"Thank you, Lord Hescox. Your kind words are appreciated. The teacakes are especially good today. We have fresh maple syrup if you would like some. Please help yourself."

"I believe I will, Your Ladyship." Elizabeth smiled at the older gentleman, but she never looked in Alex's direction. After a careful discussion of the side gardens and the state of the weather, she rose. "I will leave you gentlemen to your discussions." She floated to the door of the room, a vision of tranquility and control, and then turned: "If you need anything, just ring. I will be tending to my embroidery." This last comment was a direct message to her husband, and Alex felt its sting as she passed by him. Elizabeth could not sew at all; her embroidery was a mess of knots at all times, a perfect example of the fact she was NO duchess. He struggled to find something appropriate to say to her.

"I will speak with you later, Elizabeth."

"I am sure you will," she muttered under her breath, but then added aloud, "Of course. Good day, gentlemen. It was a pleasure to meet you."

She twirled and was gone in seconds.

Lord Symthe cleared his throat, completely taken by the woman's charm and beauty. "Your wife is a lovely woman, Alex. Keep her close. The rakes will be circling when you're not looking." He gave a discreet cough as Alex nodded.

"I apologize for the earlier part of your visit," Alex said as the gentlemen turned his comments aside.

"There is nothing to apologize for, Alex," the Prime Minister said. "She is delightful."

"This way, gentlemen." He led them to his library.

Lizzie fumed in her bedroom, changing back into the maid's garments. Chauncey was tied to one of the posts of her bed; he was drying in the sun. The scrapes on his body had been tended, and he was enjoying the pieces of meat that Lizzie offered. "I think you are part Airedale or maybe, part sheepdog, but you are so skinny that a stiff wind would blow you away. You certainly don't belong in the stables. Your pedigree won't stand there with all the championship bloodlines. Believe me, I know the feeling." She shook a finger at the great thing. "Keep out of Alex's way, or I don't know what will happen to you. I can only protect you so far." Lizzie leaned down and kissed the dog's furry head as Mary, her maid, came in.

"The beast's a charmer, that's for sure," Mary said as the dog's tail wagged.

"What was broken?" Lizzie asked.

"It was a blue and white ceramic urn, a rather old, ceramic urn. I think it was quite valuable," Mary said, "but I don't know much about these things."

Lizzie pursed her lips. "Can we glue it back together?" she asked wistfully. "It was probably Blue Ming, and it doesn't belong on a table in the hall where just anyone can run into it and knock it over."

Mary agreed. "I'm afraid it is beyond repair."

"I'll make a note that I need to pay for its replacement. I'm sure it will take some time for my pin money to cover it." Lizzie quickly picked up a pen and wrote something down in her notebook. "Perhaps the Duke won't notice it is missing.

"I doubt that, My Lady, but I'll put something else on the table, so it is not as noticeable."

"Thank you, Mary." Chauncey was now asleep on his side on the floor of Lizzie's bedroom. She locked the door between the Duke and Duchess's chambers. The dog could remain here until she figured out what to do. It was NOT going back on the streets. Alex would just have to deal with that. She had never had a dog of her own.

Alex escorted his guests out to the front of the Hall. "Thank you for coming, Prime Minister. There is a possibility now that we can get the legislation passed."

"It was an interesting afternoon, Alex. I thoroughly enjoyed it," The Prime Minister smiled. "I can see why you find it difficult to leave Winterbourne Hall. Your wife is enchanting. Please tell her we said goodbye, and I hope to see the two of you at the Grand Ball on Saturday evening. My wife is looking forward to meeting your Duchess." He added, quietly: "Did you know that Estelle is back in London? She has been talking about you."

Alex shook his head. "No, I did not know she was back."

"I thought you should know. She is with Viscount Myers now, and she is questioning your account of your breakup. She has hinted that you did something unscrupulous. There is nothing any worse than a woman who feels scorned. Watch your back, Alex. You will see her in a few days because she has finagled an invitation to the Ball."

Somewhat abstracted by that news, Alex looked both ways to make sure the giant dog was nowhere to be found. "I will see you soon, then," the Prime Minister said. The men waved and cantered away. Alex called over to one of the servants, "Is there a large furry dog in the stables?"

"No, Sir." Thank God, Alex thought. What was Elizabeth thinking? He went back in the house and up the stairs to his bedroom. Thinking to talk to her, he tried the door between their rooms. It was locked. A slow burn began somewhere in his mid-section; no wife of his would ever lock him out.

He came out of his room and saw Mary, the upstairs maid, in the hall. "Do you know where the Duchess has gone?"

Mary blanched. Lizzie had put on her boy's clothes and gone for a ride to cool her temper before meeting her husband. She had given explicit orders that the dog was to stay in her room. "I'm not sure, Sir, but I believe she might have gone to the gardens or perhaps for a walk?" Alex's forehead wrinkled—*or a ride, he thought.*

"Thank you. You may go about your business." The maid moved away quickly before she could be asked any more questions. The Duke could be a scary gentleman when he was angry. The entire staff had fallen in love with his young, new wife; she never stood on ceremony. She had actually baked sweets and scones with them in the kitchen that very morning. She was a true lady who managed to put everyone she spoke with at ease. Mary would do anything to help her as would the others who served her. She opened the door to the Duchess's room only to discover Chauncey contentedly chewing on the Duke's new boots. Alex had left them in the Duchess's room the night before. "Oh no," the maid thought. There was no fix to this. The Duke would be furious.

Alex walked quickly to the stables. Sure enough, her horse was missing, but surprisingly, not one of the stable hands could remember saddling the animal. She had gone bare-back. Her well-being could be at risk, and she clearly didn't understand that she was now a Duchess. There were rules. Alex had his own mount saddled and set out to find her, but the devil's luck was with the lady; he spent two hours searching and found nothing. It didn't help his already dark temper.

CHAPTER 13

Lizzie cantered miles from home before she pulled up her favorite mount. The sun was beginning to sink in the sky, and she knew she should turn around; the freedom was heady. She wondered if there was a shortcut she could use to get home more quickly. Time was of the essence, and Alex was already angry. Thinking that, she remembered a fork in the road that might lead to a quicker way home. She slid to the ground and tied off the horse's reins. Lizzie searched for a tall tree and began her climb to the top. If she could get high enough, she should be able to see the split in the road and the shortcut home.

She had climbed about thirty feet making sure that she hugged the tree only to find her foot caught in a break in the tree bark. It was firmly wedged, and she couldn't easily bend down to release herself. She wobbled precariously when she tried to release her foot. She jerked and pulled and twisted, but she could not break free. Her foot was now aching, and she hoped she wasn't bleeding.

Her mind now in turmoil, she tried once more to push her arms down low enough to force her foot. When she moved, her perch in the tree became precarious. She almost lost her balance, and it was a long way down to the ground. Her heart hammered until she had herself straight once again. Thank goodness the branch beneath her feet was wide and her hands held on to the trunk in front of her.

Alex turned his mount and was about to head for home, swearing as he did so. He hoped that his errant wife was there, waiting dinner for him, but a sense of unease surrounded him. He stopped the animal and called her name as loudly as he could. The sound echoed. "Elizabeth! Can you hear me?" He waited for any reply. "Elizabeth. Answer me."

Lizzie thought she heard someone yell her name, but how could that be? "Here. I'm here. I'm caught in a tree." She screamed and listened intently once more.

Alex thought he heard a woman's voice, but he couldn't make out the words.

"Lizzie! Call my name and keep calling it." Then he heard it—her faint reply.

"Alex."

He turned his horse towards the sound of her voice. "Keep yelling, Lizzie. I'm coming."

It seemed like hours and her voice was scratchy from screaming, but still, she kept yelling. It was getting dark now, and Lizzie was afraid. She couldn't stay awake all night and if she fell asleep, she could break her ankle or worse yet, fall to the ground. She heard the sound of horse and rider coming. "Alex." It was last time she could utter anything.

Alex found her horse tethered below the tree and looked up. In the failing light, he could see a small body hugging the tree for dear life. He took off his jacket, grabbed a rope from his bag, and quickly scaled the lower branches, edging his way towards the top. "Lizzie. I'm coming up. Hold on." Lizzie looked down towards the ground, only to see her husband quickly climbing towards her. She was never so glad to see anyone in her whole life.

"Alex. My foot is caught. I can't free it." She could barely speak, she was so hoarse from yelling.

"One thing at a time, Baggage. For now, your job is to hold on." When he reached her, he carefully took the rope and tied it around her body, making sure she could not fall. Her arms would have to be tired. It was labor intensive, but he felt much better when she was secure. His hands slid down her leg to where the boot was stuck in a scar of the tree bark. Her foot didn't move when he pulled on it. He moved to the lower branch, working the boot back and forth until he heard her cry out in pain. He stopped immediately.

"It hurts. I must have twisted it as well." That complicated things, and darkness was coming. They had to be out of the tree before that happened.

Lizzie whispered: "Did I tell you how very glad I am to see you?"

"No, you didn't, but I am very glad to see you, too, Baggage. You certainly have a fascination with trees. Oh, and just so you know, my life hasn't been boring at all since I met you."

There was a moment, and then her small voice responded; "That better be a compliment, Alex." The man smiled but knew better than to say more. He slipped out his pocket knife; he would have to cut the boot off.

"You must stay very still, Lizzie. I'm going to cut through the leather and free your foot."

"You can't do that. These aren't my shoes. I borrowed them. They belong to one of our maid's brothers"

"We'll replace them, Lizzie," Alex countered.

"I'll need to add that to my pin money list then," she responded.

Alex was confused. "What?" What was she talking about? Was she becoming delirious?

"Never mind. I'll hold very still."

"You do that." Using his fingertips to find the top of the boots, he slid the sharp knife into the leather, making sure his hand was between her foot and the boot. He sawed slowly, pushing the leather to the side to make his path.

"It feels looser. Do you want me to try to pull my foot out?"

"Yes, Baggage. You'll feel my fingers near the bottom of your foot. I'll help you, but you must do it slowly." She pulled up on her foot and felt his fingers brush underneath it. He pushed, and she pulled, and her foot finally gave, almost causing Alex to topple from the tree. The boot, however, remained stuck, a lasting monument to her adventure.

"Oh. That feels so good," Lizzie said as she wiggled her toes.

"Let's get you down, now." He carefully untied her from the tree trunk and maneuvered her body down from branch to branch. "How's the foot feel?"

"Not too bad. It's just very sore." Alex jumped to the ground and reached up to lift her down, holding her in his arms for the first time since he found her, hugging her tightly to him. He finally allowed the fear that he held inside him to dissipate. God, she felt so good in his arms. "Alex? You're suffocating me."

He didn't let go immediately but finally pulled her to face him. "Don't do that again, Lizzie Baggage—never run away. You are making me old beyond my years."

"I'm just keeping you in shape, Alex. You don't want to get old." Lizzie said soberly. "I thought you were angry with me." She was suddenly very quiet. "I've never had a dog of my own, you see."

Alex wilted at her forlorn tone, capitulating on the dog before he could think logically. "You can keep the monster if that will make you happy." Lizzie hugged him tightly, and her lips caught his in a warm kiss.

"Can it stay in the house?" Alex nodded. When Lizzy finally broke the embrace, she added in a hoarse voice: "Did I tell you how glad I am to see you?"

"Be quiet now, or you're going to hurt your throat more. That, I can't allow." His kiss on her forehead said he wasn't at all upset. "It will be long trip home." He wrapped his jacket around her and helped her up on her horse. "Don't put much weight on that foot until it can be checked out."

"Yes, Sir."

They turned their horses towards their Winterbourne home.

Halfway through the journey, Alex lifted Elizabeth from her horse and placed her before him on his mount—her mount was tied behind. His woman was falling asleep. There was only a single light in the window when the Duke carried his sleeping beauty up the steps of Winterbourne. He had to smile; he was in laboring clothes, carrying his young duchess who was dressed as a boy into the great hall, not his version of a Great Duke. His faithful butler was there to open the doors, tut-tutting over their appearances. To make matters worse, Chauncey met them at the door, tail wagging, body wiggling and tongue hanging out with one of the Duke's chewed boots in his possession. Alex gave up then and just laughed; he felt lighter than he had for a week. Lizzie mumbled his name in her sleep and turned her head tighter into his chest. His father would have been appalled, but somehow, he felt his mother was cheering.

The butler closed the door behind them. "Welcome home, My Lord. I shall put the beast outside."

Alex stopped and faced the man. "No—he will come with us, and he is now a part of this household."

"My Lord. You have pedigreed animals galore in your stable. This dog is a mongrel."

"I have an affinity for mongrels tonight, I guess. He is My Lady's pet, and he stays."

Graves nodded in a deferential manner. Wait until he told the other servants; they would all be amused, and most of them had already bonded with the large dog. He made a mental note to order the Duke new boots—perhaps several pairs—as discretely as possible.

"I have ordered a hot bath for your room, Sir. Would you like one for her ladyship? Do you require Mary, her Ladyship's maid?"

"Thank you for the bath, and no, one will do. I'm going to examine Lizzie's ankle more closely; if I have need of a doctor, I will let you know. I've treated ankle injuries in the war, so I may be able to make do for this evening. I will see to her ladyship. Thank you, Graves."

Graves bowed and left as Alex carried Lizzie upstairs to his room. The dog padded along behind him. As they entered, he lay the sleeping woman on the bed and turned to the dog. "We must come to an understanding. For whatever reason, she loves you, and you will stay. But you will be polite and well-behaved, or you will answer to me." Alex stopped and thought how ridiculous it was to be having a discussion with a dog. Chauncey sat down and wagged his tail; then he lay down at the foot of the bed and put his head down on Alex's boot. "I am happy to see you are being reasonable about this."

Alex stripped down to his pants and set about undressing Lizzie. She opened her eyes and smiled warmly up at him as he worked to free her from her filthy clothes.

"Um-mm-mm, My Lord. Do you plan to have your wicked way with me?" she croaked. Alex laughed softly and swept his mouth over hers in a touch of a kiss.

"Wicked way? Maybe later, Baggage." Her arms came up and circled his neck, pulling him off-balance and onto the bed beside her. He looked her up and down. "You are a very dirty woman tonight."

Elizabeth intentionally misconstrued his words. "You taught me well, My Lord, and I have need of you and your wonderful body. Then you may make me clean again." Her mouth nibbled down his bare chest before he could quite contain her.

His hands caught her head, and he held her still. "You are tired and scraped and hurt, Baggage."

"I am reviving, hot and wanting, Alex. I need you," she mused with a smile, "for other things." Now she pulled his hands away and hoisted her small body on top of him, her fingers running though his hair. A small grimace crossed her face when her swollen ankle brushed his leg.

"We will see, My pretty Lady. First things first—a bath, and then I must see to that ankle. I am capable of waiting for a good thing. Are you?" He swept his fingers up her bare leg to tease her womanhood.

Her body came awake with a vengeance. "I suppose, My Lord, I can wait. But patience is not one of my virtues." The hot bath appeared; then they were alone once more.

Alex picked her up and placed her carefully in the copper tub lined with linen. He added a medicinal oil to his hands and slicked them down and over her small frame treating every bug bite and scrape before taking a cloth and systematically cleaning her with a scented soap. Her eyes followed his every movement, and damn her, she made him want like he had never wanted anything in his ducal life. He had to turn his thoughts to something else.

"Do you have any virtues?"

That teased a smile from her. "Oh yes, Sir. I am a quick learner in all things, but you already know that."

Alex frowned at her. "Just remember that I am your only teacher. You will soak here for ten minutes. Then I will tend to your ankle. I am going to wash myself here at the washstand, so you had better listen, Lizzie Baggage. I will not take kindly to your climbing out of that tub."

"Oh, the mean Duke has reared his ugly head." She pouted. "Send the Duke away; I want Alex back."

"Don't toy with me, Sweetheart. I will always win in the end."

"I may be the end of you, Alex. You will throw me back into the lake where you found me before you were the Duke."

Now he looked directly at her. "I have always been the Duke, Elizabeth, and you are now my Duchess. I won't let you forget it, and don't ever go running off again." He struggled to find the words. "I could have lost you—and not just for the night, Lizzie. You could have died out there." He clenched his hands on the thought.

Lizzie mulishly set her lips and circled her hands, making designs in the hot water. It did feel delicious to be clean once more, and her ankle hurt less. Alex ignored her to let his words sink in. He soaped his upper body and attended to his lower body as well, by removing his britches and smalls. He glanced over at her at her one time as she gazed intently on his naked form. He wiped the soap from his body and rinsed. When he dried his body, her eyes were still on him, and his need for her escalated; he should keep his hands to himself—she was hurt.

"Stand up now, but don't put your full weight on that ankle. I'll steady you," Alex cautioned. Lizzie rose gracefully, holding on to her husband's upper arms. He reached for a drying cloth and wrapped her up, wiping the water gently from her face and shoulders. His hands lingered on her breasts, but he went back to the business of drying her torso and long legs. Picking her up, he carried her to their bed and knelt to look at her ankle. The swelling had subsided a bit, but it was still angry-looking. He used linens to wrap it tightly, making sure it was not too uncomfortable. Lizzie waited for him to look at her.

When he did, she gave him an apologetic grin. "I'm sorry, Alex. I didn't mean to climb up a tree; I was looking for a shortcut home. I will be more careful in the future." She awaited his pleasure, only fidgeting a little bit, hoping he would forgive her. When he finally stood, his body language told her that his patience had run out; his need was too great.

"We must go slowly, Baggage. I would not hurt you, but I have great need of you. Apology accepted." Lizzie opened her arms to welcome him to her.

"I'm sorry I ran, Alex. But you were so angry with me. I won't run again, if you will have me tonight."

Alex smiled. "I, too, owe you an apology for my own behavior. You must forgive me, as well." When she nodded her acceptance of his words, Alex gave Lizzie the night of her dreams. It might have been because he thought he had lost her, or it might have been because he needed her. Whatever the reason, the love was there—a slow build, a stunning release.

CHAPTER 14

Lady Estelle stood at the garden gate of the spring tea sponsored by Lady Bertram. It was Estelle's first foray into the English social scene since she had gone to Cyprus three months earlier. She had left England feeling elated that her plans to bring down the Duke of Winterbourne were in place and would be successful. The first letters and missives from her English friends had told her in no uncertain terms that the Duke had landed on his feet. There had been a grand wedding with the Queen in attendance, and the man had purchased the land tracts that he desired. How could that have happened? Her plan and timeframe had been foolproof.

The woman who was said to have captured the Duke was a cow, poorly dressed and puritan in her nature, lacking social necessities, and even unable to dance. Estelle had seen her at various balls; Alex must have been frantic to save himself. And how could it all have been arranged so quickly? It would be only a matter of time until she met Lady Elizabeth, and Estelle could give her some choice words. Elizabeth had obviously schemed to have the Duke marry her; this for the Duke who wanted everything in his Duchess. That was laughable.

At least Estelle could be sure there was no comparison made between Elizabeth and herself. With Estelle's fair skin, blue eyes and blonde hair as well as her stunning figure, no one could hold a candle to her. Geoffrey, Lord Sinclair carefully bowed out of marrying her, not wanting to make an enemy of the Duke; Viscount Myers stepped right in. He said he objected to being married abroad, wanting the wedding to be held in London. Estelle had acquiesced, thinking that it would bring more pain and dismay to the Duke when he was forced to watch her marry another. The Duke would be pitied wherever he went for losing her; of this, she was sure. She was now engaged to the Viscount. His land holdings were not nearly as vast as Alexander's had been, but her money could purchase the best of most things. She found the trade-off acceptable.

From the accounts of her friends, the Duke's wedding had been spectacular, the bride appearing in a stunning white gown with a long train and wearing a flowing veil. The woman was said to be of a small stature, but Estelle knew that could not be so. Lady Elizabeth's unflattering gowns had proclaimed her to be rather rotund. Estelle had come here today to gather information on how to wound the new Duchess and vicariously, to strike at Alexander as well. The Duke would hate any gossip, especially about his newly wed Duchess.

Estelle accepted tea and small sandwiches and sat in one of the chairs in the shade with two of her friends as they gossiped about all who were present. There was a disturbance at the entrance to the gardens that caught Estelle's attention; a stunningly beautiful, dark-haired woman in a striking blue brocade dress had just entered. She was being treated like royalty. Who was she?

Estelle leaned over to Lady Gretchen. "I see we have some new people among us since I left. Who is that woman just coming into the luncheon? Do you know?"

Estelle's friend glanced towards the garden entrance. "Why, everyone knows her, Estelle. That is the Duchess of Winterbourne, Lady Elizabeth. She has friends everywhere in London; she is known to be rather unorthodox, but all the men rush to her side and speak of her beauty and humor; even the Grand Dames have given their tacit approval."

Estelle's chin dropped. This was Alex's new bride? The woman was exquisite, her dress just right for an afternoon outing. And she greeted everyone with a smile. This was not the Lady Elizabeth that Estelle had seen at social gatherings parading about in gaudy clothes. Estelle's face darkened as she wrestled with how to get the Lady Elizabeth alone. Rumors of Alexander's infidelity could bring a deadly blow to their brief union, and Lady Estelle had just the tongue to do it.

When Elizabeth slipped into the retiring room, Estelle saw her chance. She quickly followed the Duchess, watching as the maid repaired a tear in a small flounce on Elizabeth's dress. The maid left to replenish her thread. "I don't believe we have met?" she said coyly, coming up behind the Duchess.

Elizabeth stiffened and turned towards Estelle. "Not formally, My Lady. I once stood in a hallway and listened to you plot the downfall of my husband, the Duke of Winterbourne. Do you remember the occasion, or should I refresh your memory?"

Estelle's chin dropped. How much had this lady overheard? She immediately defended herself: "You were never invited to my home, Lady Elizabeth. Your story cannot be true."

"I wasn't invited, but I dropped in anyway. Your revenge against Alex was poorly timed and even more poorly executed. I would have expected better from you." Elizabeth selected a cool, wet towel and wiped her hands with it. "You wanted him to be disparaged. Isn't that true? Did you think to catch me here and tell me tales of my husband? You don't know my husband at all. If you did, you would never have let him go. Of that, I am sure."

"I slept with your husband." Estelle threw it out there.

Elizabeth let out a laugh. "You silly thing. If you had, Alex would never have let you go. That's the kind of man that he is. You lie once again, Estelle. Don't you get tired of making things up?"

The Duchess walked the few steps that brought her into Lady Estelle's personal space. "Do you want to do this here, Estelle, or should we just pretend to be friends and move on with our lives? I will not allow you to hurt my husband in any way. Make note of that. I am not someone you should cross." The woman stood defiant, but Estelle saw only the woman who would become her new target.

Estelle backed up a step. "Well. Look how brave you are. You will never hold Alex. Newer clothes have made a small difference in your appearance, but he will tire of you. There is more to the story of the two of you than I was led to believe." She paused striving for a reaction to her words. "Were you seeing Alexander behind my back?" Estelle's tight smile indicated that she thought her innuendo was correct.

Elizabeth blatantly ignored her. "You were planning Alex's downfall even before you left England; I have to wonder if the Viscount is a part of your scheme as well. Were the two of you intimate, Estelle, forcing you to run from your marriage to Alex? He would never have accepted an impure Duchess, would he? Oh, that would make a wonderful story for the ton, but it would also bring down your Count. Or doesn't he matter, either? Is he just the means to an end?

"You wouldn't," fumed Lady Estelle.

"Don't underestimate me. I am very pleasing in bed. Are you, Lady Estelle? Perhaps I can ask the Viscount." The arrow struck home as the two faced each other. "Think long and hard before you attack my husband. I won't hesitate to respond in kind, and I know a great deal about your thirst for revenge. I have done more research on your complaints against his family." Estelle became very quiet as she contemplated what Elizabeth said. "Is there anything else to say before we rejoin the ladies?"

"Do not get complacent, Lady Elizabeth. I have friends in high places."

"Yet your soul remains in the gutter. I will make everyone see your true colors if you proceed against Alex in any way. Be forewarned. I am an unconventional woman, and I might just challenge you to a duel. I am adept with a sword and a firearm; I was never a pampered woman. Think before you attack me or what is mine, and Alex is mine."

"You will need to give him an heir. I can see to it that you will never carry a child to term," Estelle fumed.

"Threats, now?" Elizabeth did smile, a true smile. "Alex and I seem to have the methods of sexual gratification down well. By the way, Alex is a magnificent lover; but if you didn't permit him to touch you, then you could never know. How is the Count as a lover, Estelle?" Her facial expression told Elizabeth all she needed to know. The lady had been to bed with the Count. "As for my child, I am more than capable of protecting it. Go away, Estelle. Marry your Viscount and stay away from me and mine. That is a threat."

Elizabeth swept out of the room, stopping to give a kind remark to the young maid who had just come back into the room.

"Isn't Lady Elizabeth wonderful?" gushed the maid to Lady Estelle. "She is the most gracious soul alive, and she is so beautiful."

Estelle could not get out of the room quickly enough.

Elizabeth found a bench near the waterfall in the garden. She needed to be by herself. She was shaking from her encounter, but she felt she had drawn a line in the sand for her enemy. Unfortunately, she didn't think it would change Estelle's actions towards her.

Imagine her surprise when she turned to find her husband patiently standing beside her. Word of Lady Estelle's presence at the garden tea had reached him, and he immediately set out to collect his lady wife.

"Alex. How glad I am to see you." He pulled her up to him and kissed her sweetly.

"It is my pleasure to attend you." He looked around at the ladies still enjoying their tea, his eyes finally resting on Lady Estelle and her friends. She did not see him as of yet. "Well, Baggage. I see Estelle is back on my home shores."

Elizabeth looped her arm through his as they walked from the garden area. "Did you know she would be here? Is that why you have come—to ride to my rescue? You need not worry, you know. I am not a true lady; I will have little trouble dealing with that viper. Maybe she knows how to fistfight." Her face lit up; Alex's face held disbelief at her comment. "She means us harm, Alex. The gossip here says she is to marry the Viscount in the coming weeks, and she is spinning a different tale of the breakup between the two of you. Of course, you are portrayed as the villain."

"I feel sorry for the Viscount, then. And to think, I almost chose to make her my Duchess, a grave error in judgment."

A soft peal of laughter came from Elizabeth's lips. "And look what you got instead, My Lord—Lizzie Baggage."

Alex looked her up and down with soft eyes. "Yes, Baggage. Just look at what I got." His eyes grew hotter as he remembered their trysts in strange places and their experiments in sexual congress.

"If you don't soon take me away from this dull assemblage, I promise I will jump into the fountain and throw water at you. Wouldn't that be a story?" She could imagine the rags writing about her fall into depravity as she cavorted in the water in front of the ton.

Alex seemed to read her mind. "It would depend on whether or not you were wearing clothes; I would enjoy your show if you were *au naturel*, but then again, I have seen you often enough that way; I would not wish to share you with others. You are a joy to all my senses, Baggage."

Elizabeth slapped his arm sharply. "You must wipe that vision from your eyes."

"That will be difficult. What exactly did you have in mind to do with me—at home, I mean?" asked Alex, pretending innocence.

"I can think of only a few things," she saucily replied. "By the way, the illustrated books in your study are very enlightening."

Alex stiffened in response as he looked at her. "They are locked away."

"You attempted to lock them away, but I am a very resourceful soul. Never forget that." She looked down at her feet. "I know how to pick locks, and I have other nefarious gifts as well which I will not enumerate. Tell me, do you have other volumes hidden away?" Her cheeks turned red at her confession to him. "I think the pictures are...."

Alex grabbed her arm and gave her a little shake. "Beware, My Lady. I will set boundaries for you." Elizabeth knew from his set expression that he would. "I'm sorry, my dear, but I do have to go. I have a meeting on the Mercantile tax. I will see you at home as soon as I can." He moved a step closer to her and lowered his voice. "I do not trust Lady Estelle, so please stay clear of her." Lizzie's quick glance to where Alex was looking showed a very unhappy, sexually frustrated Estelle gazing daggers across the yard at her husband.

"If looks could kill, I think I might be dead," Alex quipped.

"Or she is imagining you in bed, completely naked, waiting for your mouth to..."

"Stop that this instant." Alex grabbed her hands and managed to command her complete attention. "No discussing our bedroom antics, remember? You have no reason to be jealous, Lizzie. She knows nothing of me, and I know nothing of her—end of story. Has she tried to speak to you?"

Elizabeth paused, avoided his eyes, and then flat-out lied. "No. She has kept her distance. And I would like to keep it that way."

Alex watched Elizabeth carefully; she was not telling him the truth. It was time for him to step into the fray without her permission. She would not be pleased, but Alex no longer trusted Estelle or her Count.

CHAPTER 15

Alex had managed to trace his wife's movements at the Garden Party easily. Women were always willing to tell a gentleman what they knew. Apparently, Estelle had followed Lizzie into the retiring room, and neither one had appeared again for a number of minutes. He sought out the young maid who was working, and she informed him that the two women had come in. Unfortunately, she left the two alone because she needed to go to the Main House to replenish the thread that she had used to fix a tear in Elizabeth's dress.

That left Alex with only one choice. He would have to visit Estelle, and he would have to do so without telling his wife. The stories that were reaching him about her accounts of what had happened between them were nothing but lies. Normally, he would let them go, but Lizzie was now involved. He also planned a meeting with Viscount Myers, sending his card to that gentleman.

Something about the Viscount's name brought up another hazy memory—when Lizzie's abductor was questioned, wasn't that the name given to him? Alex was sure of it. He remembered the man saying that the Viscount planned to marry Lizzie. The man must have a need for money, and now he had caught Estelle. But the information was second-hand, and there could be a mistake in the identity of a Viscount.

The search became two-fold—to stop Estelle from spreading her lies and to bring the Viscount to judgment for his attempted kidnapping of Lizzie. The man would have to confess to his part in the abduction and making him do that could be challenging.

Alex arranged to visit the men who had been charged with the attempted abduction in Newgate Prison. He was ushered into a small room off the prison, and he recognized both men when they stood sheepishly before him. They had admitted their parts to the constable who had arrested them; their statements were on record, but The

Viscount's surname name had somehow been removed. Alex wondered how much of a bribe that had taken.

"Gentlemen." He addressed the two prisoners. "I'm sure you recognize me. I want to talk with you about the plan to kidnap Lady Elizabeth Weston." He pointed to one man. "You, I believe, told me that the woman was to be delivered to a Viscount Myers, that he planned to marry her and then keep her on his property while he made free use of her dowry money. Do I remember that correctly?"

The man looked at the other. "Are you a member of the constable's department?" he questioned. He obviously didn't realize that Alex was a Duke.

"I am not. I am a friend of the lady's family."

"I got nothing more to say. I'm in enough trouble as it is, and I been told to keep my mouth shut on account of them. They will be taken care of as long as I keep my yap shut."

Alex questioned the prison guard, "Can you tell me who has been to visit these two men?"

The officer picked up his notes. "Says here that they had family visit them and then a lawyer from town, a Mr. Joss Symonds."

"Is the lawyer connected to Viscount Myers by any chance? Alex asked.

"I believe so. I can check," the man said. Alex nodded.

He turned to the two men. "This is your last chance to tell me what I want to know. If you do not, you are complicit in the kidnap attempt, and I will see you both transported. If you are looking for mercy, however, I am your man."

Now, it was a waiting game. Alex settled in and poured a drink.

Lizzie was on the move again, the horse between her legs running full speed. She bent low over the saddle and laughed. She had managed to escape the poor groom who was assigned to go with her; she would make sure that he didn't get into any trouble if she were seen riding astride by her husband. He was still under the mistaken impression that she could not handle her own affairs, and he still believed that she could be the perfect Duchess. Lizzie knew better.

Alex hadn't learned about her run-in with the constable when she tried to help a woman who was being evicted from her small cottage. She had actually struck the man, forgetting that she was incognito as a young, aristocratic youth. Only her coin had saved her and the old woman. Lizzie paid her taxes for the next two months and promised she would look into the situation. The constable was less than pleased, and he began asking questions that would lead him back to, what he assumed, was her aristocratic father. She just managed to escape when he was talking to his deputy.

The social cage was closing around her, and she felt stifled. There were dances, at-home teas, the opera and theater, and house parties almost every other day. The house ran itself, and aside from putting personal touches on various rooms, she had little to do. She could run a household blindfolded. She cooked whenever she could, but the kitchen staff seemed alarmed at her interaction with them. She guessed it was because that wasn't on the list of the Duchess's duties. Ordering linens was tedious at best and determining the meals each day was not exciting. Alex became more and more the Duke, and not her soulmate—she missed his teasing and his sense of play; she missed the man. She dearly missed the freedom to pretend her life was different, that she could make a difference. Women did not have that luxury, but she had managed to go about as a young lad, learning new things and meeting new people—that had been severely curtailed since she married.

What if Estelle had come to the wedding, and Elizabeth was now a free entity with a fortune at her fingertips, but without Alex. What would her life be like? There was no baby so far, and she was sure it was because of the constricted environment in which she lived. She could conceive in the wild place where she had first met her husband. It was not for want of trying for a child; Alex was a sexually motivated man, and he knew his way around a woman's body. She was delving into the books about what a man needed, and her small attempts to scandalize him were working. She often caught him watching her in wonder, the question on his lips but never asked. How did she know to do that to him?

Lizzie had planned this escape for a number of days. Now, if only Alex would take the bait. She was on her way to the very spot where he had first seen her—the lake. It was where she wanted them to be when they created their first child together. But getting her husband away from his governmental and ducal duties was like prying a dog from its favorite bone. He continually talked of duty, and he never had time to just 'be'. Well, it was her duty to give him a child, and she wanted to be successful; even more, she wanted him to love her not only as a man loves a woman but also in the spiritual sense of connection. She wanted all of him.

Lizzie pulled up her mount and looked at the peaceful setting below. Her missives to her husband were just now being delivered. She wished that she could see his face as he pondered her words.

Dearest

I am Lizzie Baggage once again and waiting for you to find me. You always seem to know what I need, and right now I need you. Think about how we met and join me in making memories that will last us a lifetime. I want our child.

I ask for your undivided attention, husband.

Lizzie

Several more similar notes had been delivered to him, in his London offices, in his gentleman's club and even in the parliament building. Would he come, and if he did, would he have any idea where she was waiting. If he truly loved her, he would. And that was really the question, wasn't it? Was she his society wife, or was she his love? The next days would answer that question.

Alex was handed another missive from his wife. The men around him tried to hide their smiles as they watched Alex receive it—they noticed a faint smile on his lips as he took in her perfume from the letter.

"How many notes does that make, Alex?" Essex teased him.

"At least six, I think," said another Lord in their meeting.

"I'm not counting," responded the Duke. "But I am going to determine what is going on with my Lady Wife." After reading it, he stood. "I will be gone for several days, gentlemen. I think you can do without me."

"And, I am sure Lady Elizabeth offers you a far better adventure than haggling over laws," Essex said. "If you don't go, I may offer to go in your stead. Your wife is…"

"Mine." Lord Winterbourne ended the conversation by walking out of the meeting. What was Lizzie doing, he wondered, as he headed towards Winterbourne. His interest was definitely piqued.

His wife was not at his townhome; that was no surprise to him. Searching through his room (Lizzie no longer slept in the Duchess's bed, but rather in the ducal chamber, (in his bed, at his insistence), he found her clothes undisturbed. The drawer holding her 'boy' clothes had been rifled, so she was riding as a young man once again even though he had threatened her about doing that without protection, and she was also riding astride. His mouth tightened. The lady was poking a stick in her sleeping husband; he would soon see to her. He assumed correctly that the poor stable hand who had been assigned to ride with her was completely out of his element and waiting to lose his job. Alex chuckled at that. He was sure Lizzie had gone to some lengths to make sure that didn't happen. The woman was sneaky; he could attest to that. And yet, his blood roared in his head as he imagined her out on his property alone somewhere.

Alex stopped by Winterbourne Manor before packing supplies for a brief getaway. He hoped his wife had done the same. Asking the housekeeper if Lizzie had said anything to her before leaving, the woman answered that she had been told to take care of the dog for a few days. No one had seen the lady leave; that was disconcerting to Alex. Unbeknownst to his wife, he had placed a tail on her for her own safety, especially after the affair in town with Estelle. He could wait for his report, but that didn't sit well with him. He would find his lady himself.

Alex pulled her notes from his pocket where he had carefully placed them. Each one spoke of where they had originally met. Could that be where she had gone, and what did she plan for him when he arrived? He thought he had some ideas, and he hoped she was ready for whatever actions he would bring to this excursion. He felt lighter and happier than he had in weeks, and he hoped he had followed her clues to the right place. He set off at once.

Viscount Myers had assigned a man with a scandalous background to follow Lady Elizabeth. When she left her home dressed as a young boy, the man noted her escape from her husband and returned to tell the Viscount. Was there trouble in paradise already? It would be a smashing story to discount her overwhelming popularity.

The Viscount rubbed his jaw. The Duke was attempting to connect him to Elizabeth's kidnapping several months ago, visiting the two men accused of the crime to question them. He had also received a note that the Duke wished to see him as soon as possible. There was no direct evidence, but that did not reassure the Count. Estelle, if pushed, could confirm what the men were saying. That could not happen; if he were charged, it would cause him to lose his inheritance. With his association to Estelle and her broken romance with the Duke, it became imperative that he have something to hold over both Alex and her. The Duke's wife and her fidelity to him could be the key to keeping both of them in line. He needed to find and hold Elizabeth to threaten the Duke.

His man had returned to tell him that Lizzie was out riding the Duke's lands, alone, and unprotected. Why she would do that was unknown. Perhaps the lady regretted her marriage and was looking for a liaison. The Count wouldn't mind being the 'other man'; he smiled at that thought. The Duchess was gorgeous, and she was thought to have her husband's total devotion. The rumors about her were many; the truth, barely known. The Viscount told his man to return to the Duke's land and to find and keep an eye on the lady; if he could, he was to take her.

Once he had her, he could arrange a deal with the Duke. After all, she was only a woman, but gossip from the gentry assured him that the Duke wanted her.

CHAPTER 16

Lizzie's eyes searched the horizon once more. Alex should be here by now, that is, if he wanted to be here. She contemplated having to contact Lord Essex about the use of his small house if Alex didn't show. She sat on the banks of the lake where she had first seen the Duke, as he ordered her from his property. The only problem was that she didn't know he was the Duke, and now she wished fervently that he wasn't the Duke. The weather was warm, and she wanted a dip in the lake to cool her heated skin.

She disrobed quickly on the shore, much as she had done the last time she was here. Her long hair was freed from its pins, and she stepped cautiously into the water. It was cold, and a shiver ran up her. She felt as if she were being watched; she glanced around, but she saw no one. Gingerly, she continued on into the water, finally dropping into its depths. She dunked her head to get her hair out of her face, and she swam a small distance. When she emerged, Alex watched her, mesmerized by her goddess-like beauty. He sat on a rock ledge along the bank just observing her; she hadn't yet seen him, nor would she until he was ready for that to happen. He wanted her as he had never wanted another woman in his life, and she was already his, here at this spot, however, against his wishes. She wanted something from him—he could sense it in his bones, and he wanted much from her as well. She had kept her reputation spotless, but seeing her now, he knew there was a wild side to her; he would tap into it whenever he could. She was like no other lady he had ever known.

Lizzie splashed her arms in circles, making waves on the glassy top of the lake. Then her merriment rang out, filling the air and scaring whatever small creatures were around. Delightedly, she turned her body in circles in the water, free of her Duchess duties once again. She stood up in the chest-deep water, and she was truly an otherworld creature, dancing in its ripples.

Alex crept down from the rock on which he had been sitting and stripped off his own clothes by hers. He moved further up the bank from where she was, hiding behind an outcropping of rocks that teased the edge of the water. He slipped into the water without making a sound courtesy of his training and the long war behind him and swam underwater towards her. The water was deeper where he had been. He came up behind her and used his arms to pull her under the surface of the water, his hands hard on her body touching her private areas. He heard her scream of surprise, but then she was beside him under the water. His arms pulled her body to him, holding her tightly as he pushed up with his feet and brought them both to the surface. She was sputtering and coughing to get the water from her lungs as she continued to fight his hold.

"Baggage." That voice was all that it took; she twisted her body in his arms and wiped her hair from her face seeing him clearly.

"You Bastard, You," she uttered. She began spouting every swear word she could think of towards him.

Alex laughed at her. "No, My Lady. Not me. I was born on the right side of the blanket—I'm a Duke, remember?"

"I wish I could forget. I want Alex, not the Duke." In her anger, Lizzie forgot that she had practically begged him to come for her until his mouth closed off all of her invectives. She relaxed into his naked body and hopped up, wrapping her legs around his waist, his skin warming hers as his hands caressed her backside. He broke the kiss, only to say: "Have I taught you nothing about your own safety? I could have been anyone looking for a willing woman."

"Ah, My Lord, but I am only a willing lady for you. I did bring my knife."

"Where is it?" His hand ran down her bare body pretending to search for the knife.

Lizzie wiggled and countered with a kiss of her own before saying, "It is by my clothes."

"And where are your clothes?" She pointed to the shoreline. "That's a wonderful place for your knife to be, isn't it?" His hand moved slowly into places that brought her even further alive under his invasive touch. Her whispered moan did things to him. "What did I tell you about being alone and unprotected?"

She changed the subject, as she often did when on the losing end of an argument. "I cannot believe that you have come for me."

"You thought I wouldn't?" He seemed surprised.

"I truly didn't know. Sometimes you seem so distant. I'm never sure what role I play in your life."

Alex met her eyes in a fiery exchange of emotion. "In the last few weeks, you have become my life. There are some things we need to discuss, though, Baggage. Your safety has become my number one concern. There are threats around you."

"I can take care of myself," she pointed out to him. His raised eye-brow said he disagreed with her. "In truth, I need more of your undivided attention. Make time for me, Alex. I don't perform well by appointment."

Alex attempted to read her face. "I know my ducal duties take me away from you far too much. I will have to work on changing that. But today, you have garnered my undivided attention, Baggage." His hands ran slowly up and down her bare body. "What do you need from me, Lizzie?" he whispered.

"I want a child, Alex. I think you know what that entails; you are a very savvy man. Nevertheless, I did bring one of your illustrated books with me, so that I could study it until you arrived in case you needed help."

Lizzie shrieked as he squeezed her breast hard and picked her up, carrying her in his arms towards the shore. "Is this what you wanted the first day we met, Lizzie?"

Her face questioned his conclusion. "Oh, no," she said. "I had determined never to marry, and you were so angry with me. The last thing I wanted was YOU in my bed. It would be like sleeping with a wild animal."

"Then, tame me, Lizzie; I mean to make you mine. You wear my ring, you said your vows." He carried her further up the bank and lowered her gently to the ground, following her small body with his own unclothed one. His broad shoulders and chest above her almost kept the sun from hitting her fair skin.

Suddenly, Lizzie stiffened, and alarm filled her. She began to struggle against him. "We're out in the open where anyone can see us."

Alex put his head up and looked all around them; then he laughed. "That's the deal, Lizzie Baggage. Nothing hidden, nothing faked. Just the two of us—man and woman. You claim you are no lady; a lady would abhor this coupling in the wild. What say you? Are you a lady who must have a soft bed beneath her and a sedate, sweet joining, or are you a woman who knows what she wants and takes it?" He was teasing her.

"You know who I am," she whispered.

"I do, Baggage. I do! You have made such a difference in my life." Alex's kisses meandered all over her naked body, never staying long in one place. Her own hands were busy as well, and her teeth marked his neck and shoulders, as he spoke. He felt the love bites, and he offered her his own, catching the tips of her breasts. Just watching her writhe beneath him, out in the open, the sun hot on his back and legs, her warm body cushioning him, made Alex feel emotion that he had never had to address before. He pushed open her legs and slipped down to taste her, holding her hands at her sides and restricting any movement. His assault caught her by surprise, and she turned her head from side to side in a thrashing motion. "What do you want, Lizzie," Alex asked through his kisses.

"I want you, Alex, any way you choose to take me," Lizzie managed to get out. "I love you."

Shock brought hot blood throughout his body, and he murmured: "Well said, Baggage." He was so close to coming, too close. The swim, the discussion of their tentative joining and her soft, eager flesh gave him a pressing need unlike any he had ever felt. This woman appealed to him on every level. Flipping her over and pulling her onto her hands and knees, a new position for her—a necessary one for him—Alex moved, finding her first with his long fingers. He slowed at her opening in order to give her time to accommodate his length and width. Once he was positioned, he pushed in slowly and deeply, pulling back her long hair to imprison her and to direct her. She cried his name out as he tunneled in and out of her very receptive body to her soft cries. Alex was all around her and in her as well. She uttered his name over and over as he drove her closer and closer to her own release; even when she screamed as her own orgasm shook her small body, he moved again within her causing her to splinter yet a second time. He was a wild animal, and she was his mate in that moment, his large body covering her small one, making them one. His last thought as he filled her with his seed was that this was beyond belief. He had caught a glimpse of Heaven in her arms. She was all woman, and she was correct about one thing. In society's view, a true duchess would never behave as she had just done. He was so blessed in his choice of a wife.

Alex lost strength and fell over her back, struggling to get breath into his lungs. His body still pulsed deep with her passage. He pulled her down beside him and finally slipped from her. His arms automatically surrounded her, pulling her in closer to his warm body, and his lips feathered the corner of her mouth as she turned her face towards him. "Oh Alex. That was marvelous." The man laid his head down on the rough earth and then stiffened.

"Someone is riding this way. There is a tremor in the ground of hooves. He quickly stood and grabbed his pants and shirt urging his wife to do the same. She could not move as quickly as he could; her legs were like rubber and would not support her. "Hurry Baggage." He reached for her hands.

She brushed them away. "I can't. I'm spent. You go."

"No, you will…"

"Alex, please. Hide yourself. It might be the only way we will both be safe." Lizzie managed to get her arms in her tunic and drag her breeches up her shaky legs.

Alex hesitated, but Elizabeth was correct. There was not enough time for both of them to run and hide without giving themselves away. He picked up her knife and put it in her hand. "I will be nearby, and I will rescue you as soon as I see what enemy we face. Don't antagonize him, Baggage."

She nodded her head, and Alex sprinted for the rocks nearby. She followed his progress until she could no longer see him. A horse was galloping at quite a rate of speed and coming closer. Who would be out here on Alex's land, she wondered. She turned to see the rider come into view, and it was someone she didn't recognize. She had just managed to fasten her breeches when the horse and rider cantered into the open area by the lake and carefully approached her, slowing as he did so. She steadied her hands and held tightly to the knife which was hidden in her tunic. She had no idea where Alex had gone, but she turned to face the new threat, taking deep breaths to settle her breathing. She was still caught in the thrall of their joining, her face flushed with memories of Alex, hot and hard behind her.

The man came forward, checking out the area as he did so. What he saw was a woman, dressed as a boy, standing on the edge of the lake watching him intently. He thought he recognized her as Lady Elizabeth. The Viscount would be pleased; he had tracked down their quarry, and what a quarry she was. Perfectly formed with long legs, a beautiful heart-shaped face, her long hair in wet curls around her face, she was quite a woman; her clothes were somewhat askew. He watched her carefully, waiting for her to run as he pulled his horse to a stop.

"Who are you?" Lizzie challenged. "You are on the Duke of Winterbourne's property."

"Are you the Duchess of Winterbourne?" His dialect assured her he was of the working class, but she noted that he carried a gun. Not many in the working class could afford a weapon like that. She hoped Alex could see it in the waistband of his pants.

"What is your name, and what is your business?" She needed to keep him talking to give Alex time to get behind him and to get as much information from him as she could.

"Ain't you a high and mighty piece. You'd best answer my question." His eyes roamed over her hungrily. "You'll soon change that tone with me." He moved his horse closer to her and dismounted. "We are going to get to know each other, Missy. You can count on that."

Lizzie stiffened her body and countered: "I don't care to know you at all. Why do you think I am a Duchess? Step back from me." She fingered the knife in her hand and concentrated on where she could hurt him the most with the blade. She could not outrun him; that, she knew.

"Don't fool with me. I been watchin' you for days now. The Viscount don't pay if I got no information on yer whereabouts. You are the Duchess."

Lizzie giggled and looked down at herself. "So, I look like a Duchess to you? You must be daft, Man."

The man wrinkled his forehead. "You look like the lady I was followin'."

Lizzie now forced her body to relax. "Well, I'm not this Duchess that you seek. You've made a mistake."

"No mistake, Missy." Lizzie changed the subject.

"I was just about to take a swim. Do you swim?" If he didn't, she could make a run for the water, and if he couldn't follow her; she might yet escape him.

"Ain't never learned how, and you ain't goin' in that water, either."

Elizabeth backed towards the shoreline, noting a movement now behind the man. Alex was sneaking up, only steps away from their quarry.

The man became more threatening. "Don't you move one step further, or I'll have to shoot you. The Viscount won't mind a little damage to you, as long as I deliver ya. You will come with me." Lizzie stalled, hoping to give Alex more time.

"I'd prefer not to get shot," she huffed. "I would not be a good patient if you shot me. I cry a great deal. I'll just put on my shoes, and then I'll come with you. You'll soon see that I am not this Duchess you seek." Elizabeth's mind was in overdrive. She knelt and reached for her shoes; as she did so, she picked up one of the round rocks that peppered the lake shoreline. She would only get one chance to distract him, so she could throw her knife. She stood suddenly and threw the stone with all her might. It missed the man completely, but it distracted him. When he turned to look at what had been thrown, Alex moved directly behind the Viscount's man; that man's attention returned to Lizzie once more as he prepared to advance. Alex brought down his pistol butt on the back of the man's head; he went down like a stone, the gun falling from his hands.

Lizzie shook now as she saw Alex and realized the danger she had been in. "Is he dead?"

"No Baggage, just out cold." Seeing her trembling, Alex came to her and gathered her in his arms, hugging her tightly and kissing her forehead. "You were quite brave, Lizzie."

"Only because I knew you would come," she replied, hugging his waist.

Alex turned her face up to his and touched her lips briefly with his own. "This was quite an adventure, My Lady." After making sure she hadn't suffered any injury, Alex took the time to tie the man up. Lizzie was still shaken.

Tears filled her eyes as she stormed: "He has ruined my adventure. I suppose we have to do something with him, don't we? We can't just let him here to die."

"I'll give him to Robert as soon as he arrives," Alex said.

Lizzie's head came up. "Robert? Why would he be out here, and how would he know…"

Her voice broke off as she eyed her husband's innocent face. "You were having me followed, weren't you? You have known where I was the whole time, haven't you?"

Alex tried to stop the tirade he knew would be coming. "I was concerned, Baggage. I can't be with you all the time. I am a busy man."

"Of course, you are, and I am your society wife, your property, and I ought to know my place by now." The woman drew herself up to her full height and advanced on him. "I suppose it never occurred to you to tell me you had assigned Robert to dodge my footsteps."

"Be reasonable, Baggage. You would not have allowed it. This incident should have taught you that you are in danger, and while you are a fair shot and you can use a knife, men have far more powerful bodies than you do. I cannot allow you to be hurt. You are my wife."

"But not your love," she mumbled under her breath. "My apologies, My Lord." Lizzie looked down and turned away from him, putting on her shoes. Just then, Robert appeared, and the two men discussed what to do with the prisoner. By the time they had him tied on his horse, the man was coming around, but Lizzie had come around as well. She gathered the remains of her discarded clothing and the few things she had brought with her and mounted her own horse. "I am returning to Winterbourne. I will be careful to avoid meeting anyone who might recognize me. I wouldn't want you to be held accountable for my unladylike actions."

Alex tried to head her off. "Lizzie. Let me escort you home."

She urged her horse just out of his reach. "No. Get this man to the proper officials. I will see you later," and she took off as if the hounds of hell were after her.

"What did I interrupt?" Robert asked. "She looks a bit 'out of sorts' if you don't mind my saying so, Sir."

"She's upset with me. I'll have to figure out what I can do to make it up to her. I'm afraid our romantic outing here was disrupted by this lout."

"Give her some time, Sir. She'll come 'round."

Alex wasn't so sure. Something had happened here, but he had no clue what it was.

CHAPTER 17

Lizzie's dream was over. Alex would never love her, and she could never be the demure Duchess that his position demanded. She couldn't stay with a part time husband. She determined to remain in his life for a brief time until she decided how to best move forward. She would research divorce in England and plead with Essex to remember his contract with her about the house on his estate. She could leave as soon as all was in place. Until then, she could become a paragon of virtue; she could play *Duchess* with the best of them, but she would still go about London as a young man, hoping to make a difference. Alex would never know, and as long as she wasn't found out, he didn't care. It was the image that mattered, not the woman.

The biggest ball of the year was in just over a month and a half; she would use that as a tipping point and disappear from Winterbourne on that night. Having made her decisions, she got a bath and went to bed in her own room. She asked Mary to tell His Lordship that she felt ill and needed to rest. After all, she told Mary, she didn't want the Duke to become ill. He was needed in Parliament.

When Alex came home that evening, Mary caught him before he entered his rooms. "Her Ladyship is indisposed, Sir. She has been abed since after dinner. She said she would see you in the morning."

"Should we call a doctor," Alex asked. "Is she that ill?"

"I think she is just very tired. I did give her a light dinner before she slept, and I offered to stay with her, but she said she would call if she needed me."

"Thank you, Mary." Alex tried to think as his wife would. She certainly could be tired after the long day the two of them had had—their romantic session on the beach was far beyond anything he expected of her. She had promised him that she would not run away, so he decided to wait until morning to talk with her, and talk with her, he would.

His bed felt empty that night for the first time since they had wed; she always slept wrapped around him. Of course, he had been away from her at times when his work demanded it. But tonight, he found it difficult to sleep at all without her by his side. In the middle of the night, he opened the connecting door of their rooms and saw her curled on her side in bed. Chauncey looked up at him, but then put his head down and promptly began snoring. Lizzie looked like a lost child in the large bed; Alex chided himself—he was getting maudlin. She was just a woman asleep, but one he cared deeply about; she had managed to inhabit his very being. He hated his unsettled feelings as he watched her even breathing, so he turned and went back to his bedroom. Lizzie heard his footsteps as he walked quietly away. She had kept very still as silent tears marked her face, not wanting to see or speak to him. The door between the rooms closed once again. The latch clicked and heralded the end to their promising relationship. She would deal.

Alex was called out early the next morning for a special meeting of Parliament. He told the housekeeper that he would be gone several days, if not a week, and he would be staying at his townhouse in London should he be needed. The issue with his wife would just have to wait until he came home. Rather than wake her, he wrote her a note, telling her he needed to speak with her as soon as he returned. As he left the house via the front door, Lizzie slid out a side door of the Great House. She rode properly, with a side-saddle, planning to meet with Essex. Her groom accompanied her as was proper. Lizzie had sent Essex a note when she arrived home last evening, and he agreed to speak with her this morning. He, too, had been called back to Parliament. She needed to be at his home before nine.

Lizzie cantered up the driveway of Lord Essex's home, and her groom helped her to dismount. Essex stood in the doorway to welcome her. He had a bad feeling about her visit, but he needed to find out what she had need of. Even though he was Alex's friend, he respected this little lady for her gumption and her composure, and Alex had never seemed happier. The only thing different in Lord Winterbourne's life was Elizabeth.

"Lord Essex. Thank you for agreeing to meet with me."

"Come in, Lady Elizabeth. It is my honor."

"You won't think that when I am done," she replied. The two entered the front parlor for their discussion. He offered her a seat and sat himself. "Would you like some tea?"

"A glass of whiskey would be far better than tea," she replied.

"You are joking, right?"

"I am not. I have need of your expertise. I am looking for a lawyer to represent me in a divorce proceeding."

To say Essex was shocked would be underestimating the occasion. 'Lady Elizabeth. Do we speak of you or perhaps a friend? I know you often work with those in difficult circumstances."

"No, John. The lawyer is for me. I need to be free of Alex, and I am gathering information about how to proceed. I am planning to live in your house for five years or so. I understand that Alex will keep my dowry."

"And any children you might have," Essex responded.

"There is no child, so that, at least, is a blessing. Alex can marry again and sire his heir as his position requires."

Essex sat quietly. "I am sorry things turned out this way. I should have stopped you from marrying Alex until you knew him better. He can be a difficult man."

"It is not Alex. It is rather the lady who sits before you who is having the problem. You can help me by not telling Lord Winterbourne what I am planning. I am counting on you to do that. I would not have you in the middle of our fight; if you can advise me of a person whom you trust to represent me, I would appreciate that very much. The circumstances surrounding our wedding may come into play, and that is a worry to me. I don't want Alex to receive any negative publicity, you see. I will contend that I was the one who perpetrated the hoax."

"How will you pay for your representation?"

Elizabeth hesitated. "Alex never spoke to my brother to ask for my hand in marriage, so he is unaware that there is another fund that I may use. It was willed to me by my grandmother for my use and my heirs; it will not belong to Alex since it was not part of the marriage contract that you and I worked out. I think that my brother will allow me to draw upon those funds. They were marked for my children, but since it is highly unlikely I will have any because I won't have a husband, it may free me from this marriage. I am leaving here to go to my brother's home to discuss the matter."

Essex shook his head sadly. "You obviously have thought this through, Elizabeth." She nodded. "Is there nothing I can say to make you rethink the situation."

"There is nothing you can do but to honor the contract that I made with you on the day of my marriage." She stood on those words. "I will stay with Alex until everything is in place for me to leave without great fanfare. This conversation will stay between us, and I will wait to hear from you concerning the lawyer you choose. I don't think Alex will even fight the dissolution of the marriage.

"My dear, I think you are very wrong on your last point."

Lizzie looked up, tears filling her eyes. "Essex, Alex doesn't love me, and he never will. He is incapable of the emotion. It is my loss, and I will deal with it." She walked towards the door of his home, and he rose to follow her. "I will be in touch with you." She stopped and turned, smiling at him through teary eyes. You have been a true friend to me, and I thank you."

Elizabeth left with a conflicted Earl staring morosely out the window after her. What in the hell had Alex done? Lizzie had asked for his help, and that included not telling her husband of her plans. He was bound by that promise. He went to his office to look up lawyers he could recommend. He would personally ask that the men do the best job that they could for her. Alex had money and prestige on his side. A good lawyer might even the scale for Lizzie.

Viscount Myers learned that his man had been captured, and by none other than the Duke himself. He was in danger of being implicated in another attempt to kidnap the Duchess. If the crown had not believed the first charge, this second one would lend it merit. The captured man would have to be dispatched and as quickly as possible. A simple note should take care of the deed.

A knock on his study door distracted him. "Sir. You have a visitor: Lady Estelle asks to speak with you. She said it concerns the wedding."

Why did she have to come at this moment when he had other pressing things to do. "Show her into the drawing room and fetch her some refreshments. I will join her shortly."

"Yes, Sir." The butler hurried to do his bidding. The Viscount needed an influx of funds and soon. Estelle could provide that, and she very willing to do so. Estelle was also a beautiful woman; she would grace any man's arm. Societal appearances mattered, and if he were a married man, a settled man, he could receive more offers of funds and more contracts from the aristocracy that surrounded him.

Lady Winterbourne was an entirely different matter. English law held that when a woman married, she was the property of her husband. Known as *coverture*, it said that the husband and wife's identities were one, that of the husband. Practically speaking, a woman could not conduct business through contracts or write a valid will without her husband's consent. A husband received the rights to his wife's goods, including property, business accounts and personal items. Her money became, for all intents and purposes, his money.

Elizabeth was a prize, and if her husband were dead, she would be a widow on the marriage mart. Any man could see to it that she agreed to a second marriage even if it were by force. He could imagine his own funds and lands if he could obtain the Duke's vast holdings. There was no heir to the marriage to stand in his way. Destiny was knocking on his door, but he would have to put off Lady Estelle until he could do away with the Duke. If he took the Duchess captive, he would achieve two results—a dead Duke and a new wife. It was not an impossible task, as long as he stayed ahead of the Duke and his retainers.

Since his new hire had been taken by the authorities, a slippery slope loomed ahead. He had to act, and there was much for him to consider. Now, to placate his intended bride and to string her along for a while were his goals. The future could yet change for him. He wondered how Estelle would take to the idea of killing the Duke in a lover's quarrel; he could blame the Duke's death on her. He could make that happen, but it would take careful planning.

Alex had spent the morning arguing the proposed law concerning debtor's prisons. A debtor could avoid prison by declaring bankruptcy, but not all Englishmen could do it. The cost for filing bankruptcy was 10 pounds; that was 10-20% of the average yearly income of a worker in 1865. The new law under debate would significantly reduce the ability of the courts to detain those in debt. Since credit and debt could be linked to a person's character, debt was seen as a moral failure instead of an economic circumstance, and it was accordingly punished often by incarceration of the man, throwing whole families out onto the streets or having children work in poorhouses. Credit could be granted to those in the upper classes, but not to those of the working class; it was perceived that those who were poorer would not repay the loans, and the interest applied was often far greater.

The debate had dragged on and on with no end in sight for several long days, and Alex was frustrated at the slowness of the procedures. Robert had seen him briefly to tell him things were going well at Winterbourne. His wife was visiting her brother and had plans to go to Tattersalls to look at some of the horses that would be auctioned off on the weekend. Robert would escort her himself. Alex chafed under the dictates of his position; he and his wife had not settled their differences, and not being able to see her was grating on his nerves. He determined that he would go to Tattersalls himself to see her; then the two of them could return to his townhouse for the rest of the weekend. He would reserve all his time to her.

Staying at her brother's home before her visit to Tattersall's, it was easy for Lizzie to put on her boy clothes and stuff her hair under her hat; she was going to visit Marie; she had need of a spectacular dress to mark the end of her reign as the Duchess of Winterbourne. She rode through the side streets of London until she reached the small shop. There were no other clients there; a note from Marie cautioned her to come after six at night. The shop would be closed, but Marie would be waiting for her. Three taps on the door would gain her entrance.

Lizzie slipped from her horse's saddle and looked about. It was just getting dark, and the streets of London were not safe, but she had need of this dress. She bounded up the stairs and knocked three times on the door. It was immediately opened, and Marie hugged her, drawing her inside.

"Where is your groom?"

"I didn't bring one."

Marie fumed. "Well, my husband will escort you home then. It is not safe for a lady to be on the streets at this time."

Lizzie laughed. "You sound just like Alex. I am not a true Lady, Marie." She pulled off her hat and her hair tumbled down, and she wiped her dusty hands on her pants. "I need a wash, but what I really need is a new creation more than anything else—something that will wow everyone."

"You want to impress the Duke that much?" Marie gave her a conspiratorial smile.

"You might say that. Can you help me?" Lizzie asked.

"Let's see what I can do." Marie clapped her hands as she began to imagine her new creation for Elizabeth. Lizzie hated to dissemble before Marie, but she could not take the chance that Alex would find out her plans to leave him. Marie urged her to disrobe, and she even managed to provide a basin and pitcher of hot water for Lizzie as well as a cloth. Lizzie felt much better after she had washed her face and hands, and Marie had such beautiful pieces of material from which to choose.

"I have something very special in the back for you, if you like it, that is. It is straight from one of my best friends in France. It is a Silk plain weave (taffeta) with printed warp, and a moiré finish—but Lizzie, the silk weave and V front with small sleeves will look lovely on you. The appliques on the back of the train are of flowers. It is basically a beautiful garnet, but the flowers and decorations are black pearls and lace. Do you think you would like that?"

"Oh Marie, I would love anything that you choose."

"Let's get it pinned then," and Marie went to work, draping material over Lizzie. "Your breasts are a bit fuller, Lizzie. I will need to retake the measurements." She giggled. "We don't want you falling out of the dress, now, do we? Alex would not care for that at all."

Alex probably would blame Lizzie if anything like that happened. It wouldn't be 'proper'; she was so tired of being proper. "No, he would not," she replied cryptically. The color of the material on her skin was just right, and the dress brought out her figure to perfection. She would be the Duchess of Winterbourne for one evening before she faded into oblivion and was never seen again.

It was pitch black when it was time for Lizzie to leave. She heard Marie cry out in the back of the shop, and Lizzie ran to see what had happened. The woman was almost in tears. "The boy didn't take this package; the Viscount will be so upset with me. He even paid ahead to see it was delivered this evening." Marie sat down, her sobs barely in check.

"I can take it," Lizzie said. "It's only a small detour out of my way, and I will look like a proper delivery boy. Let me do this for you, Marie."

"Lizzie, I couldn't ask you to do that."

"You aren't asking; I'm volunteering." She picked up the carefully wrapped package and read the name. "Viscount Myers is expecting this?

"It is a peignoir and nightgown set for one of his ladies made in French lace."

"I thought the Viscount was going to be married to Lady Estelle." Lizzie pushed her long hair under her hat. "Are they not engaged? Is he still seeing other ladies, then?"

"I believe so. The set inside is of the sheerest French design with appropriate cutaways, something for a paramour, rather than one's intended, I would think."

"Do men continue to visit their paramours even when they are about to be married? Do married men continue their liaisons? I have been told that most of the men in the aristocracy do."

"To my knowledge, Alex has been faithful to you since you married, Elizabeth. There has not been a whiff of indiscretion about him. He remains loyal to you."

Lizzie wasn't so sure he was doing that; she quickly changed the subject. "Do you know if packages go to the front door or to the servant's entrance?"

"Deliver it to the front door, and then promise me you will go straight home."

"I will. Your husband can wait for me on the street while I do it."

CHAPTER 18

Etienne Flaubert was a small man, a Frenchman who was devoted to his talented wife. Lizzie had met him only once before, but he was eager to ride with her to make sure she arrived home safely. He told her it would help to pay the debt to Alex that he owed.

The streets were not busy, but Lizzie was glad that she had someone riding with her. They approached the Viscount's residence in short order. Lizzie hopped down. "I won't be a minute."

Making sure to adjust her walk to that of a boy, she climbed the steps to the townhome. She could hear yelling inside, having to knock twice on the door before the shouting stopped. The front door swung open, and a disheveled man stood before her.

"Package for Viscount Myers."

"This was to have been delivered far earlier this evening." He raised his hand as if to strike the boy, and Lizzie stepped quickly back.

"Madam Flaubert sends her apologies, but she rushed to have the outfit finished," Lizzie mumbled.

The man hesitated and then grabbed the package from her hands, saying "Give it here." She could hear a woman shouting wildly inside. The man threw a coin at Lizzie and slammed the open door. What could be happening? Was Estelle there? Was she the woman who was yelling?

Lizzie turned and ran down the steps of the house only to hear the front door open again, and a lady come barging out. "You will have to give me more money and I want it in writing. I know what you intend," she shouted over her shoulder. "You think about it." A carriage drew up out front as soon as she came out. Lizzie moved out of her way, but as the woman passed, Lizzie did not recognize her. She was from the demimonde from her dress.

Lizzie climbed on the back of her horse and rode a little way, only to hear another carriage come rumbling to a stop at the Viscount's home. Lady Estelle was helped from the carriage by her driver, and the

Viscount came down the steps to greet her. He had put on his coat and was smiling affably.

"I have a gift for you, Sweetest. Come in, and you can model it for me before I take you." He kissed the back of her hand and then Lizzie saw his other hand move to squeeze her breast.

Estelle laughed in a coquettish manner, snuggling into the Viscount: "But of course. It's about time you gave me another gift. The wedding is coming; it's almost upon us."

"We will talk of that when you come in," the Viscount replied. "I have a suggestion for you to consider." As the door closed behind them, the Viscount's hand cupped her bottom, and he ushered her into his house.

Elizabeth turned to Etienne. "The Viscount is up to something. The Duke needs to watch his back."

"I will pass that along to him, Duchess. Lord Winterbourne sent a note to escort you to his townhome. He was concerned for your safety when you were not found at your uncle's." When they arrived at the Winterbourne residence, Etienne helped her down from her mount, and one of the stable hands came to take the animal. She bounced up the stairs, deep in thought, yelling over her shoulder, 'Thank you.' Just as she grabbed the door handle, it opened under her hand, and she was pulled right into her husband's hard chest. Had he not caught her, she would have bounced right off it. "Alex!" Genuine surprise laced her voice.

"Welcome home, Baggage. It's a bit late to be out, isn't it, and in such a fetching attire." Lizzie swallowed hard, as Alex waved goodbye to Etienne. "At least you were accompanied. I notified your brother that you would be staying with me. He is sending your things." Alex closed the door behind her, but he never let go of her. "Since you were with Etienne, I assume you were at Marie's. Is that a fair guess?"

"It is," she stammered, her heart beating wildly in her breast. It couldn't be because of Alex; it must be because she had been caught—again. He pulled her into his body, and his mouth came down softly on hers. Maybe he wasn't too upset with her. Her arms wound around the back of his neck of their own accord. It felt so right.

Alex knew that it had been too damned long since they had been together, and a disagreement tonight was not on his agenda; their falling out still stretched between them, but her softness under his assault tore away any emotional distance that he might have felt. All he knew was that he wanted her, and he would die if she would not have him. He backed slowly away from her, running his fingertips up and down her cheek, and he kissed her hard.

"I am staying," he announced, "just in case you were wondering." Lizzie nodded her head and smiled.

"It is your house, Husband."

"Have you eaten?" She nodded yes. "Then let us retire My Lady Duchess. I have great need of you." She didn't want to feel for this man, but he had a way with women; no, he had a way with her, and she had so missed him. The next few weeks would be all she could have of him. Perhaps it was time to make those days count.

"You could always have a taste of me, Sir," she teased. "But I prefer Alex to the Duke; could Alex come to me tonight?"

"I plan a veritable feast, Baggage. Alex it is." His hand slid under her tunic top to find her bound breasts. "Oh, Lizzie. This will never do." He began systematically to unbind them, and they eventually slipped into his willing hands. "This is much better, I think." His fingers teased the tips, manipulating them carefully to her sharp intake of breath. "I would have more of you, Baggage. Bear with me."

Alex carefully stripped her breeches, stockings and shoes from her before he moved both of them up the stairs together. "I don't think a bath would go amiss. You smell a bit like horse, Lizzie, and while I like horses, I like your scent better." He nuzzled on her neck, and she giggled.

Winding her hands around his neck, she played with the hair on his collarbone, so happy once again to be with him. He picked her up, and she unwound his cravat and threw it on the steps. Buttons were next on the agenda, and before they reached the top of the stairs, his shirt and jacket were both undone and slipping off his broad shoulders. "I have missed you so, Alex."

The man stopped to consider her words. "It is all my fault. I should have moved you here while parliament was in session. There is no excuse for my not doing so. I am sorry, Lizzie."

"I am sorry, too, Alex, for everything. Remember that." Her words were filled with some emotion that Alex didn't completely recognize.

Then neither of them could speak. There was just a reconnecting. Lizzie found rapture in Alex's embrace as he worshipped her body with his hands and mouth. He filled her completely with gentle love and care. There was no tension in his embrace—that eternal drive to find sexual fulfillment; there was a slow loving and a giving of self, pure and simple. Elizabeth reveled in it, memorizing each touch, each kiss for the dry days to come. And when he allowed her to climb atop him and ride him as she rode her favorite mount, he welcomed her ingenuity and her drive as a wanton. This was the side of her that he loved the most. She was unpredictable, spirited and determined, and she was his.

Alex left the townhouse early the next day. He had meetings scheduled all morning. He ran into Robert, his land manager as he walked down the front walk. "Robert. What brings you here today? Do you need me?"

"No, Sir. I've come to find the Duchess, and I was told she might be with you here. The new supplies for the school have arrived, and I want to make sure I do what she wishes."

Alex's forehead furrowed. "Supplies?"

"We did as you asked and made desks from lumber on the estate, but the books, paper and ink, and writing utensils as well as lunch pails had to be ordered. The shipment arrived and is waiting for her direction," answered Robert. "My children are so excited about this school. The applications for the teaching position are only awaiting your perusal. Interviews will be scheduled around your parliamentary duties."

"I get the say on the teacher?" Alex asked.

"Yes, Sir. Lady Elizabeth said that you were to see them."

"I see. How many children will the school hold?"

Robert now frowned. "The Lady didn't tell you? She has offered schooling to anyone on your estate who seeks it. We have twenty-five children as of last count, and the Lady is looking at schedules that will allow the children to complete their work as well as go to school. Some of the men and women on the estate also asked for schooling. I'm not sure how we are going to accommodate them, but your Lady-wife seems to be looking into it."

"You signed for the goods?" Alex asked seeing his wife's hands all over this.

"At her Ladyship's request, yes, sir, I did." Robert was sensing something not quite right with the Duke. "We're refinishing one of the buildings on your property that was no longer in use. It's all right that I did that, isn't it, Sir? I thought…"

Alex smiled. "Of course, it is. I will be interested to visit the school, and I'll get right to work on staffing it adequately. There was no cost incurred to my workers, was there?"

"No, Sir. The women are making clothes for the students to wear as we speak. The material was donated from a merchant in town who has asked that his son be allowed to attend.

Alex chuckled to himself and spoke aloud. "Ah, Baggage. You are always one step ahead of me, but not for long." He turned to Robert. "If you have any problems, don't hesitate to ask me, Robert. I assume the funds for this undertaking are already paid."

"Lady Elizabeth said something about her 'pin money' being the source." Now Alex did laugh out loud. Lizzie's 'pin money' covered everything from his chewed boots to a shattered Ming Vase and everything in between. It would take her a lifetime to pay it all off if he demanded. But he held her vouchers, and he was always amazed at her termerity.

Alex continued down his walk. "Lady Elizabeth is still abed, Robert. Just ask for her to be awakened. She will be upset if you don't."

Robert watched Alex as he mounted his horse. The man was really content today for some reason. Might the Duchess be upstairs asleep in his bed?

When Lizzie received Robert in the front parlor, she hesitated to ask him if he had seen her husband, but she needed to know how much trouble she was in.

"Hello, Robert. Would you care for some tea and cakes?" she asked as any good Duchess would do.

"Lady Elizabeth. I've already had some while I waited, thank you." Elizabeth sat daintily on the front of her chair, ankles and wrists crossed at just the perfect angle. "You haven't seen the Duke, have you?"

"Yes, My Lady. I did. We shared a discussion about the new school." Elizabeth looked startled at what he said. "My Lord seemed pleased at our progress. He is anxious to help you choose the teachers to be involved." Elizabeth chewed on her lip hard. "And, he added that any additional expense should be brought to his attention. He seemed concerned about your 'pin money'."

"Ah, yes, well, I'm glad he is planning on taking a more active role." She swallowed. She had just signed any bill that came before her with the Duke's name; Alex could take it out of her pin money for the rest of her natural life.

"Lady Elizabeth, did you even tell him anything about this project? He seemed confused when I first mentioned it."

"I told him all about it one night before we slept." She didn't add that it was after a frenzied bout of lovemaking that had tired her poor husband out. He had been mostly asleep as she had expounded on it. Since he hadn't disagreed, that meant he was for it, right? That counted as telling him.

"I hope you aren't planning on coming to help us continue building the inside of the school on Friday. We really can do it without you." He hesitated. "That fall you had scared all of us, Lady Elizabeth.

"Well, if I were permitted to wear my boy clothes, it wouldn't have happened; the skirt got caught as I was coming down. And my ankle is doing just fine. I will be there."

"That's what I was afraid of, My Lady." Robert looked upset. "Will His Lordship…"

"Oh, don't be a downer, Robert, and don't mention anything to my husband about my building or climbing skills. He is well aware of them." Robert had to smile at her. Elizabeth always got her way, by hook or crook, with one or two exceptions. Lord Winterbourne was at the center of those.

"Yes, My Lady."

She flashed him a beautiful smile.

CHAPTER 19

Lord Winterbourne had just returned from giving his speech on the creditor legislation. He had worked on it for some hours that afternoon. He was exiting the building when he saw everyone running. Something was happening. A man pushed by him, and Alex clutched at his sleeve. "Do you know what is happening here?" he asked.

"Someone said it is an altercation between a Lord, his driver, and a street urchin. It involves an old, beaten down horse." No, thought Alex. It couldn't be. Lizzie was still in his townhome. Nevertheless, he joined the masses heading down the street and veered towards the left. A huge crowd had gathered around a horse that was staggering in its traces, pulling a far too heavy load for it. Its driver was striking with a whip over and over to the cries and screams of the street urchins who chided him and tried to stop him by kicking at him and pelting him with stones.

Alex pushed his way through until he had a better line of sight. A burly man who was the driver of the overloaded conveyance was striking a young boy with his whip; the Lord of the realm urged his driver on; it was the horse that was supposed to be struck, but a lad had placed his body in front of it, taking the blows on his back and shoulders as he turned away from the whip. The horse could barely stand and was near collapse.

Alex measured the boy in his head—he was Lizzie's size. The boy was protecting the animal. Several of the street boys continued to attack the driver, kicking and punching him wherever they could as he screamed obscenities at them. Alex forced himself through the bystanders and grabbed the man's arm, jerking him back from the animal and the boy. "Stop this. You are causing a scene and backing up traffic." The boy staggered and almost fell; the Lord grabbed the boy's sore shoulders and held him, even as he tried to break free.

"I'm calling a constable to have this boy arrested. He is interfering in the delivery of my goods," the Lord cried.

An onlooker then yelled, "Nay, Governor. The man was beating the horse and wouldn't stop. That boy tried to stop him from killing it."

Alex felt anger break over him as he took in the boy and the flagging horse. The animal was dying on its feet. "Put a price on the animal." His own voice said the words aloud.

The Lord recognized the Duke and made a low bow. "Your Lordship. I am sorry for the traffic backup. The horse is worth at least fifty pounds."

"It is not, Sir. I hate those who cheat, but I will pay you your fee if you let the boy and the horse go. That's the offer, Sir."

The Lord looked uncomfortable for the crowd had definitely turned in favor of the boy and the horse. He nodded, and Alex counted out his money. "Let the wagon on the side of the road; you can get it later and bring a team of horses that can pull it. It is far too heavy for one animal." Alex reached across the man and pulled the boy to him. In a low tone, he chastised the man: "Don't ever let me see you abuse an animal or a boy like this again. I will make it my business to ruin you if you do. Do you understand?"

The crowd's dissent was growing louder, and two of the urchins rushed to unhook the beaten animal from the wagon to the crowd's roaring approval. The boy who had defended the animal kept his face away from the Duke. "You. Come with me." He latched on to the boy's shirt.

The lad winced and shook his head. "No need, Sir. I'll be fine." Drops of blood stained his back and arm from the whip strikes. "I'll just go along home."

Alex felt a trembling in his body as soon as he touched the boy, a familiar awareness. He motioned to two of the street boys. "Go to the Winterbourne townhouse and bring the head stablemaster. Tell him I have an injured horse that needs immediate treatment.

"Yes, Sir."

"If you do a good job, there will be work for all of you at the new horse complex that I have started. You obviously care for animals," he looked at the injured boy, "and those who would protect them. I am the Duke of Winterbourne. Give this card to the stablemaster." The boys ran off to do his bidding. Alex watched the bleeding boy begin to stagger; he was in some pain now. The Duke reached down, turned and tilted the boy's face to his own—only to stare into the green eyes of his wife. She was definitely injured.

"If you kiss me, I will kill you," she whispered. "People are still watching you." She grimaced as his hand caught one of the welts. "You will make all the rags, then, and not in a nice way."

Alex tried to maintain his distance from her, but all he wanted to do was scoop her up and hold her close and kiss her senseless. His voice was rough as he said, "Can you stand, Boy?"

"I can." And she did although not without difficulty. His stablemaster arrived in a matter of minutes with another stable hand, and the crowd began to drift away. "Sir?" His eyes wandered over the distressed horse.

"Get this animal the help it needs, and when it is ready, move it to my stables for further care. I need to take this boy to get some help as well."

"Yes, Sir." The stable boy went immediately to the horse's head to comfort it and to remove the traces and yoke from the wagon.

"He needs a drink, Sir, please. He is so hot." Lizzie's voice was labored and small.

"I'll see to it. I promise you the animal will be cared for. Now, you are coming with me. I'm going to sit you on the horse that brought Nathaniel to me. Your back is going to hurt badly until I get you some care." She nodded. "Nathaniel, I'm taking your horse back home. Can you help me get the lad up before me?"

The two men worked diligently to get the 'lad' on the horse. A low moan came from the boy's lips, but then they both were seated. Alex directed the animal to move slowly. Spots of blood appeared on the white tunic the boy wore, and Alex cursed at the sight of them. "You can add the fifty pounds I owe you to my 'pin money' account," Lizzie said through gritted teeth.

"Oh Baggage," he whispered. "Just be quiet and try to rest until I can fully see the damage." She struggled to sit up straight; she failed, and then she snuggled into him with a soft sigh as the world began to spin.

Three hours later she was situated in bed, her wounds dressed, and the doctor had examined her. She had lapsed into unconsciousness because of the pain medication to keep her drowsy given by the physician. The wounds on her back and upper arms were welted with several breaks in the skin. These, too, had been treated. Alex sat by her side and held her hand. The incident was sure to hit the rags quickly, and he shuddered to think of what they would say. Mary, her maid, sat with her.

"I'm going to go down and see to the horse. I will be right back. If she wakes, send for me immediately." The maid nodded.

Alex entered the stables to find the battered horse in one of the last stalls. He had been cooled down and his wounds carefully tended. He was given water periodically to quench his overwhelming thirst, and oats and hay were available to him. "What do you think, Nathaniel. Will he make it?"

"He will if we can just keep him eating. I'm going to walk him around in a bit to see if he is stable on his feet. His hooves have been treated, but he is in deplorable condition. The man who had him should be shot. How is the boy?"

Lizzie's face came into his mind. "He's going to be all right with some rest and care."

"The people there told me of his bravery, how he stepped in front of the whip and begged for the animal to be spared. That bloke never even paused. I would have punched him had I been there," Nathaniel said.

"I wish I could have done that but being a Duke…" and Alex stopped to consider what he was about to say. He hadn't acted because of his ducal affairs—what did that say about him as a man. He had allowed two men to strike and browbeat those who were 'beneath' them and expendable, an old horse and a young street urchin. It was not a pretty picture of himself that he saw.

Alex grinned at the thought of Lizzie's pin money. It would take her years to pay him back. She was an heiress in her own right, and he had been given her money for his use; he returned only a tiny fraction. Those laws should be revisited as well.

Alex swore to advocate for the animals being used on the streets of London; he would search for ways to protect the working animals and to punish those who would abuse them. He promised himself that he would; it would be one way to pay back his wife. His anger was at those who oppressed Lizzie, but it was also at himself; he had led her to believe that her behavior was the problem, rather than his. He petted the horse as it labored to stand in the stables. "Come on old man, you've got to get better. My married life might depend on it." He fed it a piece of apple which it ate with sad eyes. Then he turned away, and Alex went back to his wife.

Lizzie awakened feeling fuzzy and way too warm. There was a constant ache in her shoulders and back that would not go away: ah, the beating would be the cause of that. She dreaded the scolding from Alex she would receive; she remembered that Alex had discovered she was out on the streets again. She was such a poor duchess to him. She felt sick in her stomach, but she managed to close her eyes until the dizziness subsided.

Alex decided that Lizzie would return to Winterbourne as soon as she could stand the trip. He would be unable to go with her at the present time, but he would join her just as soon as he could possibly get away. She needed his protection now until he could ascertain the fallout from what had happened today.

He would cancel their plans for the gala tonight even though he had replied and accepted the invitation; the gala was to commend him for his new venture into the horse complex. He couldn't go by himself; he would have to find some excuse.

Alex stood at his desk, a glass of bourbon in his hand, when he heard a slight sound. He turned to see his wife in long, white nightgown bouncing from foot to foot at his door. "Lizzie. Why are you out of bed?" He came quickly to her and led her into the room, sitting her down on his couch; a shawl was laid carefully over her shoulders. "You'll catch your death of cold, and where are your slippers?" He knelt down and covered her freezing feet with his warm hands. "Your feet are like blocks of ice."

"I just came to ask when we are leaving for the gala. My dress is still at Marie's, and I need to send someone to pick it up. That's why I was in London today, to pick it up."

Alex found another throw, sat and put her small feet in his lap, and covered them. "We are going to send our apologies."

"Why? The gala is for you. We are going to go." she said mulishly.

"You're not up to it, Baggage. I can't in all good conscience make you do that."

"Are you ashamed of me? Don't you want me to go? This is a good way for you to put me aside."

"Elizabeth. That's not true. Your back...have you seen your back? You would be in some pain to sit and dance all evening."

"Why don't you just call one of your Ladybirds and ask her to go in my place. I'm sure she would be thrilled to be your partner," she sniped. She slipped out of his hands and stood suddenly. "I want my dress, please, and I will be ready to go at 9:00 this evening. I trust you will escort me. If you do not escort me, I will go on my own." Alex's mouth fell open at her defiance. She did a perfect turn and went through the doorway rubbing her shoulder as she did. He had no ladybirds, so from where did that come?

Retreat was in order; Alex called for one of his men to go and pick up her dress at Marie's establishment. Then he sat down and wondered how he had been outflanked.

CHAPTER 20

The Duke of Winterbourne stood in his entryway, looking up the long stairs waiting for his wife. He had her dress delivered in an hour, but he had yet to see the woman in it. He was not a patient man, so he paced and walked and nursed his drink. The clock told him she still had an hour to appear.

"Are ye waiting for the lady, then, Sir?" asked his butler. "She is in the barn with the new horse."

Alex considered the words he heard; of course, that was where she would be.

"Thank you." He turned on his heel and headed for the door. Perhaps he could yet dissuade her from this folly. She was not well enough to go out this evening. He would put down his foot, and she would obey.

Pulling open the barn door, he strode confidently into the interior and saw her immediately. She stood on the second rail of the poor animal's stall, and she petted the horse who stood on the other side. Occasionally, she offered bits of apple to the animal, and it fed contentedly from her hand. It stood patiently and allowed her to play with its mane and pat its neck where there were scars. She chatted to the animal in a sweet tone, one that he hadn't heard from her in some time when speaking with him.

"You are a prince among men, and I need to find a name that will suit you. Do you have any suggestions?" she whispered into its neck. A long peignoir hid her undergarments from her husband; he wondered if she knew how alluring she looked. His anger grew at the fact she was here practically undressed for his stable staff, but she was a beautiful sight. He wanted her; he reminded himself that she was his for the taking, but not tonight. Tonight, she was fragile, and yet she demanded that she go with him to the Gala.

"Baggage. It is nearly time for us to go. Do you intend to wear that to the Gala? I find it very engaging, but I'm not going to advocate that you share it. Such sights are for my eyes only. You would be far too tempting to my colleagues."

Lizzie turned at the sound of his voice. "I know. I'm going. I just wanted to see him, to make sure he is doing well. He seems so much more alert tonight, and I am pleased. I never did thank you for rescuing him and bringing him here. Oh, and thank you for rescuing me, as well. You must have been very surprised to find me there."

"It was a surprise." She began to ease herself from the rails of the pen. "Let me help you, Lizzie." Alex moved quickly to steady her as she climbed down. "I have been told he is doing well. He needs time to heal, and we can give him that here. He will be well looked after."

"I know he will, Alex, and I'll think of a name for him, too. I'll go and finish dressing now." His arm came carefully around her waist. He had to touch her, and he quickly kissed her cheek as well. "We have plenty of time. It won't start without me, I promise." The two of them walked quietly back into the Manor, each deep in thought.

When she reappeared at the top of the stairs some time later, she was resplendent in a gown of ivory taffeta, her bodice adorned with small appliqued flowers of a soft pink. The embellishment adorned the train of her gown and her small sleeves. Dainty pink shoes peeked out from her skirt. She wore her hair down; soft ivory gloves covered her arms. She was the Duchess of Winterbourne incarnate. Alex stepped forward to meet her. The dress discretely covered her wounds from this morning. "I think I am ready," she said, endearingly, and then, as if seeking his approval, she added: "Do I look all right?"

"You have to ask?" Alex inquired. "I am overwhelmed, Baggage. You manage to do that to me all the time; there is something new to be found in you every single day."

Lizzie laughed. "So now you are telling me I am an enigma to you?"

"I am."

"Sir, the carriage has arrived." Alex nodded to his butler as he opened the door for the couple.

The ballroom was filled with elite ton of English society. Alex was to be honored for his horse complex project. The King himself was interested in the management of the animals. All England was abuzz with this new way to create the perfect horses for racing and for hunting.

"Stay by me, Elizabeth. If you should feel ill, I want to be near you," he whispered.

"I will try, Sir," she replied.

They were quickly engulfed by the members of society as they entered the ballroom. Every nuance and every move would be marked by the critics. Elizabeth knew this to be true. She buried her true personality behind that of the Duchess. She smiled enchantingly and danced the first waltz in her husband's arms. She never faltered. The Queen spoke briefly to her as she was led into supper by Lord Essex. Talk was of horses and balls and the summer away from the countless entertainments and back to the manors that were often forgotten while the Season was in play.

In the retiring rooms, Elizabeth overhead catty comments about the fact that she was not increasing yet. If they only knew, she thought; there would only be weeks before she left the Duke. She spent as little time as possible there in that poisonous atmosphere. Returning to the ballroom, she was stopped by several older ladies, asking for an opportunity to speak with her about some charitable ventures. She smiled and replied that she would be happy to help them if it was at all possible. Lady Greene promised to be in touch with her for the next meeting of the group.

Viscount Myers managed to catch her arm and turn her towards him. "I would like a dance if that is acceptable to your ladyship." She was a delectable morsel, far more beautiful than he had known. "A waltz, perhaps?" She could be his wife if all worked out as planned.

Elizabeth noted his stance before her, and she sensed a threat; she was no innocent when it came to men like him. The man was arrogant to offer for a dance without Alex's approval. She smiled sweetly and said, "I only have a quadrille left on my card, and my waltzes were all claimed by my husband. Would you like the quadrille, Sir?"

The Viscount did not, but he nodded graciously and placed his name on her card. "I will look forward to being with you." The quadrille would keep that from really happening. She smiled to herself. Alex should be warned about this man.

When Alex saw his wife with the Viscount, his concern grew. He knew that the Viscount had been named in her attempted kidnappings, but she did not. He moved quickly to her side, and she turned to him as the Viscount moved away. "The Viscount has asked for a dance, a quadrille. I know you will have no issue with it."

Alex looked Viscount Myers in the eyes and nodded. "He will enjoy your company, Elizabeth, but he will return you to me." A line had been drawn in the sand, one that Elizabeth didn't quite comprehend; she would have to ask Alex about it later.

Alex moved her away from the Viscount. "Beware Baggage. The Viscount is not to be trusted. Do not leave the ballroom with him, please."

"Of course, Alex, but you will explain this to be at a later date, won't you? Is it because of Estelle?" Alex shook his head no.

"How are you feeling? You must be in some pain by now."

"I am, but it is bearable. I can do another hour or so."

"Let me get you a drink, Baggage. I'll escort you to the refreshment table." She agreed, and they made their way to the table. Essex joined them there.

"I see the Viscount is here. Where is his intended, Alex? Do you know?" Essex continued to look over the large gathering.

"I have not seen Estelle, nor do I wish to," Alex replied. "The Viscount has obtained a dance from my fair lady." Essex raised his eyebrows at Lizzie.

"It's only a quadrille, John. I think I will survive."

"There is some news on his marriage front. The Viscount has pushed off his wedding to Estelle—it is now to be in six weeks instead of next week," John said.

"Did he say why?" asked Alex.

John shook his head. "He said there were extenuating circumstances, but a wedding would proceed at that time."

"I don't like this," said Alex. Just then the Viscount approached Elizabeth for his dance. The quadrille was forming. She smiled at Alex and left with the man. Alex watched their departure and moved so that the couple would always be in his sight. He hadn't counted on Estelle coming over to talk with him, taking his attention from his wife.

"Well, Duke. I assume you are still speaking to me?"

"Why should I, Estelle? You wronged me by not telling me of your marital concerns, or was it something else I did or even something my father did? It's over, Estelle and I have married another. I know that you are spreading rumors about me. It will stop, Estelle. I have information on you that you would not like the public to know. My father made every attempt to save your mother's holdings. Your father would not listen."

Estelle's eyes turned dark. "That's not true; Alex. I will never believe you. You have far too much power over everyone, so making you pay was never an easy task; but to be fair, you are correct. I lost the game, and you have won. It is over, and you are married."

"Were you seeing Viscount Myers behind my back, Estelle, or perhaps it was the man you sailed to meet in Cyprus? Had you already bedded one of them, and was that a major issue for not appearing at our wedding—your lack of virginity?" Her eyes told the tale. "Never mind. That is none of my concern now. I have moved on, and I suggest that you do the same. Be warned. I will support my wife in every way."

"Your wife isn't increasing yet, is she?" Estelle probed. "Isn't she as good in bed as you had hoped." The cut to his wife went deep, especially since the opposite was true.

"Really, Estelle." Alex's anger exploded. "Did you think you would be better? I'm assuming Viscount Myers would tell me if I asked." The woman bristled at his words.

Lizzie's eyes found Alex in deep conversation with Lady Estelle. What did she want with him, or had he looked for her. The Duchess closed her eyes and concentrated on the steps of the dance. Alex searched the dance floor in vain for his wife as soon as the music ended, moving Lady Estelle out of his sight line. His wife was nowhere to be found; Viscount Myers was also missing. Alex pushed Lady Estelle aside and rushed forward to find his wife.

Elizabeth had walked through the steps of the quadrille, and when it ended, she expected to be returned to Alex. Instead, her arm was grabbed roughly by the Viscount, and she was pulled to one side of the room as she tried to get his attention to stop. The pain in her back fired up as he tugged on her already injured muscles. Another man, swarthy and tall, joined him; Lizzie didn't recognize him. He grabbed her other arm, and she was unceremoniously pulled through the double doors that led to the garden. She opened her mouth to scream as soon as she understood what was happening, but it was already too late to summon help. The rough handling caused her back and shoulders to twist in more pain, making her barely able to fend off their manhandling.

Lizzie still had her small knife on her, secreted away in her glove. She managed to pull it out, and she swung her dress around and slashed one arm that held her viciously. He was a brute of the first order, but no match for her. He immediately let go of her, bellowing out in pain as blood ran down his slashed muscles. "Stay away from me. The next time it will be your ugly face," she threatened as she moved gingerly away. The Viscount had lost his step when his comrade let go of the woman and had almost fallen. Elizabeth had time to turn on him and punch him in the face with her fist. He, too, fell to the ground, holding his bleeding nose and crying out. Lizzie pushed him out of her way and kicked him hard somewhere in his groin area; she had been told that men were sensitive there. Then she picked up the skirts of her gown and tore off into the gardens with the Viscount and his friend staggering slowly along behind.

"We have to catch her," the Viscount said, and the two men set off in pursuit. "She can't get far in that gown. The carriage is waiting in the alley."

The full skirt of her beautiful dress impeded her sprint. She dove into a dense group of trees, selected one and pulled herself up on its branches until she was nearly half way up. Her entire body was on fire, and her breath was almost non-existent from her desperate run. Her ivory gown made her a sitting duck if the men looked up. Where was Alex; did Estelle still hold him captive?

Lizzie heard the thrashing of the two men as they beat at the vegetation; they thought they had brought her to ground and that she was hiding there. She managed to climb a few feet higher, and then she pushed herself against the trunk, holding on for dear life. Still the men searched below. "Come out, come out, Elizabeth. There is nothing here to hurt you," the Viscount coaxed. "I just want to talk to you."

"Like hell, you do," she murmured to no one in particular.

Another gruff voice could be heard just inside the house patio doors: "Who is calling Elizabeth?" Both men who were chasing her ducked into the bushes and waited.

The doors to the patio exploded, and a stronger voice called out: "Elizabeth. Are you out there?" It was Alex's voice.

"Here, Alex," she yelled. The relief on Alex's face was palpable. "I'm hanging in a tree again. She muttered to herself. "We really have to stop meeting this way, or you will be the death of me." Her sweet voice reached him in a soft moan, and he was running. Hearing Alex crashing through the vegetation, the Viscount took off along with his henchman heading towards the back gate of the property just as quickly as they could. Lizzie went on, musing to herself: "How does a fall out of a tree feel? I think it might be on my upcoming adventures."

Alex's frantic voice came from below the tree where she was. "Where are you? I can't find you."

"Look up. I'm in the tree and oh," her voice cut off as she took in her ragged dress, "just look at my beautiful gown. It's totally ruined—again." Alex climbed rapidly once he located the ivory dress in the branches. As he reached her, she commented: "I hurt everywhere, Alex. I don't think I can climb down. I'll just stay here. You can come and get me when you leave."

"I'll get you now, Baggage. Just hang on. I'll deal with the two men later. Did they hurt you in any way?"

"I'm OK," she sniffed with tears running down her cheeks. She looked up as Alex moved to the branch just above her.

Alex smiled at her: "You are not staying in this tree."

"I can't come down. I will ruin you socially if I do. 'Duchess of Winterbourne enjoys gala from tree'; I can see the headlines in the rags. Just go. I can hang on until everyone leaves."

A small crowd now formed at the terrace of the mansion, wondering what all the noise was. Essex hurried back to them. "Folks. There is a white cat caught in the tree in the garden. The Duke is trying to extract it, and his wife is trying to comfort it. They ask that you go in and enjoy the rest of the gala. The quiet will help with their capture of the kitty." He gave them all a kindly, forceful smile.

The group slowly turned and moved back inside the double doors. One matron squinted her eyes as she looked: "That seems like one big cat." Another of the matrons said she could see a flash of white in the tree as well. "I am so glad the Duke is willing to rescue it. Let us know when it down, Essex."

"I will." When the patio was cleared, Essex hurried back to Winterbourne and called up. "How can I help?"

Alex was standing beside Lizzie now. "She is in pain, John. She says she's going to stay here until everyone leaves. I can see that the wounds on her back have opened again; she's bleeding. I'm going to try to place myself to her back between me and the tree, steady her, and ease her down the trunk. Then I'll lower her down to you."

"All right. I'll be ready."

Alex placed his hands around Lizzie's waist and held her. "Let go, now Lizzie. I have you."

"No. I'll embarrass you, and we have to save the kitty."

"Lizzie, there is no cat."

"No cat? Well, that's disappointing. I like cats."

"Just hold on, Baggage." Placing his own body against her, he felt her relax her weight into him, and they navigated the trip down with Alex keeping her from falling. Essex reached up to grasp her legs as she was finally near the ground. Alex jumped down and helped Essex.

Alex's arms came around her, and he sat her on the bench at the base of the tree. Her face turned up to his. "I'm down. Did everyone already go home?" She wobbled in his arms. "You are fading in and out. I hate to do this to you, Alex, but I'm going to faint. It's not a Duchess-like thing to do, but that's what you got when you married me." With a sweet smile, she promptly fainted.

Essex went for the carriage as Alex held his limp wife in his arms, kissing her mouth and rubbing her cold cheeks. At least she could no longer feel any pain. The two men carried her into the conveyance. "I'm going back in and tell the cat story. Get her out of here, Alex. Just go. I'll give your regards to your host and hostess."

Alex nodded and climbed into the carriage himself. "Thank you, Essex. I owe you one." Essex thought of what Elizabeth had in store for the Duke and berated himself for promising the lady not to reveal her plans. But a man was only as good as his word.

Lizzie was put to bed and asleep before an hour was gone. Her wounds had reopened in her attempt to flee the Viscount and his man and in her climbing the tree; they had been treated and still, she slept peacefully. Her beautiful ivory gown was ripped to threads. Alex would owe her yet another dress—he needed to up his monetary account for clothing for his Duchess. She had a habit of destroying her dresses or maybe, it was him. He no longer knew, but he had allowed his attention to be drawn from her, causing the incident. He crawled into bed beside her and wrapped his arms carefully around her. His warmth surrounded her, and she relaxed even further into his body. He had failed her again, and he wondered if Estelle had played a part in the attempted kidnapping. If she were involved, she would pay a dear price. He would see to it.

Something was changing in him—it was Lizzie who was making the transformation, and even if he hadn't agreed to the change, the cold demeanor he had always used as a shield to the world—the rules and regulations—had irrevocably broken. He was seeing the world in a whole new way. He watched her sleep in some wonder.

CHAPTER 21

Lizzie awoke to a small, soft, furry body on her chest. It was white and fluffy and had such a dear little nose as her sight centered on it. Its china blue eyes stared at her as if assessing this new person in its life. Alex sat in the chair beside the bed and just watched the two—the lady and the kitten.

Lizzie slowly pulled herself up to a sitting position in some pain and took the tiny thing in her hands. "Oh, Alex. Look. It's a kitten. How did it get here?" She rubbed her nose across that of the little cat's, and it purred.

"Essex brought it this morning. It's a gift from the Queen. She heard the story from the gala last night of your attempts to rescue a cat. Apparently, this little one was found in the drawing room late last evening, and our hosts assumed it was the one that we were after. The Queen wanted her sent to you." Lizzie looked confused. "She also suggested a name for it—Victoria."

"I must have missed something, but I love the cat." Her mind began to work. "I stabbed someone." Her nose wrinkled. "I won't get arrested, will I? The man deserved it."

"No, Baggage. I would never allow that. With your predicament of being caught in the tree, Essex put about the story that I was rescuing a white cat."

Peals of laughter came from the tiny woman in the bed. "Oh, how delicious." She rubbed the kitten's fur, and it purred again. "I love her."

"You are turning my house into a home for wayward animals, Lizzie…first the dog, then the horse and now a cat. I hope you don't plan on rescuing an elephant any time soon."

Lizzie looked him directly in the eyes: "My plan, My Lord, is to rescue you from your life as a stuffy old Duke," she said cryptically.

He looked confused. "I don't need rescuing, Baggage."

Her sad smile gave him little to go on. "Whatever you say, My Lord." She managed to get up and go to him, taking his face in her hands, and kissing him on his unshaven chin. "I am going to get up and see to my pets."

"Well," he replied as he, too, stood: "This pet will see you at dinner. Stay safe, Baggage. We will be going to Winterbourne at the end of the week, and I will accompany you. We will return for the Grand Ball at the end of the month. Does that suit you, Lizzie?"

"Oh yes, Alex. It does. It will mean weeks of being together without the circus. I should love that above all things." It would be the end of her grand passion with her husband; she would lose him after that, but for three weeks, he would be totally hers. Alex kissed her mouth sweetly and left.

The Duke's physician stopped by to see Lizzie. He found her in the barn with the rescued horse. "Well, Alex's idea of horseflesh is certainly unique," he quipped. "That's quite a specimen."

"Don't pick on him. He is a very special man." Lizzie fondled the animal's ears and kissed his snout. He continued to chew on the fresh hay in his box.

"You obviously like him more than you like me. I've come to check out my patient. Shall we go to your room, Duchess?" She nodded.

As they talked, she bit her lip. "I had a bit of a setback last evening. It's a long story, and if you truly wish to hear it, you should speak to my husband."

"In other words, you are more injured today than you were yesterday. I saw you at the gala with Alex. You looked like you were holding up. What happened?"

"Talk to Alex." She climbed gingerly down from the fence and struggled to maintain her balance. "I'm just a little dizzy today." She gave him an impish smile and took his arm. The doctor walked slowly beside her and gave her a speculating look.

Alex returned for lunch to find his physician just leaving his townhouse. "Alex."

Alex turned. "Fred. How's the patient?"

"She is improving, but not as rapidly as I had hoped. She mentioned that she had another problem at the gala last night, but she also told me that I had to get the whole story from you."

"Viscount Myers tried to take her from the dance with a henchman of his. I'm tracking him down as we speak, and there will be consequences. She escaped him but ended up in a tree. She overused her muscles and her back was damaged again."

"I hadn't heard that. All I heard was that you were dispatched to save some cat. Really?"

"It's close enough."

The doctor became serious. "Why does Viscount Myers want your wife? Do you know?"

"I think it's a ransom thing. The man needs money, and he hates me as well. Stealing my wife would be a coup, and Lady Estelle is now his intended. She seems to have a vendetta against my family according to Lizzie. You do know that Estelle stood me up on my wedding day. Elizabeth came to my rescue and married me." Alex needed to remind himself of that again and again. "I'll have to sort it all out and place extra protection on Elizabeth. She will not be pleased to be further harnessed by me."

"Your wife was a little dizzy today," the doctor said.

"She fainted last night after her ordeal. It's probably related to that."

The doctor glanced at Alex and smirked. "Are you sure it isn't something else? Could your wife be increasing?" Alex looked thunderstruck, trying to recall the date of her last menses. He could ask Mary, her maid, but it certainly hadn't been in recent weeks. He was unable to wrap his arms around that thought.

"Surely, she would have told me," Alex argued. He thought of the whipping and the tree climbing last evening. Could that have affected his child if she were expecting?

The doctor went on: "I'm not sure Elizabeth has any idea. Keep an eye on the little lady. In a matter of weeks, we will all know the truth." His friend clapped him soundly on the back. "She is in excellent health, Alex. You'll make a great father." Then the man walked away whistling. Alex couldn't move with the thoughts that raced through his head. How could he keep her safe from herself as well as from those who would harm her? A child—his child—it was almost too much to consider.

Elizabeth had a note from Essex that the lawyer to handle her divorce wanted to see her as soon as possible. She had to find some time to escape Winterbourne and go to Essex's estate, and that wouldn't be easy with her husband on the premises. She would ask for a specific time for the meeting. Lizzie had been advised by Essex that she could apply for a divorce, but only through the passage of a private act of Parliament could it be granted. The remedy was new and was only offered to the very wealthy. A court heard divorce cases, but only one court in London could grant divorces and the burden of proof was unequal—the husband held most of the rights. In addition, any children of the marriage would belong to the father. Lizzie didn't have a child, so that point was moot for her.

In the meantime, she had three weeks to enjoy Alex in every possible way, and she had several new thoughts about that. He was such a different man when away from his ducal responsibilities. If only he were Alex, a businessman, and not the Duke of Winterbourne. But, as Alex had pointed out—he was both. The more time she spent with Alex, the more deeply she cared for him. Even though it was clear to her that he preferred Estelle, she wanted him to enjoy his life just being with her--Lizzie. Seeing Estelle and him together at the dance had brought it all home.

Perhaps if she talked first to Alex about the wedding and the fact that he didn't choose to marry her, he would offer to divorce her; her reputation in society would be shattered, but the matter would be resolved, and Alex would not be embarrassed and could move on with his life. That would be the best option, she decided. She chose not to think about how she would feel when he was gone from her life. But she could never be the Duchess he wanted.

Lady Estelle confronted her intended, Viscount Myers "What were you thinking? Why in the world would you try to steal Alex's wife? She has no money; Alex has it all."

Viscount Myers stammered his reply: "Ransom, my sweet. We felt sure that the Duke would feel obliged to ransom his pretty wife for a huge amount. He would not chance being looked down upon by the matriarchs in the ton; they love the girl."

"You are fortunate that no one who was at the gala truly knows what you intended. The investigative arm of the police has been called on you; you can go nowhere until the Duke is able to question you about the incident. It is very hush hush, but my brother has influence, and he has heard of an investigation. I cannot marry you if you are under a cloud of suspicion."

Anger crossed the Viscount's face. "You will do as you are told, my Sweet. Your reputation as a fallen woman could hang in the balance if I choose to tell all I know about your innocence and how you planned to get even with Winterbourne. He would not have welcomed your lack of virginity. I am going to Bath for a brief time to plot my next move. You will become charming and helpful and needy to the Duke. Feel him out. Find out what he suspects and what he knows. That would be helpful. Tout my innocence to the world, Estelle. If you do not do so, you will pay a very dear price."

"Alex is too smart for my playacting; I will approach him as a friend and have him turn to me when his Elizabeth is gone. He has said nothing of the incident in the garden; the world thinks he was helping a kitty out of a tree. But he has told others in high places in no uncertain terms that he will call you out. I will put together a story for you."

"You are a great little liar, Estelle. Do it quickly. Winterbourne hates me."

Alex came into his townhome in the early afternoon and ordered all of his servants out—they were to go and have a paid evening of release. Their rooms were housed in another building on the townhouse property, and they came and went as needed, so they would not be required at all that evening. Then he ordered flowers delivered to Elizabeth—wildflowers, huge arrangements of them.

"Your Lordship. Your dinners are in the warming tray in the kitchen should you choose to have them," his Butler said.

"Thank you and thank the staff as well. I will expect you on duty in the morning then."

"Yes, Sir. Should you need anything, just send for me."

"I will."

Lizzie was standing on top of the desk in Alex's office trying to reach a volume on one of his upper book shelves. The books that had been placed up high intrigued her; were they her husband's array of tantalizing sexual volumes? Not one of these books could be found in the lending libraries that ladies had access to. If she could just stretch two more inches, she might be able to knock down the book that she wanted. "What are you hiding from me, Alex?" she whispered. She only had three weeks to gather all the carnal experiences that she could.

Her life after that would be one of a lonely woman with her cats. She wanted more pets than just cats, though. She would take her dog, her old horse, and her cat.

"What in the deuce are you doing?" The Duke's voice bellowed across his library as he strode towards her; Lizzie turned far too quickly; she lost her balance and fell, but thankfully, into her husband's waiting arms. He clutched her closely to him as his heart beat frantically in fright. He righted her and shook her hard. "Baggage, you owe me ten years. That's how many I lost watching you topple off that desk. Whatever were you doing up there?"

Lizzie ignored his frightened words having a full-blown discussion with herself. "I'm going to take falling from a tree off my adventure list. It was rather scary to see the floor coming up to meet me." She looked at him then with a smile. "Thank you for catching me."

Alex shook her lightly again and growled. "This isn't funny, Baggage. I don't want you more than one foot from the floor."

"Why ever not." Her laughing face caught him. He wanted to scream at her *because you might be carrying my child,* but the look on her face was so young and so full of life—she was a lover of adventure. She would make carrying a child such a special event, just as she embraced everything in her life. She had no idea she might be pregnant; he was sure of that.

Alex went on: "I'd like to live to see 35, and I'd rather not have to scrape you off the floor for my celebration," he added in a dry voice.

"Oh, what a lovely thing to say," she gushed, and she reached up and kissed him, even as deep down inside, she wondered if he meant it. Might he want her to stay? God, he was wonderful, and she loved him. The admission finally found the light of day, and her eyes clouded over with the thought. It was too little, too late—but she had three weeks to fill her memories of the Duke book. No, make that—The memories of Alex book. She already had so many images in her mind of the two of them together. She loved the man. She really did.

Lizzie felt Alex's arms pull her even closer, and his voice whispered in her ear: "I want you, and I want you now, Lizzie. The house is ours tonight—no interruptions, no other people, just you and me." He kissed her then, his tongue invading her mouth as his hands played at the buttons on the top of her dress. "I don't know what you were looking for on that shelf, but I have some idea. Perhaps actions will steal the place of those thoughts. Next time, just ask, and I'll get the book down for you." She colored at what he had surmised.

His mouth suckled one nipple through the thin material of her dress, making it peak from the pull of his lips, and his hand manipulated the other to her gasp of surprise. "That's what I want, Baggage, your mouth gasping in anticipation, not crying out from falling bodily from high places." She twisted into him, her arms wrapping around his waist, seeking more. He didn't disappoint.

Alex's patience was almost overcome with his need for his woman. He tore the buttons on the top of her dress and reached his hand inside her bodice. He captured the warm flesh of her breast only to find that it was fuller and more sensitive than before. She jerked as he stroked it with his thumbs. Her lower body was pushed against his, and she could feel his rampant need. Her fingers found the fall front that guarded his manhood, and she deftly undid the buttons that would release him. Her nimble fingers quickly traced his length and breadth as he continued to explore her covered body.

Then her skirt was gone, the bodice removed, and she lay in his arms on the steps to the upstairs in only her shift and stockings. Alex slowed to savor her flesh, kissing her legs and thighs as he removed the remainder of her clothes. "You are too covered," she implored. "I need to feel your skin against mine, Alex. I want to do to you what you do to me with your mouth. Please." Alex was taken aback by her sensual utterings…no woman of rank knew of or how to do such things. His little baggage had become well read and even better informed. Now to make it all reality.

Alex stood and pulled off the rest of his clothing, making short work of his pants, stockings and shoes. His lean body was bared, and then he slowly eased over her once more until they were skin to skin. Her hands ran brazenly through his hair. "Have you noticed, My Lord, that we are on the staircase of your townhome; if anyone opens the front door, they will get an eyeful," she said with a knowing smile.

Alex smirked. "I've had a fantasy of taking you in the dining room on the large table. I plan to make a meal of you, Baggage. Are you up for that?"

She gave him a sultry look. "The question is, are you up to it, Sir?

"You doubt me?" He swatted her behind as he picked her up in his arms and walked down the hallway towards the dining room.

"I would taste you, too, Husband." She nibbled on his chin and chest as they moved already planning what she could do to him. He was very aroused, and she had just begun.

Alex feasted on her body, his mouth on her core as she trembled in his arms, crying out her release; she, too, managed to get her mouth on him, turning the tables as she pushed him to his back. Looking down on him as she brought him to climax with her mouth was beyond belief to the Lord. She was untutored in the practice, but he would teach her what he craved as their trysts went on. She was a lady with a mission—to taste every inch of his body.

How had be gotten so lucky?

CHAPTER 22

The master and mistress's shenanigans were on the lips of all who worked at the Duke's Townhome. The servants tiptoed in and out of the kitchen in the morning, hoping that both were abed. The suppers had been sampled, and there were copious wine glasses on the first floor. But there was not a sign of the couple.

The bell went off for the master's suite. The butler straightened his cuffs and his jacket and went slowly up the stairs. He motioned to the staff to get busy at their duties. Tapping politely on the door, he heard the Duke's distinctive voice bid him enter. He pushed open the door to find both the Duke and Duchess on the terrace overlooking the gardens.

He glanced at the Duchess with surprise on his face. "Would you like your maid to come?" he intoned to Lady Elizabeth.

She giggled. "Not right now." Alex gave her a look from where he was shaving. She reached out her hand to grasp that of her husband's. "I would like some tea if it's not too much trouble."

"No, Ma'am. No trouble at all." He bowed to the two of them and backed from the room closing the door softly behind him.

Lizzie burst into peals of laughter. "I shall never be a true Duchess. That poor man couldn't find anywhere to place his eyes but on the floor. I embarrassed him." She tried to reason through his actions. "We are dressed, well, nearly dressed." She fingered Alex's robe that she wore; there was nothing else under it, and a long expanse of her bare leg was clearly visible outside its coverage. Alex stood with a bath sheet wrapped around his waist. He was just finishing his morning ablutions. His fingertips found her long tresses and raked through them, tilting her head back for his plundering kiss.

"My servants don't usually find women in my room, Baggage; he thought you would be in your own room; he'll just have to get used to us. By the way, last night was one of the best nights of my decadent life," he said.

Lizzie frowned. "I fear I still have much to learn, but I do try." She whispered an additional thought to herself. "As a matter of fact, I am very trying." Her body was satiated from her husband's unending attentions, and small bruises could be easily seen on her hips and neckline from the pressure of his hands if one looked closely. Over all, it had been a remarkable night, and Alex seemed genuinely relaxed.

There was another discreet knock on the door, and a whispered, "Your Lordship. You have a visitor."

Alex replied, "At this early hour? Who—pray tell?"

"It is Lady Estelle. She said you were expecting her." *Only Alex was not; the lady was spinning tales again, he thought.*

He frowned, but said, "Tell her I'll be down soon. Put her in the front parlor with some refreshments." He whisked the remainder of his shaving cream from his face and grabbed for his shirt and pants. Lizzie watched him with some unease. Why did Estelle always have to intrude on her liaisons with her husband. It must be because Alex allowed it, and why wouldn't he? Estelle would be the perfect Duchess for him. She would never love Alex, but she would play her role well.

Alex turned to her, kissing her on her forehead. "Don't come down, Lizzie. You deserve some rest. I'll entertain her." He grabbed his coat and left.

"Of course, you will entertain her," Lizzie grumbled after her husband had left. The entire household would leave for Winterbourne in two days. And when all was said and done, Alex would return to the woman who had deserted him at the altar. Lizzie wrapped the robe more tightly around herself and opened the door between their bedrooms. She had been reminded once again of her temporary position in this household.

Alex noticed Lizzie's coolness towards him, but he couldn't begin to fathom what he had done. She was always engaged in shutting down the house or in packing for their move. When he sought her out, she was too busy or on her way in or out of the townhouse. He wracked his brain as to the change in her, but he could only trace it back to Estelle's visit—he had no idea why that lady had come to see him. Her reasoning was suspect at best, questions about investing and animal stock. He told her to seek out her intended, just as he was trying to do. She laughed softly and told Alex he was mistaken in the Viscount's business at the gala. She claimed that the Viscount had never intended to take Elizabeth—rather, he had planned to warn her about abduction from another.

On the Friday of the move to Winterbourne, Lizzie surprised Alex even further. She decided to ride rather than go in the carriage with him. She sat a horse beautifully in her riding outfit, the sidesaddle not giving her any difficulty. He then opted to ride as well, but it precluded any serious discussion between them. She chatted to those who were riding along side of her, Robert, in particular. Alex couldn't be jealous because he knew Robert was happily married, and that Lizzie was fast friends with the man's wife.

They started early in the day and reached Winterbourne in the early afternoon, stopping several times on the way. Lizzie asked for a meal in her room and declared that she wanted to sleep for a week. She did look tired, and Alex once again wondered if she were expecting. She had no older lady with whom to discuss pregnancy. He would encourage his physician to visit her in the next weeks. Perhaps the man could suggest the idea to her.

When Alex tapped lightly on the door connecting their rooms, he opened it to find her fast asleep in her bed. He didn't see the tear tracks on her face. She needed her rest, so he closed the door quietly. He would have to find out what had gone wrong between them.

The next two weeks were highs and lows for Elizabeth. She worked on the school house that her husband supported after her impassioned plea to him to allow anyone on his estate to be educated. Planned as a school for children of the workers, she soon saw adults seeking education. Another impassioned plea won her the right to allow those people to come to school as well. Alex enlisted at least four teachers for the up and coming experiment. He often came to the building to offer his help as well. He could build with the best of them. He offered advice that saved them money and still met the requirements of the project. The workers were always stiff when the Duke came in to the building, but by the end of the day, he had won them over. He never dressed as the Duke at these gatherings, and some of the workers never knew that he was the Duke.

Having Alex there was a blessing and a curse. He made sure she was not one foot off the floor, asking others to take over her chores if she disobeyed him. Her hair fell out of her pins and flowed down her back, and her vivacity enlivened many a discussion. He seemed to have his eyes on her no matter where she was, but he never once chided her for her appearance or for her laughter. She hammered nails, delighted when they went in straight, and she washed shelves and cupboards. When the boxes of supplies arrived, she was the one hanging on the back of the wagon to sort them; when they were opened, she was the one to pull slates and writing utensils out as well as to roll the maps out on the floor, so she could see them.

And the nights became hers as well. Alex spent every evening with her, sometimes just doing estate work as she worked beside him in his library, and sometimes instructing her on the many pleasures of being a wife and a woman. The man was a brilliant teacher, or maybe she was just an eager learner.

Still Estelle appeared at least once a week with some problem that needed to be addressed riding over the estate to take up his time, and Alex always seemed to have time for her.

The mornings were becoming an issue for Elizabeth. She was often ill, losing her breakfast before ten o'clock. But then she felt fine and filled with energy. Her maid, Mary, gave her dry biscuits and unsweetened tea to settle her stomach; she also gave her ginger cookies. When his wife had been sick for the fifth time in a week, Alex suggested that he call his physician to make sure there was nothing else that could be done to make her mornings better. Elizabeth was sure it was because she was eating everything in sight—she was gaining weight much to her dismay.

Dr. Pearson would arrive at noon, and Elizabeth had to get to Essex's property to meet with her lawyer. It was going to be a tight fit, time-wise, but she could do it. She informed Mary that she was going for a ride and to tell the Duke she would return to meet the physician. By the time the message was relayed to Alex, she had already gone. He hoped that Fred would tell her of her condition. It had been a hellish week trying to make sure she didn't injure herself in her many projects. The days were passing swiftly, and Alex found he was enjoying himself immensely as he worked on his estate-from digging wells for watering crops to playing ball with the children of his tenants.

Essex met her at the door the moment she entered. She rushed into speech: "I hope you have told this gentleman that this is to be kept very quiet. It wouldn't do for Alex to be accosted with the news that his wife is looking for a divorce. I need to have his word on that." She peeled the gloves from her hands.

"I have made the situation quite clear to him, My Lady. I've told him that you are seeking information for a friend of yours. Your work with the ladies' societies has not gone unnoticed. You could be asking for anyone of them."

"Thank you, Essex. Would it be possible to see the little house that will be mine in a couple of weeks? There might not be time for it today because I need to be home by noon," she said.

"That will not be a problem, My Lady. It is, however, a half hour away from this main estate, so we will need an afternoon to explore it."

Lizzie smiled at him. "That sounds wonderful." She swept into his library to meet the man who would take her away from all that mattered in her life, but Alex would be able to have what he wanted— Lady Estelle and a proper Duchess of Winterbourne. She had heard from the Housekeeper that Estelle planned to ride with Duke in the morning to her nearby estate. Who knew what they would do there. She didn't want to think about Alex's hands on another woman.

"Good Morning. I am Lady Elizabeth. Thank you very much for coming; I have a number of questions for you, Sir."

The graying man stood, bowed, and kissed the hand that she offered. "I look forward to doing what I can to help, Your Ladyship." He went on to explain that the Act passed in 1858 moved the legal view of divorce from one based on a sacrament to one based on a contract between two people. Any issue from a marriage would go to the husband, however. And she was warned that the process might be long and difficult unless the man was in favor of the dissolution of the marriage. Men would be treated differently than their women counterparts. The doctrine of nullity stated that a marriage could be annulled for several reasons and treated as if it never existed. Among them was that if one party did not consent to it, the marriage could be made null. This annulment could be applied for, at any time after the marriage.

That was it, Lizzie thought. Alex did not consent to the marriage; it was forced upon him, and he went through with it to protect his name and Dukedom.

Elizabeth rose and said she would give it her full consideration and get back to him as quickly as she could. She had already made plans to leave Alex the night of the Ball in London, and then, there would be no going back. She planned to see the small home Essex had promised to her during in another visit. The Duke could use this part of the law to obtain an annulment; the marriage would never have existed, and she would move on.

CHAPTER 23

Lizzie barely made it home before twelve, and Dr. Pearson had been shown into the front parlor. She rushed to get her hat and gloves off, stopping only a minute to straighten her skirt and pat down her hair. Then she ran into room and slid to a complete stop as she saw him patiently waiting. She walked sedately the last few steps: "I am so sorry to have kept you, Doctor." She dropped into a beautiful courtesy.

He stood with a wide smile on his face. "No problem, Duchess. I had a lovely luncheon and tea, courtesy of your staff." He went on while motioning her to sit, "I've come to check you over at your husband's request."

A frown marred her face. "I am fine. I don't know why the Duke is worried. Do I not look well to you?"

"I think this might be about your illnesses in the morning."

Lizzie waved her hand and laughed. "It goes away very quickly, and I haven't had any issues in the last few days. I guess I was making poor dinner choices. I am so sorry that Alex made you travel all this distance to see me."

"Would you object to my looking you over? It will make the Duke feel much better, and it would make me feel that my trip was worthwhile."

She hesitated, but he had made the trip. "I have no objection. Perhaps we could adjourn to my room." She rose, called for her maid, and the doctor followed her up the stairs. Within fifteen minutes, the doctor had finished his examination. Mary helped her to button the top of her dress.

"So, your breasts are tender; you sometimes have issues with your food, especially in the morning; and you feel like you are gaining weight even while you are losing your breakfasts."

"I am also quite fatigued until I get moving at the beginning of the day, and I always want to nap. What is it? What's wrong with me?" she implored.

The doctor looked at her with a huge smile. "Lady Elizabeth, I think you are carrying the Duke's child. There is nothing wrong with you…"

The doctor's words came from a great distance, bouncing around in her head; the light around her faded turning into a black wave that plunged her into total darkness, and suddenly, her legs gave way. Lizzie fainted dead away. Chaos ensured from all around her; the Duke was summoned from the fields, the maids went running, and the melee continued with a frenzied dog, barking madly. Lizzie missed it all.

The room around her finally swam into focus, and she was met with Alex's concerned face as he held her hand and rubbed his fingers over it. She was lying on the bed in Alex's bedroom, well, her bedroom, too, since she slept every night with her husband. "Lizzie?" His voice was filled with anxiety. "Can you hear me?" Other concerned faces were at his shoulders, her maid, Mary, and the doctor. Many of the staff stood just outside the bedroom door. All looked concerned.

She nodded and asked for water. A cup was immediately secured and placed in the Duke's hand. He gently held her head up and placed the cup to her lips. She drank to ease the thirst in her mouth, wetting her dry lips. What had that doctor said—that she was expecting a child—Alex's child—the next Duke of Winterbourne? Her extreme interests in how men and women shared themselves with each other had certainly borne fruit…oh, God! Why hadn't she thought of that before falling in love with her husband? Her hand moved to cover her abdomen where a new life lay. A child. Her child. She could never leave it as she had been left by her mother when newly born. Her eyes met Alex's, as a lazy smile lit his face. "I am so happy, Lizzie Baggage, so happy." He gently squeezed her hand and then kissed her full on the lips; she kissed him back as everyone applauded.

Her plans were in ruins.

Once she had given birth to his heir, Alex would be able to have as many mistresses as he wished, but she would have her child. Would that be enough to make up for the loss of her husband? She had seen other women of the ton take their own lovers after their birthing duties were done. Leaving might still be the best option for her and the child. If it were a boy, however, she would deny him his birthright. That, she couldn't do, but she also could not allow him to be raised as his father was; he would be a child with days and days of no expectations.

"What? What did you say?" Lady Estelle's strident voice could be heard screaming a county away. "Don't tell me that. Lady Elizabeth is not carrying a child. No. It has to be a lie. I don't think the Duke has even touched her. She cannot give him what I could have if I had married him." She threw the vase in her hands at the wall where it crashed into a million pieces. "He would not replace me with her." Her plans had gone up in smoke. The Duke had escaped the ridicule from the ton that he deserved, and now he could tout a new heir in the spring. She would have to get the information to the Viscount; this changed everything. Of course, Elizabeth would have to be alive to give birth to the child, but accidents did happen.

Or, the Duke would have to die. Then Elizabeth could marry the Viscount and have the child to cement the ownership of Winterbourne. If it were a girl, there were no problems. The child could be sent off to school or parked in the countryside until she was ready to make her bow to society.

If it were a boy, then the entire estate would pass into the child's hands, and Lady Elizabeth would be declared the child's guardian. That simply could not happen. Estelle paced up and down the hallway. What if Elizabeth died after the birth of the child. Then the boy could come to the Viscount and her, and they would be the guardians of the child and command the entire ducal estate of Winterbourne. She laughed at the thought; she would have everything then, and there was nothing that Alexander could do about it. She had much planning to do.

Essex paced the hallway waiting to be admitted into Elizabeth's room. He had come immediately when the summons from Alex had arrived. What did the man know about his wife's plotting, and how would he react to John's role? The door opened, and the maid welcomed him into the room. Lizzie was sitting on the couch in the bedroom, and Alex sat beside her.

"Essex," Alex said. "You have to congratulate me. I am to be a father. Lizzie is expecting." Lizzie watched the emotions pass over Essex's face—concern, fear, joy and then confusion. She gave him a dazzling smile and reached out her hand to him, but there was caution in her look.

"How do you feel about it, Lady Elizabeth," John asked.

"I am ecstatic, Essex. It was such a surprise, and it puts a new light on many things," she said cryptically. "There is much now to consider."

"I would say so," Essex said as he mopped his brow. "I am very pleased for you, My Lady." She thanked him as Alex kissed her cheek once again.

"I think you should rest until dinner, Lizzie. Essex and I will go down to the library and have a cigar and some whiskey with the doctor to celebrate the grand occasion" She nodded her acceptance. Essex was the last to leave the room, and he turned to Lizzie.

"We will talk later, Essex. I have to think. But for now, the lawyer must be told that circumstances have changed." Essex nodded.

"I never thought you should leave His Lordship. He cares deeply about you, Elizabeth."

"If you say so, John. I know you are great friends with him, and looking back, I never should have asked you to shelter me."

"The time may come when you will need a place to stay; the house is yours, just as I promised, Lady Elizabeth. Don't forget it. We will visit it sometime this week before you leave Winterbourne. Alex said he has a meeting in the town about the repairs to the church. We will go then, just so you know where it is."

"All right. Thank you."

In minutes, her world had turned upside down, and she had no idea which way to go. Her priorities had changed to the small being now growing inside her. A soft smile crossed her face; she might not be a good Duchess, but she felt she would be a fantastic mother.

Alex could not believe that Lizzie carried his child. He hoped it was healthy and that she would have an easy birth. He would be a much better father to it than his own sire was to him. Lizzie had shown him the shortcomings of his upbringing; he had never enjoyed life before her. And she had turned his whole staff in a new direction. They laughed and smiled and went over and above what they were asked to do. The aura of fear and pomp had been lifted from Winterbourne. Lizzie was the reason.

The strictures on her because she was a Duchess didn't seem to matter to her. People mattered, animals mattered, the earth mattered. She flouted society's rules but mostly, that was not intended. She would laugh at herself and sweetly apologize. How had he not seen that she was beloved by everyone on his estate and even the Grande Dames in the ton had smiled on her; the Queen had recognized her for her kindness and refreshing stance on life.

And now with God's blessing, she would give him a child—a daughter who was just like Lizzie or a son who would love Winterbourne and nurture it. All was right with his world except for the residual fear he held that she could be abducted or hurt in some way.

Alex was startled as he saw Lizzie racing across the front yard, skirts held up in her hands, so she didn't fall. A flash of slim ankles could easily be seen; she was yelling angrily at someone. She had obviously seen something from the garden where she had been planting flowers. He jumped to his feet to follow when he saw her shake her fists and yell again at two older boys who had been walking on the road that went by Winterbourne. A smaller boy was being forced down while the two taunted and kicked at him. The Duke quickly followed his Lady and sprinted to the confrontation that was taking place.

Lizzie grabbed the arm of the larger boy who was punching the small boy. His cohort grabbed her by her shoulders to pry her off his friend saying: "She's a beauty. Grab her ass. We can have some real fun." The larger boy threw a punch in her direction, slightly grazing her arm and knocking her off balance; the same boy who was trying to pull her off was immediately firmly grabbed from behind by strong hands. Alex picked him up and shook him like a dog with a rat, furious at what just happened.

"What do you think you are doing," he bellowed as the irritated lad turned and tried to fight back. Lizzie had now grabbed the arms of the other youth, but he continued to strike at her. In seconds, a huge dog entered the fray, grabbing the boy's shoulder and jerking him from his mistress. Robert came up the road in a rush, grabbed the boy's body and slammed him to the ground, placing his knee on the boy's chest. Then he called off the dog. Alex subdued the lad who struggled with him. "Who are you?" he demanded.

"I'm Baron Cumber, so you'd best get your bloody hands off me. My father, the Viscount, won't take kindly to your manhandling me." The child on the road was now being gathered into Lizzie's arms as he cried; he was only a child of eight. Lizzie knelt down on the road and hugged him. Baron Cumber went on: "That cunt over there tried to stop me from having a little fun with this child. She'll get hers for even touching me."

Alex bristled. "You are on my lands and subject to my governance. I am the Duke of Winterbourne and that woman you just maligned is my wife—the Duchess."

The boy gaped at Elizabeth. "She isn't a duchess. Just look at her. You're a liar," the livid boy sneered at Alex. His anger no longer in check, Alex grabbed the boy and twisted his arms behind his back until the boy screamed in pain. "Please. Please. You're hurting me."

"I haven't begun to hurt you. How does it feel to be outnumbered and set upon by someone larger and stronger than you? Let's see how your father feels about his son taunting an eight-year old child and abusing him as well as a Lady of the ton. Some man you are." Alex turned his attention to the other culprit. "What is your name?"

Robert still held the other boy down on the ground under the watchful eyes of the huge dog; the youth's eyes said that he believed Alex was the Duke as he claimed to be. "I'm sorry, My Lord. We were just having a little fun with this boy."

"Name?"

I'm Baron Westmoor from Westmoor Crest."

"I've had dealings with your uncle. He would never approve of what I just saw you do"

"But he's only a worker's kid." the boy argued. "We didn't really hurt him much."

Lizzie stood as she held the little boy's hand. "I'm going to take Charles to the house to clean him up. He is Susanna, the Cook's, grandson." The little one had a black eye and multiple bruises on his legs and mouth." He no longer cried, but sniffled.

Lizzie turned in cold anger on the two young men. "You should pay for what you have done to this little one. You are cowards, and I will tell everyone what sniveling bullies you are to beat up an eight-year old. No woman would want boys like you since you find women playthings. Shame on both of you. You will never be welcome in my house." She had dirt on her nose, her hair was falling from its pins, and now there was dust on her entire outfit from kneeling in the road. She was indignant at the boys who had punched and kicked the child.

Alex motioned for Robert to march the two to the stables, one still defending his right to have a little fun. The Duke would return them to their guardians personally. He stopped the first boy and snarled: "One more thing. Don't you ever refer to any woman as a 'cunt' or see her as a plaything. It only shows the people around you what a totally irresponsible imbecile you are." Alex paused. "If you ever lay a hand on my wife again, I will not be responsible for my actions. Do you understand me?" Two nods were his answers.

Three hours later, Alex pulled his gig into the stables. The boys had been returned, and Alex let it be known in no uncertain terms that he would not permit them on his estate unless their guardians accompanied them. The families were barred from his home. He asked how the two had grown into such pitiful specimens of manhood. Both the Uncle and the Father heard his story without making a sound, but both looked mortified. "My wife was disparaged by your son. He owes the Duchess an apology, and if you will not see to their upbringing, I will make it my duty to make sure that you and your families are never received anywhere in polite society. You have much to answer for their attitudes. Do we understand each other?"

For once in his life, he relished being a Duke. With apologies ringing in his ears, Alex left with the tacit understanding that each of the boys would be severely punished and reeducated as to the value of those who worked for their estates. Their abuse of the fairer sex would also change. The expressions on the boys' faces as he left spoke volumes. They had made a dangerous enemy in the Duke, and there would be further repercussions; both boys knew that.

Alex found Lizzie in the side parlor, her lap filled with his shirts that needed buttons. The woman did horrible embroidery, but she made up for it by making sure everything the man owned was mended properly. He walked slowly over to her, only to have her burst into tears and cling to his legs. He knelt down immediately. "What is it, Baggage? Are you feeling well? Did those boys hurt you in any way?"

With tears streaming down her face, she replied: "One said I wasn't a Duchess. I told you I would be a poor duchess, but you didn't listen. Neither boy would hear me, and I felt helpless. It is not a pleasant feeling, but I am unhurt."

"There is an accounting for bad behavior, Lizzie. This was about them, not you. And you really shouldn't run like that. What if you had fallen?"

She smiled through her tears. "I would have gotten up." Alex shook his head as she went on: "What if we have a boy, and he believes that he's entitled to strike another child just because of his birthright?"

Alex's lips set in a hard line. "That won't happen, Lizzie. I would never let a son of mine grow up to do that." She wiped at her eyes with her sleeve. "Privilege comes with responsibility, but I have learned from you that a child must also have time to be a child. Kindness goes much farther in the world than I thought it did." He became thoughtful. "Learning to protect himself might be a part of my son's education. Could you live with that?" Lizzie looked thoughtful. He gathered her into his arms and rocked her. "You will be receiving an apology from both boys for their behavior."

"That's not necessary."

"It is. They need to learn there is a right way, Lizzie. They need to atone for what they did, so they never forget the lesson."

She melted into him, and he felt very proud of her. No one would be allowed to hurt her; he swore it would be so.

CHAPTER 24

The carriages pulled up in front of Winterbourne House in London. Lady Elizabeth's stay in the countryside was over. She disembarked with the help of the driver and smoothed her fashionable skirts out of her way. The house looked the same; the city was the same. She was once again dressed to the height of fashion in a lovely traveling dress trimmed in braid. What she longed for were her breeches and shirt and a fast ride astride her horse. Alex was supervising the unloading of their bags. The weeks had passed far too swiftly for her, and tonight's Ball was to have been the end of her marriage to Alex.

She walked slowly into the front receiving room and tore off her bonnet. She was not a fan of bonnets except on the heads of other people. She took off her jacket, as Mary came in, telling her she would have tea in a matter of minutes. Lizzie hated tea, but she wouldn't upset her maid. She would much prefer a strong drink, but the babe precluded that. She sat in the window seat overlooking the gardens, remembering her tour of Essex's house that was hers for five years if she needed it; it was located a half hour or so from Winterbourne. John, Earl of Essex, had been as good as his word; he collected her one morning when Alex was gone and took her to see the small estate.

It was nestled in the woods, well off the beaten path. The dirt road leading up to it was surrounded by vegetation and only wide enough for a small wagon or conveyance to pass. She was entranced as she exited the woods to see the beautiful gray stone of the exterior. A small lawn and flower gardens surrounded it. "Oh Essex. How lovely it is," she remarked as she climbed down from her horse.

The ground floor had two small parlors for guests, a dining room and a larger room with a huge fireplace. The wooden staircase wound its way up to a second level with four bedrooms with sitting rooms and a library of sorts. The rooms were well-appointed with curtains and rugs and antique furniture. Off the main bedroom, a terrace opened up; it could be accessed through glass doors. From the terrace, one could see small fields of crops and a stable and fencing for six or seven horses. There was also a large kitchen and laundry in the right wing.

Essex introduced her to the caretaker and his wife, the cook. They, along with four other workers, maintained the entire estate. "It is breathtaking, Essex, and I love it. If I had the wherewithal, I would purchase it from you. Her hand touched her abdomen knowing that her child had taken away that option, but she could have lived here and loved it.

"Here's your tea, my Lady."

"Thank you, Mary. Has the dress been delivered yet?" Marie promised it would be the best of her creations, and Lizzie could hardly wait to see it. It wouldn't be long before she would be showing, and her dresses would fit far more loosely.

Alex came in, a smile on his face. "Baggage. You looked like you were far away just now."

"I am regretting leaving Winterbourne already. There are fifty calling cards and invitations on the front table."

"Let them go for now. I have to go out for a little while. Will you be ready by nine tonight for the Prime Minister's Ball?"

"I will."

"Then I will see you then." He crossed the room and kissed her forehead. "I'm looking forward to it."

Estelle looked across the table at Viscount Myers. He had slipped into London in the dead of night and was now comfortably sitting on the Lady's sofa. "Are the plans in place?"

"They are. The Duke will be taken at the dance and moved into the countryside where he will be shot. I'll make it look like thieves did the bloody deed. Then Lady Elizabeth will be told her husband has been hurt, and she is needed. When she comes to his aid, she, too, will be taken and hidden away until she becomes cooperative. When the time is ripe, I will marry the lady and claim the guardianship of the unborn child. After it is born, Elizabeth will meet with an accident, and you and I will wed giving us access to the entire estate that is Winterbourne. We must be very careful in the next two months until all is ready. The woman must be kept happy, Estelle. Remember that. She must not lose the child—it is the key to our getting what we want. My guardianship of the child, regardless of its sex, will allow me to manage the funds it will receive."

"What do you want me to do at the Ball?" Estelle asked. "Should I stay close to Elizabeth?"

"That would be helpful. The plan is in motion now."

Lizzie gasped in delight. The dress was wonderful. It was a garnet red in color, and it brought out the blackness of her hair and the purity of her white skin. Marie slipped it over her head, and it fell around her in a flow of soft material. It covered her fuller breasts and highlighted her small waistline while it emphasized her diminutive stature. Its train was a small one, but she found she liked it better than a full one. Black diamante decorated its neckline and its hem and train adding sparkle as she moved. She felt like a princess in it. Well, she was supposed to be a Duchess, so that was only a step or two upward. She sighed as she looked at herself. This was NOT who she was, the graceful, soft woman with the striking good looks and a secretive smile. This woman must be her alter-ego. "Is there a place for my knife?" she asked Marie, striving to hold on to the Lizzie that you knew.

"Of course. It will fit nicely in a small slit in your long, black gloves. I could have made a leg holder for it if you would prefer that."

"No. The glove will do. Thank you, Marie. It is a beautiful creation." She pulled her gloves on and surveyed her appearance in the mirror in front of her. Her hair was down, caressing her shoulders and bare neck. When she looked in the mirror again, Alex stood behind her in his dress clothes. He had opted for a black ensemble.

"I think you need some jewels, Elizabeth." He opened the case he held and took out a garnet and diamond necklace, earrings and bracelet. You are so beautiful that you really don't need them, but I would like you to wear them."

Lizzie blushed, but she allowed him to put them on. She was truly thankful. Alex kissed her neck gently as his hands touched her shoulders. He whispered in her ear: "Well, Lizzie Baggage, I guess we should depart." She nodded, and the two turned together to walk to the carriage. "Promise me that if you feel ill in any way, you tell me immediately. We will go home." Lizzie nodded again.

They arrived at the Grand Ball to an influx of all the aristocracy of England. Lizzie put a smile on her face and tried to relax her already tense muscles. She did not like huge gatherings, and this one was huge. Alex stayed by her through all the introductions, only leaving to get her a glass of warm punch. The taste of it made Lizzie almost gag. She danced the first waltz with her husband and felt even more faint in the crush of people. She asked to sit down for a few moments, and Alex hurried to comply. As she was seated, Alex was distracted by Estelle. She had need of his immediate assistance. Lizzie raised an eyebrow as he stewed over her request, finally granting it because he was a gentleman. He told her he would be right back.

Three men stood outside the garden windows in the darkest area waiting for Alex to be brought outside. The Viscount had given them the approximate time to be ready. Estelle captured Alex 's arm and talked with him always moving him towards the patio doors. He kept looking over his shoulder for his petite wife, but he couldn't see her. Essex had agreed to be with Lizzie whenever he could.

Feeling totally overwhelmed with the heat of the room, Lizzie headed towards the patio to cool off. It was then that she saw Estelle pull Alex onto the patio and then onto the dark walkway. Well, no woman was going to take her husband without a fight. She had been longing to punch Estelle in the face for weeks now. Lizzie picked up her skirts and quickly followed the two of them.

Inside, the Viscount was frantically searching for Elizabeth. He was to keep her entertained until Alex had been taken. Lady Elizabeth had smiled so charmingly at him when he offered to get her a cool drink.

"Allow me to get you some refreshment, Duchess."

"Thank you," she said with a small smile. "That would be lovely."

As soon as he left to get the horrid stuff, Lizzie got up and ran in the opposite direction. That's how she saw Alex and Estelle venturing out into the garden. Now what did that creature want with her husband? Estelle turned to Alex pulling him to one side of the walkway as he argued with her that he needed to return to his wife. Three burly men jumped out of the bushes and grabbed him, pulling his hands behind his back and quickly covering his mouth. A gun butt came down on the side of his head, and he fell to the ground.

"Red, get him in the carriage at once," Estelle said.

The man called 'Red' replied. "We haven't much time." Estelle watched the proceedings and then began her return to the Ball. The Viscount would have Elizabeth in hand; then it was only a matter of time before the note arrived for her to attend her husband. Only, her husband would already be dead.

As she processed what she was seeing, Lizzie thought she should get help for Alex; she turned towards the patio. The men were moving, and she decided that she didn't have enough time to summon someone. A diversion was needed to draw attention to the garden area. She took seconds to circle around Lady Estelle and putting both hands against the woman's back, she shoved as hard as she could, toppling Estelle into the deep pond on the property. "Take that, vile creature that you are," she shouted as Estelle hit the water.

Lady Estelle's high, terrifying shriek and splashing motions alerted her men in the garden. They also made several guests look to see what the problem might be. Red doubled back to the abductors, urging them to leave and telling the others that he would meet them at the rendezvous. The note to Elizabeth still had to be delivered requesting her to come to her injured husband. He had planned to do that much later in the evening, allowing his friends time to kill the Duke. He didn't do dirty work. The entire time plan would have to change. He searched for the Viscount who was supposed to be taking care of the Duchess.

Lizzie managed to follow the other men as they labored to carry Alex. One down, two to go. At the waiting coach, the men tied Alex's arms, stuffed a rag into his mouth and pushed him inside on the floor; he was clearly unconscious, and he might be hurt. There was no way to reach him without being seen. The carriage door was pushed shut; both men climbed up to the outside to guide the horses.

As they had worked to confine Alex, Lizzie scooted over to the other side of the coach weighing her options; when the men climbed up to drive away, she navigated the baggage rack on the back, holding on to the straps. The coach set off at a sedate pace because the men didn't want to raise the watch. Lizzie hung on for dear life, waving her hands to anyone who saw the coach go by, hoping someone would help. She had two enemies to face, and she was worried about her husband. She managed to secure herself onto the back and then she ripped off pieces of her petticoats and let them go when she saw anyone walking. Her cries were muffled by the pounding of the horses and the sway of the coach. A quick pace brought them outside of London and into the countryside. It was dark on the road, but the coach did not slow. Lizzie's arms grew tired and leaden, but her mind was active. The pitch and pull of the coach made her head hurt and her stomach roil, but still she hung on for dear life. She had to save Alex—but how?

Inside the party, many people were now searching for Lizzie. Essex became more and more concerned when he couldn't find her. The Viscount was still in his sight, so he didn't know what to do next. When Estelle was hauled in from the gardens dripping with water, John knew that something had gone terribly wrong. Several of the men rushed to Estelle, asking her what had happened. She couldn't say that she thought Elizabeth had pushed her; she had to convince Elizabeth to go after her husband. To add to the confusion, Estelle's hired man, Red, came into the hallway into Estelle's sight. The lady decided to blame him for her mishap.

"That man pushed me." Her finger pointed to Red. An audible gasp came the group, and all attention was turned to him. Several men surrounded him.

Red stammered: "No, Miss. No. You're confused. I got to give a note to the Duchess of Winterbourne." He held up the note that the Viscount had written, and he realized he had just made a colossal error. That note was to have been delivered much later.

Essex called out. "Give me the note," and everything went downhill from there.

The Viscount tried to thread his way around the outside of the room planning to make a run for it. He was stopped by Robert and another friend of Alex's at the front door; freedom was so close. Instead, he was held fast and pushed back into the gathering. It was only a matter of time before he would be prosecuted by the Duke—that is, if he still lived. Why couldn't Lady Elizabeth just do what she was supposed to for once in her life.

The driver of the carriage containing the Duke turned to a less traveled road branching out from the main one. Something was going to happen soon. Lizzie felt it. She marked the road turn with one of her last petticoats. It flew from the back of the carriage and landed on the turn, settling onto the dirt road in a pile of material. She hoped it was enough to mark their way. Pieces of her clothing decorated many of the streets of London and the road leading away from it. Now, she only had her gown, and the red wouldn't show in the dark.

The coach continued on for another half hour or so and finally pulled up, stopping at an abandoned farmhouse alongside the road. The men were laughing and joking now, one pulling out a jug and imbibing its contents. The other man jumped to the ground and tied the team. He walked some fifteen feet up the road from the carriage and looked around.

"There's no one here. Let's get a small fire going. It doesn't matter when we shoot him, does it?"

Shoot him? They were going to shoot Alex?

The other man climbed carefully from the carriage so he that didn't drop the jug. "I could use a drink or two or three." There was more talking, and the jug was passed back and forth. Lizzie carefully climbed down from the back of the coach and slid into the bushes. She could hear snatches of the chatter as the men lit lanterns and made a small fire. The horses had been tied in their traces; as she moved, she had to be careful not to spook them. She could not be discovered.

The men continued to drink heavily as she debated what to do. The carriage door on her side seemed jammed, and she couldn't risk being seen on the other side. One of the men got up and walked back to the coach to pull open the door. Her heart caught in her throat, and she crouched low. Lizzie watched as he dragged Alex's body out onto the road and pulled him in the grasses at the other side of it. The man stood: "Here's to ya, Governor."

He pulled out his gun and cocked it before she could react. The shot went straight into his captive. The explosion reverberated in Lizzie's mind over and over, and she trembled as she watched the spot where Alex lay. Her husband didn't move, and a dark spot was now spreading on the front of his white shirt. Lizzie's heart slammed in her chest.

Alex was dead.

The man turned back to his friend. "It's done. The Viscount will be here with that Duchess in the next couple of hours. All we have to do is wait, and then we're going to be rich men." He returned to the small fire, and soon both men were snoring.

At the Ball, Estelle pretended a faint, hoping to garner more time. Essex removed the note from her man's fingers and unfolded it, reading quickly. "This note says that His Lordship has been taken by robbers and that he is hurt. It requests that Lady Elizabeth come to care for him. This man is to lead her to him." Now men did grab Red's arms, and although he struggled, there was no escape for him. "Where is the Duke? Your life may depend on your answer."

"I'm just a working stiff, Sir, and I was given coin to deliver the note at this party. I ain't involved in nothing else. I didn't push this Lady in the lake neither," he added. "I done my job, and I want to go now. This here 'Lady' can take you to the rendezvous spot. She showed me this garden and His Lordship; she's directly involved." A gasp of horror echoed in the room. "I didn't touch nobody."

In shock, Lizzie crawled towards her fallen husband, tears threatening, her breathing ragged. The dark color of her dress made it difficult for anyone to see her. *Be alive, Alex, she thought. Please be alive.* If Alex did not live, she would have to escape. Her thought was for their child and her need to protect it. But she couldn't leave without knowing if Alex lived.

Lizzie slipped quietly to his side and pulled the filthy rag from her husband's mouth; she cradled his head in her lap, and she kissed his face, willing him to respond; he was still warm to the touch as she tried to find a heartbeat. She was afraid to say anything to him that might carry on the night air, and she kept her movements minimal.

Rubbing his hand with her own, she leaned down and whispered in his ear: "Alex. If you can hear me, just move your finger. We are surrounded by enemies, and we must be very quiet."

She thought his lashes fluttered, so she tired once again. "Please, Alex. If you can hear me, wiggle your finger." The wound seemed to be in his right shoulder, and it was bleeding, but slowly. Could the man have been such a bad shot then, or had Alex moved to deflect it? A little finger moved in her palm, and the Duke opened his eyes to gaze on his young wife. His head felt like someone had stomped on it, and there was a burning in his shoulder, reminiscent of his time in the war. His hands were numb and restrained. He was confused as to how Lizzie was with him, but she needed to get away from here.

"How did you get here, Baggage? You need to go." His voice was weak. He knew that she and his child were in danger, but he didn't know who had targeted them.

She grinned at him. "And miss all the fun. I don't think so, Alex." He took in her disheveled appearance.

"Looks like I owe you yet another gown. You're going to bankrupt me, Baggage, but I have to confess that I have never been so glad to see anyone."

"Then you won't send me away. We are in this together? Right?"

He hesitated, but only for a moment. "God help me, yes, Baggage. We are certainly in this bind together. What happened to your dress?"

"I tore pieces of my petticoats to leave a trail for the Watch to follow. There are parts of my undergarments on the road all the way to London." She was proud of her clandestine acts. Alex wondered how he would ever explain the lack of most of her underclothes on his Duchess. "I tried to garner attention to our plight by yelling at those who passed by, but when no one paid attention to me hanging on the back of the coach, I had to do something."

"But, of course you did." Alex managed a smile at her. "And removing your undergarments, piece by piece, was the answer."

"They were very white, and they are a trail, of sorts," she replied, but that didn't matter. Alex was alive. Lizzie covered her mouth to stop the joy that welled up in her, threatening to escape from her mouth. She whispered once again: "Alex. I'm going to get these ropes cut." She pulled her knife from her glove and carefully sliced through the ties. His arms were finally free.

In London, the Viscount's man, Red, turned to run as he watched the crowd turn against him; he had blabbered on and on, but since Estelle had given him up and blamed him for her attack, he had had no problem telling the assembly of her part in the plot to kill the Duke. "The Viscount and Lady Estelle ordered me and my men to take the Duke and kill him. We was supposed to escort the Lady Elizabeth to her husband then. The Viscount said he was going to lock her up and force her to marry him—to control her fortune and that of the Duke's, too."

Robert grabbed the Viscount's arm and hauled him over to where Estelle was seated. "Where. Where was this to happen, and where have you hidden the Duchess?" No one seemed to have an answer for that.

All eyes turned on the Viscount. "I don't have your damned Duchess. I have no idea where that lady is. I swear she is part ghost," the Viscount replied, thinking of her disappearance in the garden before.

The snoring around the campfire was getting louder. Lizzie leaned down to Alex to hear what he was saying.

"I have a small derringer in my coat pocket. We will need it, I'm afraid. Do you know how many men are here?"

"There are two, Alex. Another man stayed at the Ball with Estelle. We were set up."

"Then our work is cut out for us, Baggage. I don't know how steady my hand will be if I have to shoot. My head aches, and my vision isn't quite right. I'm going to try to move my body to see where things stand." Lizzie nodded, and Alex pulled his arms slowly from behind his back to the front. His wound began to bleed more freely.

"Stop Alex. I need to get this wound bound to stop the bleeding." She cut a large piece from the bottom of her chemise and began to carefully cut strips of cloth with her knife, making as little noise as possible. The men were clearly sleeping, but she kept careful watch on them. "I can't see your wound very well, but I'm going to try to wrap it. "She fashioned a heavy pad of material and opened his bloody shirt. The wound, from what she could see, was small. She wondered if the bullet was still in there. She placed the pad on the wound with pressure and began wrapping the strips tightly around it, tying knots as she went. "Alex?" There was no answer. Her voice now held a frightened note in it. "Alex!"

His eyes opened. "I'm doing all right. It would have to be my right shoulder. I am right-handed. Can you help me to sit up?"

Elizabeth pushed gently on his shoulders to get him into a sitting position, still listening for any changes. So far, her movements had been undetected. Alex felt the world careen around him, but he forced himself to sit still. He closed his eyes against the pain and whispered: "We don't have much time left. We need to disable these two and hide before the Viscount comes. We may have a chance then to escape into the woods around here." He thought of his time in the war. "We'll set a trap and cause a disturbance. When they come to investigate, we will take both of them out. I can fire the gun if I get a clear shot, but that lets another one to deal with."

"They don't know I'm here, so I might be able to surprise one of them," Lizzie said. "I need something heavy to strike him."

Alex nodded, pointing to a rock. "You also have your knife if all else fails. Use it. Look woman, you have to be safe. If this falls apart, I want you to promise me you will run and get away. I will do everything I can, but I need to know you are safe."

Lizzie smiled: "I will," but her eyes said otherwise. She intended to stay and do battle with him and for him.

"You're such a lousy liar, Elizabeth." Alex's look caught and held her eyes, and they were moments from their confrontation. His hand caught her chin: "I love you; I'm sorry I waited so damn long to say it, Lizzie Baggage. It has been a wild ride, and I've enjoyed the blazes out of every minute with you. It's like I wasn't alive before I met you."

Lizzie smiled and kissed his hand. "Not bad for two people who weren't committed at all until the bishop asked for our vows." Her lips met his in a sweet kiss. "I love you, Alex. Oh, and we will make it. I have a long story to tell you that I know you will enjoy. I was planning on divorcing you tonight."

"What?" Alex's voice was a cross of wonder and anger. "Divorce?"

"Well, I was going to have you divorce me. We can talk about it later. Right now, we need to concentrate on taking out these men." The funniest look crossed Alex's face, as her hand caressed his cheek. "Don't look at me like that; I changed my mind—about the divorce, I mean."

"Well, that's something in my favor, I think." Alex replied.

"I don't think I could live without you, Alex. Let's do this."

Lizzie gathered middle-sized rocks from the pathway on the road; this would become their diversion. Alex moved slowly to get into a position to take a good shot. The moon flitted between the clouds, making seeing somewhat difficult. A slightly larger rock would be used to disable or knock unconscious, the second man, and hopefully, then to capture him.

Lizzie crawled to the opposite side of the road from Alex and prepared herself. At his nod, she threw the stones between their location and the fire. The drunken men clawed their way upright. "What was that noise?"

"Don't know, but I better go and see. Probably just some animal." The man staggered to his feet, pulled out his gun, and walked towards where the noise had occurred. He tramped around a bit but found little. "Nothin' here, Jake." Lizzie crept silently up behind him and brought the rock down on his head. He was too tall for a direct hit. He slumped forward, but the blow did not knock him unconscious. He turned and looked at Lizzie. "See here, you." Her heart in free fall, Lizzie brought her knife down in an arc and plunged it in his upper shoulder, kicking him in his private parts to his loud scream. As he clutched himself, she bashed him on his head again with the rock, and he collapsed at her feet. "One down," she murmured.

"Hey, Fisher. What's going on? Where did you go?" The other man meandered to where he had last seen his friend. He found Lizzie leaning over Fisher's body, ready to hit him again if he moved. "Well," he drawled. "Looky, looky, looky what I found. Where'd you come from, Woman? Was Fisher hiding you from me?" Lizzie jumped up and turned, backing up. The man followed her with his eyes and with his menacing steps until she stopped. She stood frozen in fear as his hands reached for her, and his stench surrounded her. A gunshot rang out in the night air, and the man's eyes rolled back in his head; he pitched to his knees and then onto the ground. Alex's shot had been deadly.

"Baggage," he called. "Are you all right?"

Lizzie swallowed hard. "I think so. I have to confess I'm not used to having dead and wounded bodies around me, but I suppose I can deal with it." She took in a huge lungful of air.

"Don't wilt on me now, Baggage. We need to tie up the other man before he regains consciousness." Lizzie nodded, but she walked carefully around the dead body on the ground, coming slowly to where her husband stood. He held out his good arm to her, and she helped him to move to the man; he was secure in minutes, his knife wound not bad.

"Now what?" she asked.

"We plan our trip home, of course. How are you at guiding a carriage." He looked her ragged outfit. Not wanting her to have time to think about the past hour, he said, "Damnation. I do owe you another dress."

Lizzie giggled in relief. "But I'm still wearing my jewels. That should count for something, shouldn't it? I didn't lose them!" Now Alex's laugh joined her own; the immediate danger was over. They turned the carriage around, and Lizzie helped her husband up on the perch. She climbed up after him, taking the reins. "I've always wanted to drive one of these."

"Slowly, Baggage. We will send men back for our two abductors." His arms went around her shoulders, and his hands went over hers to help keep the team together, even as he grimaced with the pain in his shoulder.

In London, the search in the ballroom for Lizzie continued without success. She was not on the premises, causing a great deal of concern. Two men reported to the Watch seeing a young woman in a gown hanging on the back of a carriage, waving and throwing something, but they had been unable to stop the conveyance, and they had no means of following it. Essex wondered if it was Lizzie. Alex had announced that very evening that Elizabeth was expecting, and he had received the congratulations of the entire ton. Essex prayed that woman wasn't Lizzie. The whole experience would overwhelm a lesser woman, and she was with child.

The Lords and gentlemen from the Gala rode out together with the Viscount's man. They were promised he would show them where the rendezvous was to occur. The man hoped that the Duke had not been killed yet; at least they could not hold him accountable for that death. They still hadn't found the Duchess. As they rode, they saw a number of pieces of undergarments strewn along the road, like bread crumbs. Essex became convinced that Lizzie was involved.

Within the hour, Lizzie and Alex heard the sound of a large group riding towards them. Lizzie pulled back on the reins, bringing the carriage to a complete halt. Both waited, hoping for rescue rather than more turmoil, but they had discussed a plan if they had to run. Alex drew his gun. The group of riders seemed quite large from the sound. Perhaps, there would be running. Lizzie followed the plan they had concocted, climbing down and getting into the carriage, ready to bolt if necessary. Alex waited, his derringer ready and loaded.

A shout could be heard; it sounded like Essex's voice; had he and his friends finally found the two of them? "Alex?" Essex called out. "Alex? Are you there, Man?"

The entire group circled the carriage, and Lizzie popped up, dressed in a torn garnet gown, still wearing her sparkling jewels, her hair a mess and her face dirty. She climbed from the carriage. "Gentlemen. It is very good to see you." The Duchess of Winterbourne sank into a low courtesy and stood before them in all her ragged glory.

Red nodded to her with a grin on his face. "You was the little lady what pushed Lady Estelle into the pond, wasn't you?"

Lizzie halted and then replied: "I am indeed. She didn't drown, did she?"

"Oh no, Ma'am. She's still kicking and mad as hell at you, Little Lady. She was spittin' nails, she was."

"Well, I guess I should be happy that she isn't dead, but I wouldn't mind her getting a dreadful chill." Lizzie put that image in her head as she reached Alex, who had been helped down from the coach. She could picture Lady Estelle with a red, running nose, pasty skin, and a nasty, hacking cough. Lizzy decided at that moment she would put restrictions on the woman and any relationship she sought with Alex. Perhaps Lizzie could practice her swordsmanship. Estelle would just have to find another man to help with her problems.

As Alex stepped forward, he said, "You're a blood thirsty woman, Baggage," but his glimmer of a smile belied his words. "Let's go home."

It had been a long night.

Alex and Essex met late the next day in the Duke's library; Alex's shoulder had been attended to, the bullet removed, and his head no longer ached. The nightmare was behind them. Lizzie was still resting, having broken down in tears as soon as she had reached their bedroom the night before at the thought that Alex had almost died. He tried to reassure her he was very much alive, but to little avail. She finally cried herself to sleep as he held her close in his arms. Alex's physician had seen to both their needs, and they had slept late into the next day.

Alex prodded Essex as to what he could get his wife for all her bravery and daring. If she had not come to his rescue, the outcome for him could have been very different.

"Buy her Glenn Marsh, that small estate on the corner of our properties. She and I visited there, and she loved it. Perhaps she just needs a place to hide away sometimes and not be a Duchess."

Alex thought about that proposal. "He could see her fishing, riding astride her favorite horse, weeding her garden and climbing trees at will. "Do you think I could talk her into not riding astride a horse in London if she had a place of her own? The lords want me to do something before their own wives demand the same privilege. I'm afraid they find me lacking in discipline with my wife, but they all adore her and even envy me. Imagine that."

"You love her, my friend, and she loves you. It's your call, Alex, but I think you might be on to something—give her a space of her own." Essex clapped him on the back.

"And what's this about a divorce?" Alex added, needing to know his Duchess's mind. "Who would want to divorce me? a Duke, mind you?"

"That's a tale for another day," Essex said. "You need to be sitting down while I tell it." The idea of divorce had just recently been legislated, and Alex wasn't sure of its reach. Lizzie couldn't possibly have been looking into that, could she?

The Duke quickly added: "As to Glenn Marsh, I'll take it." After all, his Duchess deserved the best. Outside the library, standing in her nightgown on tiptoes, her ear against the door and listening to her husband's words, Lizzie tried to keep from laughing out loud. She was going to give the Duke the ride of his life, and she would love every minute of it.

A stern voice came from inside the library: "Lizzie Baggage. If you are listening out there, go to bed."

Her small voice whispered into the door: "Yes, Sir. I'll be waiting."

EPILOGUE

Alex watched from the library window as Celeste, his nine-year-old daughter, shimmied down the tree from her school room window; it was a thirty-foot drop to the ground. Her long black hair was loose and flowing down her back as she did so, and the white pinafore, gown and stockings that she wore were already dirty and ripped. She was a natural climber, just like her mother, and she was supposed to be studying with her governess this morning. Alex was not worried, however. It was just another day at Winterbourne Manor.

Alex weighed his options. He loved that little girl with all his heart, but he needed to be a strict parent to her lest she get herself into more scrapes. She had gotten herself lost in the maze on the property, and she spent several hours locked in the mill when she wanted to figure out how it ground the wheat. Lady Celeste needed to have boundaries set. He sighed as he got up and went out the patio doors to the garden, where he found her examining a small nest of new bunnies that lay near the rose bushes.

"Cece." That's what he called her. "What do you think you are doing?" He made his voice stern.

The child smiled up at him with an impish grin trying to decide how frustrated he was with her before she answered. Her mother was in the kitchen planning the Harvest Ball with cook, so there would be no help from that quarter. Her father waited patiently for her answer, and she knew he would continue to wait until she replied. He had boundless patience when she was in a bind.

She stood up and walked to him, putting her arms around his waist in a big hug. "Miss Barnes is very dull today Father, and I thought I would learn more by going out into the gardens and observing wildlife."

Alex could barely manage to restrain his smile; what a winsome child she could be. "Then I guess I shall have to let Miss Barnes go and look for someone new."

The little girl's face clouded up and she exclaimed loudly: "No, Father. She is a good governess, especially to my younger brother and sister. Cece's violet eyes beseeched him to reconsider his edict. She was a child who cared passionately for others and would do no harm to anyone. Cece mumbled on, and Alex could barely hear her. "She needs to stay, please."

"Then you need to go back to your classroom, apologize to the lady for your escape, and get to your lessons. I will not have a child who is uneducated just because it is a nice day to be outside. You will have the entire afternoon to explore."

She moved closer to him. "Will you come with me, Father? I want to go down into the cave that is on the property. Maybe there is treasure there." Her eyes lit up with the thought. She had discovered the cave on her wanderings on the weekend, and she had been told to stay away from it if she valued her life. Her eyes met his with her challenge to her father.

Alex debated the wisdom of giving in to her request. If he went, he could supervise this excursion and see just how dangerous the cave might be. If he said no, then he was sure his delicate daughter would be there on her own within hours, probably dragging Hunter, her older brother, along with her. The boy was twelve and very mindful of his role as a protector to his sister. Nevertheless, Hunter would enjoy the excursion just as much as his sister would. He was a daredevil in his own way, thoughtful, intelligent, and patient with everyone and quick to laugh. He was well-suited to become a Duke.

Alex caved. "Ask your mother to make a picnic basket for the four of us, and we shall go and explore this wondrous place. The twins can stay here. Now back to your classroom."

Her face lit up, and she was the most beautiful thing he had ever seen. He would have to beat off the men when she came of age to marry. He wasn't sure if that was on her agenda or not. After all, her mother had almost divorced him some thirteen years ago. She placed a kiss on his cheek and ran towards the door of the Manor: "Oh, I can hardly wait to tell Hunter!" Now, she was yelling. "Hunter!" Her feet scrambled across the garden, skirts flying "Hunter! Guess what?" And she continued to yell at the top of her lungs as she ran, hair blowing wildly, as she ripped across the lawn in a very unladylike manner. Alex lamented the man who would take his daughter on.

The Duke stood and watched her go, only to observe his wife coming towards him. "I was just coming to see if you needed rescued. Cece can be a handful when she chooses."

"Ah, so says the woman who wrote the book on being a handful." His wife's delighted laughter pealed out. Her arms came around him, and she pulled down his chin to kiss him firmly on the lips. Alex returned the kiss possessively and then continued: "We already have four children, but this is a very large estate, and I'm sure a few more..."

Lizzie slapped his chest but then put on a cunning face: "You know I am always up to trying new things in delightful unusual ways," she taunted. Her hand moved slowly down his trim, yet muscled body.

Alex did know. She had been well educated now in pleasuring both herself and her man. "What are the twins up to," he asked to change the subject. The twins had been a surprise; they were now five years old and into everything.

"We were making cookies in the kitchen this morning. You were supposed to be working on the estate books, I believe. How did you ever get Cece to go back to the classroom of her own will?"

"I threatened to fire the governess."

Lizzie was aghast. "Alex, how could you do that? Miss Barnes is doing such a good job preparing both of them for what lies ahead."

Alex gave her a devilish smile. "It worked, didn't it? She will never allow anyone to suffer for her own behavior or lack thereof."

"You are a sly old dog. I'm going to have to make you pay for your male superiority complex." Lizzie said it with a smile on her face; suddenly she looked quickly around, and without warning, she tackled him to the ground, her skirts flying as Alex fell, the agile man making sure she landed on top of him and wasn't hurt. She draped her body strategically over his, settled on him and licked the inside of his ear, whispering tauntingly: "We are out in the middle of the front lawn, Alex. I am ready and very willing..." Her lips teased his with their magic, her hands working at his buttons.

Alex reacted strongly, placing his hand inside the bodice of her day dress and freeing one breast to taste it. He let go, only when she squirmed beneath him obviously seeking more. "I am always ready and willing, Wife." His other hand crept underneath her skirts and petticoats, and he touched her intimately. She moaned under his soft caress.

Lizzie tensed when she saw movement on the porch of the great house. "Alex! Hunter is coming this way. We have to stop."

Her husband was enjoying her discomfort. "Why? He will be learning soon enough about the ways between a man and a woman."

Lizzie pounded on his shoulder, as she tried to push herself from him, and she meant business. "Alex. Behave! Pretend you're a Duke."

"Pretend I'm a Duke? Well, this is a change." Nevertheless, his hand stopped its upward movement as he broke out in a fit of laughter, finally pulling it free of her skirts. "I love this body, Baggage." Lizzie pushed her bodice up with shaky hands and attempted to put more distance between her body and her husband. Their oldest son walked steadily towards them in a nonchalant fashion, but his grin said he knew what they were about.

"Father, Mother. It's a grand day for rolling about on the lawn, isn't it?" Hunter smirked at his parents, the esteemed Duke and Duchess of Winterbourne. "Is this a new game I should know about? It looks engaging."

Alex still hadn't allowed Lizzie to escape; she was still held atop his body. As she smoothed her skirts down around her, Alex proceeded to kiss her softly. "You will learn it soon enough, Hunter. But I will say this: beware of marrying a woman similar to your mother. She will lead you on a merry chase, and you will have stand tall to tumble a woman like her in your bed." Lizzie's face colored as he added: "But oh, what a life you will have."

"Don't listen to your sire, Hunter. You find someone you love, and the rest will follow."

Hunter's expression was intrigued as he eyed the two of them. "I will be just like you, Father; I can promise you that. I will search for the right woman." The young man turned away but not before he caught his father's eyes and mouthed, "I want to be just like you."

Alex looked up at his wife as Hunter walked away whistling and said for her ears only: "I pray, that you capture a woman just like my Duchess. In fact, I'm afraid that I must insist on it."

56650628R00113

Made in the USA
Middletown, DE
23 July 2019